"With deft att⋯⋯⋯⋯tion with the forbidden ⋯ ⋯tisfy romance fans." —*Publishers Weekly*

"A must-read . . . Carew definitely knows how to turn up the heat." —*RT Book Reviews*

"Carew brings erotic romance to a whole new level. . . . She sets your senses on fire!" —*Reader to Reader*

"You might find yourself needing to turn on the air conditioner because this book is HOT! Ms. Carew just keeps getting better." —*Romance Junkies*

"A dip in an icy pool in the winter is what I needed just to cool off a little once I finished this yummy tale!" —*Night Owl Reviews* (5 stars)

"Whew! A curl-your-toes, hot and sweaty erotic romance. I didn't put this book down until I read it from cover to cover. . . . I highly recommend this one." —*Fresh Fiction*

"Carew is truly a goddess of sensuality in her writing." —*Dark Angel Reviews*

"Carew pulls off another scorcher. . . . She knows how to write a love scene that takes her reader to dizzying heights of pleasure." —*My Romance Story*

ALSO BY OPAL CAREW

Big Package
(e-novella)
Nailed
Meat
(e-novella)
My Best Friend's Stepfather
Stepbrother, Mine
Hard Ride
Riding Steele
His to Claim
His to Possess
His to Command
Illicit
Insatiable
Secret Weapon
Total Abandon
Pleasure Bound
Twin Fantasies
Swing
Blush
Six
Secret Ties
Forbidden Heat
Bliss

A Fare to Remember

Opal Carew

ST. MARTIN'S GRIFFIN
NEW YORK

A FARE TO REMEMBER. Copyright © 2017 by Opal Carew. All rights reserved. Printed in the United States of America. For information, address St. Martin's Press, 175 Fifth Avenue, New York, N.Y. 10010.

www.stmartins.com

The Library of Congress Cataloging-in-Publication Data is available upon request.

ISBN 978-1-250-11668-0 (trade paperback)
ISBN 978-1-250-11669-7 (e-book)

Our books may be purchased in bulk for promotional, educational, or business use. Please contact your local bookseller or the Macmillan Corporate and Premium Sales Department at 1-800-221-7945, extension 5442, or by e-mail at MacmillanSpecialMarkets@macmillan.com.

First Edition: April 2017

10 9 8 7 6 5 4 3 2 1

To Mark,
the love of my life!
Thanks for the
inspiration.

Acknowledgments

Thank you to Rose Hilliard, my wonderful editor and one of my favorite people in the whole world. Thanks to Emily Sylvan Kim, my awesome and dedicated agent who always goes that extra mile. And as always, thank you to Mark, Matt, and Jason for their loving support.

A Fare to Remember

Chapter One

Stevie turned on the wipers as the small splatters of rain turned to huge drops bombarding the windshield as she drove, blurring the lights of the city street.

Finally, she'd caught a break. It had been a slow night, leaving her alone with her thoughts, and with what had happened with Hank today . . . Her stomach clenched and she fought back the tears she would never let fall.

She just wanted to stay busy and keep her mind off it.

Immediately, a businessman waved her down. She pulled over.

"Good evening, sir. Where to?" she asked.

He gave her an address about five blocks east, then stared at his phone the whole trip, tapping away. Probably catching up on his e-mail, or maybe texting his wife or girlfriend. Probably the former. Everybody who got into her cab seemed to want to fill every minute with useful time. Never taking a moment to just look out the window and enjoy the sights. To see life.

She dropped him off, then a couple blocks later another man flagged her down.

"Fairmont Hotel on Bleecker," he said.

He wasn't a bad-looking guy. He wore jeans and a leather jacket, but she could tell the jeans were two hundred bucks at least, and the jacket—real Italian leather from a designer label—would have cost him a bundle. He tapped on his phone for a bit, then stuffed it in his jacket pocket and leaned back in the seat. His gaze locked on her picture, then shifted to her rearview mirror.

"A lady cabbie. Been driving long?" he asked.

"About five years."

He nodded, his gaze lingering on her face in the mirror. "Are you near the end of your shift?"

"No, sir," she said simply. She knew where this was headed.

"What about a break? Maybe we could get a drink or something."

"I can't drink on duty, sir, and I don't have a break for a while."

"Okay, well, I've heard it can be pretty tough to make a living driving. Maybe I could hire your cab for a couple of hours and you could . . . uh . . . perform some other service for me."

She sighed, glad they were almost at his hotel.

"Thank you for your concern, sir, but if you'd like a woman to have a drink with you or . . . whatever . . . just tell the concierge you'd like to meet Rita. I'm sure he can fix you up."

Rita wasn't a person, but a code of sorts. A way of asking for a hooker without asking for one.

She pulled up in front of his hotel.

"Sure but . . . a lady cabbie. That's hot. Are you sure—?"

"I'm sure. That'll be eight dollars."

He handed her a ten and his business card with his room number scrawled on the back and told her to keep the change.

"If you change your mind, call me. I'll make it worth your while." With a wink, he left the cab.

She sighed. At least this guy was polite. Some of the guys who tried to pick her up were insulting and even got physical when she turned them down. She could take care of herself, but it became tedious.

The rain had stopped and she drove around for a while, then finally decided to stop for a coffee. She settled back in the cab and sipped her latte.

Her cell phone rang and she pushed the button on her console to accept the call via Bluetooth.

"Hey, Stevie," Jon, one of her best friends, said over the speaker.

"Hi, Jon."

"I heard what Hank did and I'm so sorry. That guy is a total jerk."

Yeah, he definitely was. She'd caught him fucking another woman in the bedroom they'd shared for almost a year. In the apartment they'd picked out together after being in a two-year relationship together. It had been one of the waitresses who worked in the diner he owned, which was less than a block from where they lived. Apparently, they'd gone up for a quickie, Hank assuming Stevie wouldn't be back before her shift.

"I heard you walked out on him. I'm so sorry."

"Yeah," she said, trying to erase the horrendous image burned into her brain.

"Where are you staying?" Jon asked.

"I don't know. I just threw a few things in a suitcase and walked out." The small case and a couple of garment bags were in the trunk now and she had no idea where she was going to sleep tonight.

"You know you can stay with us until you figure things out."

Her heart swelled at Jon's generous invitation, but she knew things had been tense between him and Derrick recently.

"It's okay, Jon. You two need to focus on your own relationship right now. You don't need me getting in the way."

"But neither one of us would want to see you out on the street."

She knew they'd work out their problems. She'd seen them do it before. They would hit a rough patch, then do what it took to get things back on track. The two men were truly in love. But she needed to give them the time and space to do that.

"I'm not crashing on your couch and that's final." She smiled. "Though I really appreciate the offer."

"Okay, but I want you to call us as soon as you know where you're staying," Jon said.

"Don't worry. I've got it covered." But Stevie knew that despite her words, Jon would worry about her.

"You don't have a passenger right now, do you?"

She grinned. As if she'd have let him keep talking about this if she had.

"No. It's just me."

"Well, at least now you know why your sex life dried up over the past few months. You thought it was because of the hours you kept, but now you know it's because Hank was getting some on the side."

The sex between her and Hank had been good—who was she kidding, it had been fabulous—and she'd mistaken that for love, but now she knew it was just chemistry. A chemistry that seemed to have faded for Hank, leaving her sexually frustrated with diminishing self-esteem.

She wished she could find something like what Jon and Derrick had. Someone who really cared about her. About how she felt and what she wanted.

"Now you can find some good-looking guy and get laid," Jon said. "That'll lift your spirits."

"You make it sound like a trip to the spa."

"Well, do that, too. But I highly recommend the man first."

Stevie heard the passenger door open.

"In fact," Jon continued, "I think you should just screw the next guy that gets into your cab."

"I've got to go. I have a fare," Stevie said hastily and hung up, hoping to hell her new passenger hadn't heard Jon's last remark.

She glanced in the mirror at the well-dressed man in

the backseat. He was strikingly handsome with thick, wavy, chestnut-brown hair, a square jaw and full lips . . . and stunning cobalt-blue eyes. He wore an expensive suit— Armani—that accentuated his broad shoulders and trim waist. The man clearly worked out regularly.

Her heart thumped as an electrical surge of attraction coursed through her. Even more than his exceptional physical good looks, there was a blatant masculine intensity . . . a mesmerizing aura of raw sexuality about him that made it hard for her to take her eyes off him.

"Good evening, sir. Where to?"

"I have two stops to make this evening, but first I need to ask you something." Then his gaze locked with hers in the mirror.

For some reason, that look—filled with calm authority and almost aggressive confidence—made her feel like an ill-behaved schoolgirl.

"And what is that, sir?"

"Does your boss often recommend that you cheat your customers?"

"Cheat?" Oh, damn, he meant Jon's comment about screwing her client. "Oh, no, sir, that's not what he meant, he . . ." Then her cheeks went cherry red. "It was just an inappropriate comment. And that wasn't my boss. He was a friend of mine, so please don't blame the cab company."

He continued to gaze at her, assessing, then finally, he nodded.

"First stop, the Hotel Maison."

"Of course, sir."

She turned on the meter and started the engine, then pulled away from the curb.

"So does your friend always suggest you sleep with your customers?" he asked.

Oh, God. Was this guy going to come on to her now?

"No. I've just had a bad breakup and he was trying to push me to move on."

"I'm sorry to hear that. Were you together long?"

The question startled her. The fact he was interested in making small talk at all, instead of just interacting with his phone, was a surprise, but to show an interest in her life . . .

"Two years," she answered.

Reid nodded. "Again, I'm sorry."

He didn't know why he was engaging with his driver. Usually, he'd use this time to catch up on e-mails and handle whatever business had come up. But tonight, he had no interest in business. It had been a rough week. A promising project in Philadelphia had fallen through and his trip here to New York to land a new, very high-profile contract had gotten off to a rocky start. He'd finally gotten in to see Raphael Allegro and they seemed to have hit it off, but Reid suspected he might have to stay in the city longer than he'd anticipated to continue building a sound relationship with the man. Raphael was the kind of businessman who only worked with people he had a good rapport with.

So Reid felt a connection with this woman, who was clearly having just as tough a week. In fact, Reid had received the same bad advice from one of the directors who reported to him. George had suggested Reid find some woman here and have a one-night stand to take the edge off the loneliness and stress of travel.

He glanced at the picture of the driver hanging over the back of the seat. Pretty, in an understated way. From what she was wearing tonight, she clearly dressed to downplay her looks, wearing a hat with the brim pulled down over her eyes and loose clothing—a smart move given her career—but in the photo he could see the high cheekbones, the full, sensual lips, and the spark of defiance in her sky-blue eyes. He didn't know what she was rebelling against, but he felt a kindred spirit in her. He'd been the rebel of his family, starting his own company at twenty-five rather than taking over one of the sub-companies in his father's vast empire. Reid's business was a huge success, with branches across North America and several facilities overseas.

He had this drive to keep growing the business. Bigger and bigger. Maybe it was a need to show his father that he could build something every bit as big and successful as his father had. But lately he was losing interest in that. It never stopped and it wasn't as fulfilling as it used to be. He just wasn't sure that's what he wanted in life.

He had women in his life—several in fact—all willing to do whatever he wanted. Whenever he wanted. But that wasn't enough.

He glanced at the woman in the mirror. She was prettier in real life than in her picture. What would it be like to be with her? What sounds would she make? Would she whimper? Talk dirty? At the moment of release, would she call out his name?

The more he thought about it, the more he longed to

know. It was crazy. He wasn't the type to pick up some random woman, especially a cabdriver.

But he *was* the type to try new things. And this woman was definitely something new and different.

"Pull over at the next Starbucks," he said.

She slowed the cab and pulled up in front of a shop with the iconic green sign.

"I'd like to go sit down and have a coffee. Join me and we can talk."

"Thank you for the offer, but I'll just wait here, or you can pay the fare and call another cab when you're done."

"No, I want to stick with you and it's silly for you to just sit out here."

"There's a rule that—"

"You're the type to follow rules to the letter, are you?" he asked with a raised eyebrow.

She frowned. "I didn't say that."

"Then come in." At her doubtful expression, he added, "I could use the company."

Finally, she nodded and got out of the cab, then followed him inside. He ordered them both a coffee and they sat by the window.

"So tell me. What happened with you and your boyfriend?"

She shrugged. "I caught him in bed with another woman."

"That's tough. Someone you knew?"

"Vaguely. She works as a waitress at the diner he runs. I assume its been going on for a few months."

He shook his head. He didn't understand why any man

would cheat on a relationship. He was the type that took charge. If he wasn't happy in a relationship, he ended it. Sneaking around and having an affair with another woman just seemed . . . lazy.

"I hope you don't let this hurt your self-esteem," he said. "It's not your fault that he wasn't man enough to end the relationship before moving on."

She sipped her coffee, schooling her face to appear nonchalant. "I'm not. The guy was just a jerk."

"True, but I can see it in your eyes. You're hurt that he wanted to move on at all. You feel that you weren't enough for him."

Her eyes narrowed and her fingers tightened around the cup. "Look, I don't need you analyzing me and my life. You don't know anything about me."

"True. But I can read people. And I'm just trying to be helpful."

She glared at him. "I don't need any help, thanks."

He smiled. She was feisty and independent. He liked that.

"Okay, let's drop the talk about relationships. How long have you been driving a cab?"

"For about five years." She sipped her coffee.

She was well spoken and seemed very bright. He wasn't sure why she was driving a cab, but maybe she had no choice. Maybe her family didn't have enough money to send her to college.

"Have you ever thought of doing something else? My company—"

"Stop right there," she said, leaning forward, her eyes

intense. "I like driving a cab. It's what I want to do. So don't judge me or try to help me out of my sad, impoverished life. I'm doing what I love. That's probably more than you can say."

He laughed. "Touché. As it turns out, though, I do love what I do. It has become a bit lackluster recently though. I could use something new to liven things up."

"Is that what this is all about?" she asked, her gaze cautious. "Asking me in for coffee? Talking to me like I'm a date? You want to screw the lady cabbie to add a little excitement to your life?"

"If I was pursuing you, it wouldn't be so I could *screw* you." He leaned in closer. "I would slowly and purposefully seduce you, then take you to heights of ecstasy far surpassing anything you have ever experienced before."

Rather than looking shocked, her eyebrow quirked up. "That would be more difficult than you think. Hank might have been a jerk, but he was the best lay I've ever had."

He grinned. "I'm sure I could meet the challenge."

Stevie couldn't believe her own words. What the hell was she doing? But this guy, he was so . . . so . . . damn, he was so gut-wrenchingly sexy her hormones were boiling over in a wild fit of primal desire.

She reached for her coffee, purposefully brushing her hand against his. Electrifying desire sparked between them. She picked up her cup, making a decision she knew she would probably regret later, but right now, she didn't care.

"All right." Then she stood up and turned toward the door.

He followed her to the cab and got in, then she pulled away from the curb in silence.

She passed his hotel and drove another couple of blocks, then pulled down a side street. It was a quiet, out-of-the-way place she would sometimes use to grab a nap if needed during a long shift. She had friends in the neighborhood that looked out for her. She opened the door and got out of the cab. Her handsome passenger followed.

"Aren't you going to come up to my hotel room?" he asked.

She walked toward him and rested her hand on his warm chest. A surge of adrenaline rushed through her.

"I think here will do fine."

"You don't like a comfortable bed?"

She smiled, loving the fact that she was keeping a man off balance for a change. She stroked up his chest, then along his jaw, the light dusting of whiskers sending tingles through her.

"I don't need a bed."

Then she cupped his cheeks and kissed him, feeling every bit in control.

Until his arms came around her and she felt herself crushed against his chest. He pulled off her hat and tossed it onto the roof of the cab. Her long blonde hair fell around her shoulders in waves. He drew back and smiled, running his fingers through the soft strands.

"That's much better."

Then she felt herself backed against the wall. He leaned against her, his cobalt-blue gaze locked on hers.

"If this is what you want, then that's fine with me," he murmured.

His hands glided up and down her body, sending tingles through her. He hadn't touched any intimate place on her body yet, other than their joining of lips, but she felt he'd taken ownership of her whole being.

Then his hand glided over her chest and he cupped her breast. The feel of his warm hand surrounding her, even through the layers of clothing, started a blaze within her. She could feel her nipples harden with need.

He kneaded her soft mound while his mouth took ownership of hers again. His tongue pushed between her lips and drove inside.

Oh, God, she was feeling out of her depth. She didn't know what she'd expected, but him being so comfortable and in control in this dark alley wasn't it.

His hand found its way under her jacket, then inside her shirt. He cupped her breast, just the lace of her bra a barrier between them now.

"You feel good," he murmured against her ear. Then he rocked his hips forward and she felt a thick bulge against her stomach.

A shock of awareness rippled through her. It hadn't really hit home what she was about to do until she felt his erection pushing against her. She was about to have sex— in a dark alleyway—with a total stranger.

She felt his fingers unfastening the button of her jeans. She sucked in a breath and grabbed his hands, then pushed them away.

Chapter Two

Reid drew his hands away. Had she lost her nerve?

Then she pulled down the zipper of her jeans and drew his hand back, then pressed it to her silky panties. Her eyes glowed with desire and anticipation.

He slid his hand over her mound, stroking over the silk. Then he pushed under the panties to find her delicate folds. He slid into them. Fuck, she was slick and wet. His fingers glided over her, the feel of her moisture driving him wild. His cock twitched, painfully confined in his pants.

Then she stroked him and he moaned. She squeezed, heating his blood, then she unzipped him and slipped inside. When her fingers surrounded him, he moaned again.

"That's right, sweetheart. Stroke me."

She glided her hand up and down. Her fingers, so delicate around him, sent need pulsing through him.

"In my room, I could do more to give you pleasure," he said, regretting not having taken control and commanded her to go back to the hotel and dragging her to a bed.

"I don't care," she said breathily. "I just want to feel you inside me."

With that, she pulled him from his pants and pressed his tip to her slickness. The feel of her moist folds against his hot cockhead made his blood boil.

She released him for a moment to push her jeans down below her hips. Then she pressed him against her again. He grasped his cock and aimed it, centering it at her core, then slowly pressed forward. She moaned softly as he pushed into her warm opening.

Her body welcomed him, opening around him. Hugging him snugly in the depths of her tight canal. He pushed deeper, entering her in a slow, steady stroke.

"Oh, God, yes," she murmured as he slid deeper.

"Do you like the feel of my cock inside you?" he asked.

She nodded, her gaze locked to his.

Was he kidding? Stevie sighed. It felt like heaven.

He was thicker and longer than Hank. The feel of his marble-hard cock gliding into her took her breath away. After several intense moments of his long erection pushing inside, he finally had her pressed hard to the brick wall, his groin tight against hers.

He just held her still like that for a few moments, their bodies joined, their heartbeats synchronized. Then he captured her lips, his tongue filling her mouth like his cock did below. He swept inside, totally possessing her. Her breathing grew erratic as her heart pounded faster in her chest.

"I like being inside you," he said once he released her mouth.

Then he began to move. His cock traveled the same path backward, dragging against her sensitive passage, triggering sparks and electrifying delight. Then he pushed forward. Deep and hard until she was pinned to the wall again.

"Tell me you like me fucking you."

"I like you fucking me." The words came out on a soft whimper.

He chuckled, then pulled back again. When he drove deep, she moaned softly. It felt so good being stretched by his thick, hard shaft.

"My name is Reid, by the way." His lips played along her neck. "And yours is Stefani."

"Call me Stevie," she whispered, barely able to talk at all with his big cock stroking her.

"Stevie." He nipped her earlobe. "When you come, baby, I want you to say my name. I want to be sure you know who it is who's taking you."

Then he drove in fast. She moaned, her muscles tightening around him.

"That's right, baby," he murmured. "Squeeze me tight."

He drove into her faster, his big cock possessing her fully. Pleasure swelled inside her, rising with each thrust of his body.

"Oh, God, that feels so good." She nuzzled his neck as he thrust again. She moaned against his skin.

He plunged deeper and faster, delight quivering through her. Then his finger brushed over her clit and she gasped as a flood of pleasure pumped through her, knocking her off balance. She clutched his shoulders as her head spun, twirling in a haze of bliss.

He drove in again and again and she moaned.

"Are you close?" he asked, his voice like velvet against her ear.

She nodded, poised on the precipice. His fingertip pulsed against her clit as he thrust faster, filling her like a jackhammer. She sucked in a breath, dizzy with delight, then it hit like a tsunami. Pleasure washing over her in pounding waves of bliss. She moaned, catapulting into ecstasy.

"That's right, baby. Who's making you come?"

"Reid," she murmured on the end of a moan.

Then he jerked against her, his thick cock deep in her body and she felt him erupt inside her. The feel of his hot liquid filling her drove her over the edge again. He kept rocking his hips against her, driving her pleasure on and on. Then he finally just held her tight, his body still holding her against the wall.

After a few moments, once their breathing had settled, he eased back. He gazed down at her, his cobalt blue eyes filled with warmth, and he kissed her. He drew his cock from her depths slowly, but continued to hold her.

"That was . . ." No matter what she said, it wouldn't do justice to what she'd just experienced. "Phenomenal."

His eyes twinkled. "Just think how much better it would have been if you'd let me take you to my room."

She laughed. "It couldn't be better than that."

His gaze locked with hers. "Try me."

As Stevie drove back to the Hotel Maison, the sight of the handsome man in her rearview mirror was a constant reminder of what she'd just done. She should be cursing herself and vowing never to do anything so stupid again . . . but she couldn't. In fact, she couldn't seem to wipe the satisfied smile from her face.

Was she really considering going to his room?

She glanced in the mirror again as he pulled his phone from his pocket and viewed it for a minute, then put it away again. The smile on his face seemed to fade.

"Is there anything wrong?" she asked as she pulled into the curved drive in front of Hotel Maison.

"I was serious that I want you in my bed."

She stopped in front of the doors, then turned and gazed at him, not sure what she'd say.

"But unfortunately," he continued, "I have an event I have to attend this evening. It had slipped my mind."

She raised an eyebrow. "It can't be that important if you forgot."

His lips compressed. "It's not important to me, but it is very important to my client, so that means it's a priority. But I'll make a quick appearance, spend an hour or so, then you'll come over afterward."

She raised an eyebrow at his presumptiveness.

He glanced at his watch. "But, damn, I have to find a companion for the event and I only have an hour."

"Are you asking me?" But she knew from his distracted gaze that he wasn't.

Fuck! What the hell had he been thinking?

"No, I may have to suffer through this boring party, but I wouldn't inflict it on you."

Her eyes flashed. "So what you're saying is that I'm not good enough to take to your snooty party? You know, I clean up real good."

He couldn't help but smile at the cute way her eyebrow arched and how her impeccable speech slipped away when she was trying to goad him.

"I'm sure you do, but I'll just go with a service tonight."

She nodded, her gaze chilling. "You can ask the concierge for Rita and he'll fix you up."

Devious witch.

He couldn't help grinning. "Actually, I think Charlene would be more appropriate."

The code word Rita would get him a medium-priced call girl who would not fit what he needed at all and would be an embarrassment at the party—which he was sure was Stevie's intent—whereas Charlene meant he wanted a high-class, very sexy woman in a designer gown. It would still lead to sex, if that's what he wanted. But he didn't.

All he could think of was getting Stevie up to his place and into his bed.

But he'd hurt her feelings and he hated that. He'd made her feel like less just because she drove a cab.

"But you know, I would rather spend the evening with you, so if you'll accept my apology, I would love for you to join me."

At her cool gaze, he took her hand. "I was an idiot. I really want you to go. There'll be great food and music. Maybe we can dance a little. Just say yes. You'll make a tedious evening so much more enjoyable."

* * *

As much as Stevie wanted to experience more phenomenal sex with Mr. Reid The-Billionaire-Guy—and she was sure if she went to the party with him, she would wind up in his bed afterward—the experience had shaken her. She couldn't believe she had been so reckless as to have sex with a passenger, no matter how gorgeous he was or how intensely he triggered her hormones.

And as if that wasn't enough, the experience itself had been . . . mind-shattering. She'd never experienced anything so gritty and clandestine. Having sex in a dark alleyway. With a billionaire stranger no less.

She had chosen that location specifically to keep him off balance, but he'd turned the tables and mastered the situation totally. She had felt possessed by him. Controlled.

And she'd *liked* it.

She sucked in a deep breath.

Too much.

But it had been a long time since she'd been to a lavish party and as much as she tried to convince herself she didn't miss it, she did.

And she couldn't think of a single reason strong enough to stop her from being with this sexy, irresistible man again.

"Okay, I'll go."

His broad smile and twinkling eyes sent need thrumming through her.

"Good. I'll be back in fifteen minutes."

He exited the cab and she watched him walk through the door the doorman held open for him. She got out and told the doorman her passenger wanted her to wait for him, then retrieved her makeup bag from the suitcase in the trunk. She applied her makeup using the rearview mirror.

A few minutes later, he strolled out the door, a large suitcase in tow. She got out of the cab and opened the trunk.

"Why do you have your luggage?" she asked as she reached for the bag to lift it in, but he ignored her and hefted the large bag up and into the spacious opening.

"I checked out this morning. The concierge was holding my bag while I went about my business today. I'm going to a new place after the party."

As he set his bag in the trunk, he eyed the small, red suitcase she'd quickly packed and the two garment bags she'd grabbed from her closet on the way out.

"It looks like one of your passengers forgot their bags," he commented.

"Oh, no. Those are mine."

He glanced her way as he closed the trunk. "Really? Are you going somewhere?"

She walked back to the driver's door and got into the cab. He settled into the backseat.

"No, I'm just . . . between places right now."

"So this breakup with your cheating ex happened today. I take it you have no place to stay tonight."

"I'll manage," she said as she started the engine.

A car honked behind them—another cab—and she eased the car forward.

"Where to, sir?" she asked.

If felt so strange, asking him the same question she asked any other fare, after they'd been intimate only minutes earlier. And she'd tagged on the word "sir" out of habit, but now it didn't feel like the polite salutation she usually used with passengers. For some reason, when she said it to him, tingles danced through her. She wasn't sure why.

He raised an eyebrow and a half smile curled his lips.

"First, we need to go somewhere to buy you an outfit to wear tonight. Then we'll head to the Barcelona Hotel."

He glanced at his watch. "We'll have to hurry, though. We're running late."

She turned left at the light. It would take twenty minutes to get to the event.

"No need to buy me a dress. I have something appropriate with me."

At the doubt in his eyes, her back stiffened. He was afraid she would embarrass him. The thought tempted her to throw on her black cotton camisole—the one with the lace on the neckline—and a black skirt and pretend she thought she was appropriately dressed. But the need to sparkle for him like a fine gem was more than she could resist.

"Where will you change?" he asked.

"Don't worry. I've got it covered."

She kept driving until they were only a few blocks from the Barcelona, deciding to keep him in suspense as long as possible, then she pulled over and parked in front of a Wendy's.

"I'll be five minutes."

She got out of the cab and grabbed one of the garment bags, then carried it into the restaurant.

Chapter Three

What the hell had he gotten himself into?

Sex with this intriguing, sexy cabbie had thrown Reid totally off balance. Something no woman had ever done to him. He wanted her in his bed . . . desperately . . . where he could explore her body at his leisure. But he had to impress his client tonight. Allegro was the type who wanted to spend social time together to ensure a good fit personality-wise. And Reid was certain that Allegro would not approve of Reid having a girlfriend who didn't fit his social standing.

A woman like the one who caught his eye leaving the restaurant.

Reid watched the stunning beauty walking to the sidewalk in her designer gown, the blue silk like shimmering water cascading over her shapely body. Her silver heels were glittering and sporting the iconic red soles of Louboutin. A necklace of diamonds with a marquis-cut sapphire pendant surrounded by more diamonds glittered around her neck.

Her blonde hair was coiled in a neat updo, with tiny tendrils cascading around her face.

What he couldn't figure out was why a woman dressed like that would be coming out of a fast-food place.

And walking toward the cab. Unless she thought the cab was available.

Then it hit him.

Fuck, that's Stevie.

She opened the driver's door and got into the cab. "Sorry I took so long."

"I . . . uh . . ."

She smiled, probably loving the fact she'd left him speechless.

"That's a very nice dress."

"Thank you. It's Givenchy." She raised an eyebrow. "Do you think it's appropriate for the party?"

"Of course, but . . . where did you get a dress like that? And the shoes and necklace?"

She shrugged. "You'd be amazed what people leave in a cab."

Stevie ignored the valet parking, not wanting to embarrass Reid that much and just parked in the underground parking. She had offered to drop him at the front door, but ever the gentleman, he insisted on accompanying her.

Or maybe he just didn't want people to think he met his date there.

They stepped into the ballroom, her hand on his elbow and the sight took her breath away.

Everything glittered. From the dimly lit crystal chandeliers and candle centerpieces, to the finely cut crystal stemware on the silver trays waiters carried around the room, to the glitter of sequins on the designer gowns and the sparkling flash of expensive jewels.

The place reeked of lavish elegance. Stevie loved it . . . and hated it at the same time.

A waiter offered her a glass of champagne from his tray and she sipped from the tall flute. Reid, also holding a glass of champagne, guided her across the room. Soft music lilted in the background.

"There's my client," he said as they walked toward a group of three couples chatting. "The tall man with the gray hair. His name is Raphael Allegro."

She recognized him instantly. His square jaw, high cheekbones, and full head of wavy gray-blue hair gave his face a classically handsome look, given character by his slightly crooked nose. His sharp blue eyes gleamed with intelligence and passion. His whole presence screamed sophistication and wealth.

Raphael Allegro was one of the best known fashion designers in the world, his creations sought after by the most wealthy and famous, from royalty to business tycoons to Hollywood stars.

No wonder Reid had been worried about who he brought to this function. If his date had shown up in anything less than a top designer gown, it would have put him to shame.

As they approached, Stevie leaned in toward Reid. "And so am I your steady gal or is it okay to admit that you just picked me up today in my cab?"

At her dead serious tone, his gaze shot to her face, then she smiled.

"Just follow my lead and we'll be fine," he said.

Raphael noticed Reid and smiled.

"Ah, Reid. So good to see you." Raphael shook Reid's hand heartily. Then he turned his attention to Stevie. "And who is this lovely young woman you have on your arm?"

His blue eyes twinkled and he oozed charm.

"This is Stefani Trivoli," Reid said. "And this is Raphael Allegro."

Raphael took her hand and held it firmly as his gaze locked on hers. "Please, call me Raphael."

"Thank you, Raphael," she said.

"Trivoli. I know this name. Have we met? You look very familiar."

"No, I haven't had the pleasure."

"Are you sure? Perhaps in Rome last summer? You were a buyer for one of the large retail chains here in the U.S.?"

Her muscles stiffened and she forced them to relax, hoping he wouldn't notice her tension. Clearly, he had met her cousin Suzanna. Stevie and Suzanna looked a lot alike, and although she hadn't kept in touch with Suzanna over the past several years, she knew that was exactly the type of role Suzanna would have pursued.

He examined her face closely. "Ah, perhaps not. Now that I have a closer look, I see you have a more radiant beauty than that other young woman. And your eyes are blue, not hazel like hers." He pressed his lips to the back of her hand, smiled, then finally released it. "But I would hazard a guess that you are family."

"No, I'm sure we're not," she lied. "But thank you for your kind words."

He smiled. "Of course. I speak only the truth."

Then he turned and introduced her to the others. His date, Francesca, a statuesque blonde, and the other four people. One of the men was a well-known Broadway actor and one woman was the head of a major cosmetics company.

"Stefani," Raphael said, "I need to speak with Reid about business, but my friends will keep you company and I promise not to keep him too long."

Reid glanced her way and she smiled. "Of course, Raphael. Take as much time as you need."

The next hour flew by as she chatted with Francesca about, of all things, *American Idol*. She was a huge fan and told Stevie she'd been devastated when they'd canceled it. She'd loved following each of the hopefuls and had rooted for them, even admitting to crying when her favorites were voted off.

One of the men asked her to dance and as soon as he guided her back to the group, another man drew her back to the floor for another dance. Then another after that.

She was in heaven. She loved to dance and these men were good-looking, charming, and sensational dancers, sweeping her around the floor, her full dress fluttering in the breeze.

The music slowed down and her partner drew her close. The music was soft and romantic and she felt a little odd slow dancing with this stranger, almost as if she was cheating on Reid.

Not that he'd really care. She was just a cabbie he'd picked up this afternoon and he'd asked her to do him a favor coming here. It's not like they were in a relationship.

Someone tapped her partner's shoulder and he stopped, gazing over his shoulder, clearly reluctant to let her go.

When she saw it was Reid, she couldn't help the smile that crept across her face.

"May I cut in?" Reid asked politely, but his voice made it clear that "no" was not an acceptable answer.

"Of course." Her partner thanked her, then moved away.

Reid took her hand and drew her close to his body, then began to move to the music. He held her snugly to him and her stomach quivered, as if caressed by butterfly wings. And her heart stammered.

She'd missed him.

Why did this man have such a profound effect on her?

"Do you feel like Cinderella at the ball?" he asked.

"Is my cab the pumpkin? If so, I've got news for you. It never changed into a fancy coach."

He tucked his finger under her chin. "No, but its driver turned into a beautiful princess."

She wanted to reply with a snappy comeback, but the warmth and admiration in his eyes made her breath catch. The thought that he found her beautiful . . . that he might consider her part of his world, even for just one evening . . . pleased her. And disturbed her at the same time.

"I think *you're* the one who's Cinderella here," she said, "and I'm the fairy godmother who made it possible for you to go to the ball."

"And I want to thank you for that," he murmured against her ear. "And for totally charming Raphael. I believe he's going to sign the deal. He said any man who could attract a poised, intelligent beauty like you was just the kind of man he wanted to do business with. He's also under the impression that you and I are deeply in love and totally devoted to each other."

She frowned. "Why would he think that?"

Reid's smile sent shimmering heat through her.

"He said it was something he saw in your eyes."

"And you encouraged that thinking, I take it?"

His lips turned up. "I didn't discourage it. But in fact, I did tell him it was a little early for those kinds of feelings. His answer was that those feelings are lying there in wait, ready for us to discover them. He's a romantic who fancies that he can read true love in people's eyes. I see no reason not to humor him."

"As long as you don't start believing it."

His eyebrow arched. "Isn't that usually the man's line?"

She tipped her head. "So you think as a woman I should be all, 'Oh, he's a billionaire. I want him to fall madly in love with me and shower me with gifts and take care of me'?"

He chuckled. "A lot of women would love that. Especially with things so difficult now. Since you drive a cab, you experience that directly."

She drew back and pressed her fingertip to his chest. "Look, I told you. I love driving a cab. I wouldn't trade my life for all the lavish parties or designer dresses in the world. I work hard for my money and I feel good about that. And

I take care of myself." She emphasized each sentence with a poke to his chest.

He grinned as he scooped up her hand.

"Please, sweetheart. People will think we're having a lover's spat."

He drew her close and she allowed him to guide her around the dance floor again.

"Raphael and Francesca are staring at us with concern," he murmured against her ear, sending tingles down her neck. "I don't want them to think there's trouble in paradise."

With that he kissed her. Just a light brush of lips, sending her heartbeat racing. Then he deepened the kiss, his tongue sweeping gently inside her mouth. Her arms slid over his broad shoulders and around his neck as every part of her melted.

When the song ended, and other couples brushed past them, she realized she was standing in the middle of the dance floor in Reid's arms, the two of them locked in a passionate kiss. As their lips parted, her eyes widened. She'd lost all sense of time and place.

She took a step back and then turned. He kept a firm hold on her hand as she walked from the floor.

"I was worried for a moment," Allegro said as they returned. "But I see that Reid was able to overcome his jealousy at seeing you with another man and you two have now made up. Bravo."

"Of course," Reid said, sliding his arm around her and drawing her close to his side. "It was nothing. Isn't that right, sweetheart?"

"That's right. Reid just gets a bit possessive at times and I need to straighten him out."

As they fell into conversation, a face in the crowd caught Stevie's eye. She focused on the tall man across the room and . . .

Her heart began to pound so loudly she was sure the others could hear it.

It was Sean Benedict.

Her heart ached at the memory of him asking for his engagement ring back, calmly explaining that it was for the best. Totally expecting her to understand.

That he could so casually tear out her heart and toss it aside, just to keep their parents happy, had wounded her deeply. She had loved him with all her heart and . . .

Sean's gaze locked on her and recognition flickered in his eyes. Then a look of determination as he started across the room toward her.

Chapter Four

Stevie's fingers wrapped around Reid's, tightening so sharply he turned to her, concern in his eyes.

"I'm sorry to interrupt," she murmured, "but I have to go."

"Is there something wrong?" Francesca asked.

As she saw Sean moving closer her stomach clenched. She had to get out of here.

"I'm sorry to be rude, but it's a private matter. Reid, please stay," she said. "I'll see myself home." Then she turned and hurried through the crowd.

When she got to the atrium, rather than heading to the elevator, she followed the signs to the stairway, dodging around the corner just as Sean stepped out the doors and glanced around, searching for her.

Once she reached the lobby, she quickly strolled to the elevator that would take her to the lower parking levels. Hopefully, Sean would be looking for her at the front entrance, assuming she'd be getting her car from the valet parking, or being picked up by a limousine.

She walked to her cab, her heels clacking on the pavement. Once in the cab, she kicked off her Louboutins and shimmied into her jeans. She glanced around to ensure no one was about and she tugged her dress over her head. She tossed the shimmering fabric on the front passenger seat and grabbed her tank top.

The back door opened and she sucked in a breath as she glanced around.

"It's not every day you see a half-naked cabdriver in a parking garage."

She quickly pulled on her top, intensely conscious of his heated gaze on her half-naked breasts. She pulled on her flannel shirt and buttoned it up, then tucked her hair inside her hat and shrugged on her jacket.

"Why did you run out on me?"

"I had to leave. Can we just leave it at that?"

She pulled on her sneakers and tied them.

"Of course."

She compressed her lips. His understanding made her feel worse.

"I'm sorry. I meant it when I said you should stay. I didn't want to put you in a difficult position."

"It's really fine."

She glanced at him and noticed his grin. "Why are you smiling?"

"Well, it's just that Cinderella is the one who runs out before the stroke of midnight, so maybe you need to reassess your role."

"You're a funny man, Mr. . . . uh . . . I don't even know your last name."

He offered his hand for a handshake. She complied and he shook firmly.

"I'm Reid Jacobs. Otherwise known as Prince Charming."

She nodded with a wry smile. "All right, Mr. Charming. Where to now?"

Stevie drove in silence for a bit, heading to the address he'd given her. She was all too aware that once they arrived at their destination, Reid would ask her to come up to his room and then . . .

Her hormones fluttered as heat flashed through her.

She coughed. "So what is this place we're going to now?"

"It's my new penthouse apartment."

"You're moving to New York?"

"No. I do a lot of business here and with this new project with Raphael, the time I spend here will be increasing. I felt I should have somewhere comfortable to stay."

"So you're just moving in." Images of him leading her into an apartment devoid of furniture, towels . . . toilet paper . . . washed through her brain. Did he intend to take her against the wall again, then they'd sleep together on the floor?

Of course, against the wall wasn't a bad thing. The memory of his thick cock gliding into her as her back pressed against the hard brick wall caught her breath.

He chuckled. "Don't worry. It's fully furnished and has all the amenities. We can even have the doorman bring up dinner if we want."

The traffic thinned as she left the center core and soon they approached the neighborhood where his new apartment was. She turned off the main street and soon approached his building.

"Turn into the underground garage. My spot is seventeen eighty-two."

"I can drop you at the front door."

"Then you can't get into the garage. No, we'll go up together."

She followed the signs to the parking garage and pulled up to the entry, beside the post with the card-reader. He handed her a keycard that she slid into the slot. The garage door opened and she drove down the ramp.

After a couple of rounds, she found 1782, which was conveniently located right by the elevator. She opened the trunk and he hefted his suitcase out, then pulled hers out, too. She tucked her dress and shoes back into the garment bag and he draped both garment bags over his suitcase.

"You know, I haven't paid you for the cab ride yet," he pointed out.

"I turned off the meter at the Hotel Maison," she said.

"You didn't have to do that."

"I stopped being just your cabdriver once we had sex in the alleyway."

"Of course. But let me pay you for the whole ride. I don't mind and I know you have to cover your gas and expenses."

She gritted her teeth. "The reading on the meter is twenty-eight dollars." Unfortunately, she hadn't turned off the meter when they'd stopped for their illicit tryst in the alleyway, but she couldn't erase it from the meter, so there it was.

"Why don't I just settle up later?"

She lifted her eyebrow. "I'd be much more comfortable handling it now."

He smiled as he pulled his wallet from his pocket. "Surely you don't think I'll stiff you for the fare. After all, you know where I live."

"I'm not going up to your apartment, having sex, *then* have you pay me."

He nodded. "Fair enough. But I would at least like to pay you enough to cover the rest of your shift, which I assume you ended early to join me."

"I'm not taking your money."

He handed her a hundred.

"I mean, after this." She reached into her pocket and pulled out some bills.

He laughed. "Keep the change."

She shook her head. "That's way too big a tip."

"I'm a big tipper." He closed her hand around the hundred. "Just take it and don't argue."

At the brush of his fingers, awareness flared through her, stealing her retort. She pocketed the money and locked up the cab.

Reid led the delightful young woman named Stevie onto the elevator, then slipped in his keycard. He noticed her fingers tightly gripping the handle of her suitcase. She was nervous and probably a little intimidated. She'd handled the party with poise and grace, but how would she react to his posh and luxurious penthouse?

Most people who weren't used to it were uncomfortable with his lifestyle and surroundings, but he wanted to find a way to make her feel at ease.

She was very proud, unwilling to take the money he offered to end her shift early. He knew most cabdrivers went into a great deal of debt to buy their cab medallion, or they paid a lot per shift to drive for a company. She could probably ill afford to lose that income.

He wouldn't push the money on her—he didn't want her to feel like a prostitute—but he wished he could find a way to ensure she didn't come out at a loss.

The elevator door opened on the foyer of his penthouse. A lush potted plant sat beside a padded leather bench and beside that a carved wooden end table with a lamp that had a sensor triggering it to turn on when it was dark and the elevator arrived.

"May I take your coat?" he asked, but she was already shrugging out of it.

"I've got it, thanks." She opened the mirrored closet door and hung up her jacket.

He watched her remove her hat and unfasten the clip holding her hair up, letting those lovely long tresses spill around her shoulders. She tossed the hat onto the shelf in the closet, then sat on the bench and untied her blue-and-white sneakers and slipped them off.

He hung up his own coat and shed his shoes, then pulled both their suitcases toward the living room. She caught up to him and took the handle of her suitcase from his hand. He led her through the open concept living/dining area and past the gourmet kitchen.

"Nice place," she said as they entered the hallway to the private living space.

She seemed impressed, but not in awe as he'd feared. In fact, she didn't seem at all intimidated by the surroundings.

They passed several doorways in the hallway as they walked to the room on the end. His bedroom.

He opened the door and stepped inside. Here she paused, looking a little intimidated as she gazed at the king-sized bed in the center of the room, the sitting area by the fireplace beyond, and the floor-to-ceiling windows offering a stunning view of the panorama below, including the lake glittering in the moonlight.

He took her hand and drew her into the room, then took the handle of her suitcase from her and rolled it and his to one side.

"Nice view," she said as he led her to the couch.

He flicked a switch and the gas fireplace blazed to life.

"It's one of the reasons I picked this place."

"Good choice." She sat on the couch, looking prim and proper practically perched on the edge, her knees tight together, her hands folded on her thighs.

"You don't have to look so terrified. We've already had sex and I think you enjoyed it."

She gazed up at him, her lips pursed. "Yes, of course. I'm sorry, this is all just so strange. I don't usually have sex with my fares. And I certainly don't go home with them."

He smiled. "I'm glad you broke that rule for me. Would

you like something to drink? I'm sure there's some wine in the kitchen."

"Wine would be nice. Thanks."

Once in the kitchen, he opened the wine fridge and actually found a couple of bottles of champagne. There was even one bottle already in the chiller.

He returned to the bedroom with two flutes and the chilled champagne bottle. He set them on the table and sat down beside her, then popped the cork and filled the glasses.

He lifted his glass. "To new and exciting possibilities."

She clinked with his, looking a bit doubtful.

When he'd brought her here, he'd planned to give her a taste of his dominant style, but he was having second thoughts. She was feisty, but a bit fragile right now, having been ousted from her home and relationship only hours ago.

She sipped her champagne, soon consuming half the glass. He settled back and enjoyed the bubbly liquid sluicing down his throat as he watched her. Her hair—long blonde tresses that he remembered felt soft and silky in his fingers—gleamed in the light of the fire.

He wished he could hurry her out of those clothes. The jeans and loose shirt did nothing to show off her body like the dress had. She had round, full breasts he longed to see. And feel again.

She finished her glass of champagne and he refilled it.

"This is nice," she said and took another sip. "It was a good year."

"You know champagne?" he asked.

"A little. My dad enjoyed wine."

Reid wondered how much, hoping she hadn't been

raised by an alcoholic, possibly abusive father. But he was jumping to conclusions. For some reason, he felt very protective of Stevie.

She eyed him watching her, then tossed back the second glass.

"Are you going to make a move, or are you waiting for me?" she asked, her glittering blue-eyed gaze locked on his.

"I didn't want to rush you."

"Thanks, but I'm good. I just figured you're more experienced at this than I am."

He grinned. "You think I bring lady taxicab drivers back to my place all the time?"

"Maybe not, but I think you're experienced with the ladies. Go ahead and dazzle me."

He laughed outright.

Oh, God, the champagne had definitely gone right to her head. Stevie wished she could pull back the words, but they were out now and there was nothing to be done about it. She blinked as she realized he was leaning in toward her, his full lips still turned up in a grin.

His arms slid around her. Her body started to tingle as she found herself pressed to his broad chest, then his lips found hers and the tingles turned to sparks. His tongue brushed her lips and she opened, allowing him in. He pushed forward, then swept around her mouth, claiming it all. She snuggled her tongue against his then rode the pulsing wave as he guided her, then drew her back to his mouth, which was cool and tasted of champagne.

His hand glided up her back, sending delightful shivers along her spine, then slid to her neck. He swept her hair over her shoulder, then his fingertips brushed lightly over her cheek. She couldn't help murmuring in appreciation at the tender, intimate gesture.

Finally, he drew back and gazed at her. His riveting blue eyes glittered in the firelight, like sparks flaring from a campfire.

"So, are you dazzled?" he asked. His lips brushed hers lightly again as he stroked her cheek.

She nodded, unable to find words.

He smiled, dazzling her even more.

Finally, she drew in enough air to be able to talk.

"You and I are an odd pair . . . you in your tailored tuxedo, me in jeans and a work shirt."

"There's an easy fix to that." He unfastened the button on his jacket and dropped it from his shoulders, then tossed it onto the nearby easy chair.

She immediately unfastened the buttons of her shirt, a little unnerved by his solemn stare as he watched her undo the garment. She shed the shirt, but still wore her tank top underneath. His gaze lingered on the swell of her breasts barely visible in the scoop neckline. She sucked in a breath and reached for the hem, then pulled it over her head, leaving her full breasts—covered only by the white lace of her bra—exposed.

She wished she'd been wearing sexy black lingerie. Or red with black trim. Anything sexier than virginal white. But she hadn't thrown any of her fancier lingerie in her suitcase when she fled from the apartment this afternoon. From the look of his heated gaze, however, he didn't seem to mind.

She bit her lip as she watched him unfasten his shirt buttons, slowly revealing the sculpted chest beneath. She longed to reach out and stroke the smooth flesh. He dropped the shirt from his shoulders and tossed it aside.

Why was she holding back?

She rested her hand on his chest, the warm skin firm under her fingers. She stroked, feeling solid muscle beneath. The man was no chair dweller. Clearly, he worked out.

Her fingers glided over his six-pack abs.

A lot.

He forked his fingers through her hair and drew her in for another kiss. The light brush of his lips reignited the sparks within her.

"If you get to touch, then so should I," he murmured against her temple.

She gazed up at him and simply nodded. His hands rested on her shoulders, then slowly glided down her chest. They covered her breasts, cupping them in his palms. Then his hands slid under them, his fingers curling around her mounds, his thumbs stroking over her hardening, now aching nipples. His gaze was locked on his thumbs as he teased her tight nubs through the lace.

"I'm going to take off your bra now," he warned, then quickly released the hooks and peeled away the garment.

Cool air washed over her nipples and they thrust forward even more. Or was it because of his rapt attention?

He stared at her breasts in awe, making her feel special and . . . beautiful.

"Do you know how sexy you look wearing just a neck-lace?"

"Oh." She reached around her neck and unfastened it, then drew it carefully from her neck and set it on the end table beside the couch.

He simply chuckled, then leaned down and she felt his breath wash over her nub, then the moist feel of his lips. When he covered her aureole and sucked, she let out a small gasp, holding his head tight to her bosom. He suckled and licked, then he switched to her other breast.

She felt his fingers work at the button on her jeans, then it released. The raspy sound of the zipper gliding down interrupted her soft moan at the tingles of pleasure as he continued to suckle.

He stood up and shed his pants, then dropped his boxers to the floor. Her eyes widened at the sight of the biggest, thickest cock she'd ever seen. She couldn't help herself. She reached for it and wrapped her hand around it. It was so thick she couldn't get her fingers all the way around.

She stroked, watching the purple head leak clear liquid. She wanted to taste it . . . desperately . . . so she leaned forward and licked him. His hand cupped her head and he stroked her hair back as she opened her lips around him and took the corona inside. She had to stretch around it and, once inside, it filled her mouth.

"Oh, baby, that feels so fine."

She surged forward, taking him a little deeper, but to

get that monster cock down her throat would take some practice, so she bobbed up and down in small strokes for now.

"I truly love what you're doing . . ." The shudder in his voice convinced her of the truth of his words. "But I had other things in mind right now."

She drew back and gazed up at him. He sat down and tucked his finger under her chin and tipped it up. He kissed her, his lips moving on hers with lingering passion before he released them again.

"First, I want to see you."

Chapter Five

Stevie stood up and pushed her jeans past her hips, then let them drop to the floor. Now all she wore were her small, white panties. She tucked her thumbs under the elastic to push them down, too, but he covered her hands.

"Here, let me."

His fingers dipped under the elastic at her hips, then slowly he eased the panties downward, his gaze locked on the V in front. As the fabric lowered, his eyes darkened. The panties glided down her hips, exposing her intimate petals.

He pushed the garment to the floor, his gaze never leaving her intimate flesh, and she stepped out of them. He stroked his fingers over her mound, then into the folds. She was so wet he glided over them easily.

His gaze returned to hers and a slow smile spread across his face. He cupped her hips and turned her around, then guided her to sit beside him. He slipped to his knees in front of her and pressed her thighs wide. As he leaned toward her, she quivered inside. She hadn't had a man's mouth on her there in a very long time. Hank always brought her to climax, but only when he was inside her. And that was so much more than she'd had with any other man. Hank was the first man to make her come. That's why she'd feared losing him more than any other reason, she realized now. Because she didn't want to go back.

But this man had already given her one mega-sized orgasm just by fucking her for two minutes against a brick wall.

What would it be like when he paid even more attention to her?

His mouth found her folds and she arched at the feel of his tongue gliding over her.

He opened her petals with his thumbs, then she felt his tongue wiggle on her clit.

"Oh, God!" It felt sensational.

He teased her clit, driving her tingling flesh wild, then he eased back and licked her slit. His fingers glided along her folds, then she felt one slip inside her. He stroked her channel walls gently, sending thrumming need through her. Then another finger slipped inside and his tongue found her clit again. He stroked with his fingers, his tongue flickering over her bundle of nerves. She gasped, pleasure pummeling every part of her.

"Oh, oh, oh!" She clung to his head, her fingers tangling in his short, dark hair.

Then it happened. A surge of pleasure so pure and blissful, she wailed out loud. She arched against him, releasing the sound like a siren, a part of her worried he would think her a freak.

She'd never let loose like this before. Chad, her first

lover, had been quite adamant that a lady did not make noise like a tramp. And Hank had seemed to want her utterances to be kept to a minimum, too.

But with this man, she just couldn't help herself.

He tweaked her clit again and her wail peaked, then she rode the wave down as he licked her gently. He lifted his head, watching her panting against the back of the couch.

"I'm sorry . . . I . . . didn't mean to be so loud."

He laughed, his eyes flickering with delight. "Don't apologize. I loved hearing you enjoy yourself."

"You did?"

He settled beside her. "Of course." He smiled. "And I loved tasting you." He picked up his champagne and took a sip. "You taste far better than this champagne."

Given that the bottle he'd brought out was Perrier-Jouet 2007 Belle Epoque, adorned with the distinctive Art Nouveau white floral design—one of the most expensive and delicious champagnes in the world—she was truly flattered.

He took another sip, then settled between her knees again.

Her eyes widened. Was he going to do it again?

He pressed his mouth to her folds, then she felt his cold tongue rasp over her. Then a delightful sensation as he released cold, bubbly champagne in a gush into her opening, then lapped it out again.

He sat beside her again with a smile. "Did you like that?"

"I did. It was . . . different."

"Then I'll be sure to do it again sometime."

He went to take another sip of his wine, but she reached

for the glass and brought it to her own lips, filling her mouth with the cold liquid. She dropped between his knees and wrapped her hand around his thick shaft, then drew his cockhead into her mouth, proud of herself when she didn't lose a drop.

She pulsed her mouth around him, swirling the bubbly liquid against his flesh. His hand cupped her head and she could see the delighted smile on his face. Then she swallowed and his eyes flared.

"Oh, God, do that again."

She started to slide off his cockhead, but his hand drew her back before she released him.

"No, I mean when you swallowed."

She swallowed again and he groaned.

"Fuck, baby, that feels sensational."

She suckled his cockhead, then glided deeper on him. When she drew back, she swallowed once again and he moaned.

God, she loved giving him so much pleasure. It made her feel powerful and . . . wickedly sexy.

She tucked her hands under his balls and fondled them gently as she glided forward on his cock, allowing it deeper into her throat. She bobbed a few more times, relaxing her throat, then drew him deeper still. She drew back and swallowed again, to his groan, then began to pump him in earnest, her hand squeezing and following her mouth as she bobbed up and down.

"Oh, baby, yeah. That is fucking amazing."

She knew he was close as his balls tightened.

"Stop."

At his commanding tone, she stopped without even thinking.

He drew her from the floor, pulling her onto his lap, then his lips found hers. He kissed her with passion, his tongue gliding into her mouth in a sweeping caress. She suckled his tongue, to his groans.

He drew back. "I want to be inside you again." Then he lifted her in his arms and carried her to the bed.

The feel of the sheet—fine Egyptian cotton, to be sure—was silky-smooth against her skin. The bed had been turned down and he pushed away the rest of the covers, leaving the bed as naked as they were. Then he knelt and positioned himself over her, his knees on either side of her thighs. His thick cock bobbed as he moved, then he lowered himself and she felt the heavy shaft rest on her stomach. But rather than drive it into her right away—like Hank would have done—he kissed her. His legs were on either side of hers, his big body hovering over her, his cock ready to burst . . . but he kissed her slowly . . . thoroughly stroking her hair from her face in a gesture so tender it almost brought tears to her eyes.

"You are a delight I intend to enjoy as thoroughly and as often as I can."

The words disturbed her on some level, but the blazing light of desire in his eyes, and the feel of his masculine presence imbuing her with rampant need, overwhelmed her so thoroughly nothing else mattered.

Impatient to feel him inside her, she wrapped her hand around his cock and pulled it to her. He chuckled and pressed it to her opening, then glided forward.

Slowly.

Easing in a little at a time.

"Oh, God," she cried, wanting him deeper. Wanting his whole cock embedded all the way inside her. "Please."

He leaned down and murmured against her ear, "Please what, baby?"

"Please . . . push . . . all the way . . . in." The words came out in short pants.

But still he eased forward in a slow, purposeful manner. Stretching her a little at a time.

"I love that you're desperate for me." He nipped her ear, sending an explosion of tingles dancing along her neck. "What would you do if I pulled out and made you beg for more?"

"No, please." She almost squealed as he started to draw back.

He laughed aloud, the joyful sound filling the room. He eased forward a little.

She clutched his shoulders. "Oh, please, fill me."

He drew back again, pulling almost to the point of slipping free, then stayed there . . . poised. She couldn't understand how he could do this. He'd been close to erupting when he'd pulled free of her mouth. He obviously had a great deal of restraint.

"Call me sir," he said.

"Sir?"

He smiled. "Like you did in the cab."

She stared at him, uncertain.

"Tell me what you want, and call me sir when you do it."

"I . . . want you to push inside me . . . sir."

This was embarrassing. She wasn't used to talking during sex, and certainly not making her needs known.

He nudged in a little deeper. She squeezed around him, trying to pull him farther in.

"Tell me more."

She bit her lip. This was obviously a turn-on for him, so she would try.

"I . . . want you all the way inside me."

He nodded, encouraging.

"Pumping into me."

"Yeah?"

"I want you to fuck me. Fast and hard."

"This is all very nice and I'm loving it, but you're forgetting something."

"I am?"

He grinned. "Sir."

"Oh, yes. Sir. Please, sir, I want you to fuck me. Fast and—ohhhh!" She gasped as he drove deep into her.

"Oh, God." Tears welled from her eyes at the sheer pleasure of him filling her so full.

He drew back and glided deep again.

"Tell me you like that."

"I like that," she said in a quivery voice. At the rise of his eyebrow, she quickly added, "Sir."

He chuckled, then drove into her again.

"Oh, sir. Oh, yes." It was like a cork had been removed and all the sounds she'd stifled over the years came bubbling out.

He thrust again and again.

"Oh, please, sir. Fuck me hard."

He pumped deep and groaned.

"Remember . . . I told you . . ." he said between thrusts, "to call my name . . . when you come?"

She nodded, her senses quivering with pleasure.

He nuzzled her ear. "Instead . . . call me master . . . as you come."

A small part of her wanted to protest, but the whole rest of her shouted it down with resounding enthusiasm.

He drove into her, his thick shaft gliding deep and hard. Her whole body quivered with pleasure and she felt light-headed.

"I'm so close, baby," he murmured against her ear.

She sucked in air, blissful sensations shimmering through her core. "I . . ." She gasped as he drove deep. "I'm going to . . ." Pleasure swamped her senses. It rose like a geyser, thrilling her senses. Leaving her gasping.

"Oh, master, you're . . ." She clung to him, her head spinning. "Making. Me. Ohhhhhh." She gasped. "Come!" The final word lingered on a long moan.

He groaned and drove deep and hard, pinning her to the bed. He erupted inside her, the feel of his liquid heat surging her orgasm to a new peak. She clung to him as he started pumping again, riding her with deep thrusts, driving her wails higher and higher.

The pleasure went on and on, his cock stroking her through a continuous barrage of unrelenting bliss. Were these multiple orgasms? Or one incredibly long, sensational O? She didn't know . . . or care. She just knew she'd never experienced anything like it in her life.

Her hands hooked around his neck as it waned, but still didn't fade.

"Oh, master, I'm still coming." Her tremulous voice was barely audible and she could feel tears streaming from her eyes.

His lips brushed her cheeks, plucking up the droplets as he continued to fill her with his thick shaft. Minutes or hours passed, she didn't know, but she lost herself in the maelstrom of ecstasy.

Finally, she found herself lying still, his body still above hers, as they both gasped for air. He brushed his lips over her temple, then rolled to his side. She drew in one more deep breath, then turned her head to face him.

"Wow! When you make a promise, you really come through."

He leaned in and kissed her again, his blue eyes filled with warmth.

"Always."

Stevie woke up ensconced in the warmth of a man's arms. Big, strong arms.

His whisker-roughened cheek rested against her temple, his breathing causing tendrils of her hair to flutter around her face.

Reid Jacobs. Gorgeous beyond belief, and with a sexual prowess that literally took her breath away.

She could get used to this—waking up in this man's arms. Better yet, going to sleep in his arms, after a rousing, sensational helping of what he'd served last night.

But even if that were possible, given the man lived in a different city, she wasn't ready for a rebound relationship. And Mr. Reid Jacobs was exactly the wrong kind of man for her.

Drop that thought, Stevie. Even if the man lived in this city full-time, she did *not* want to get involved with him. Mr. Reid Jacobs was the last man on earth she'd want to fall for.

Even though what she'd felt in his arms was more compelling than anything she'd ever experienced with a man before. They'd connected on a deeper level.

While with him, she'd felt she was a truer version of herself. She'd never realized how closed off she'd been with other men. Right down to holding back the sounds of her pleasure.

But with Reid . . . oh, God, she'd let loose like she never had before. And he'd told her he loved it. With other men, she'd felt the need to hide, but with him . . . she could just be herself.

It was just too bad he was from a world she wanted to avoid.

There was nothing wrong with having a one-night stand with a billionaire. As long as she was smart enough to walk away afterward. She already knew firsthand that that wasn't a life she wanted to have anything to do with.

And Prince Charming here had some kind of Christian Grey, dominance stuff going on. That seemed a little kinky.

But memories of calling him sir—and not in the same way she called her fares—sent tremors through her. He'd even insisted she call him master. The very thought physically aroused her. She could feel a rush of heat bloom between her thighs.

God, the idea of being dominated by him actually turns me on.

She realized that was another way he was good for her. He was helping her discover new things about herself. She never thought she'd enjoy calling a man master and letting him take control. But with Reid . . .

A musical chiming sound filled the room. He murmured, his arm tightening around her, then he rolled away. The sound stopped.

Then he rolled against her again and kissed the back of her neck, sending delightful quivers down her spine.

"Good morning," he murmured in a sleep roughened voice. "Sleep well?"

"Yes, thanks. And you?"

God, she sounded so stilted, but he just chuckled deep in his chest and gathered her closer.

"With a soft, sweet body like yours pressed against me all night? Oh, yeah."

He drew her back until she was lying flat on the bed and captured her lips.

"But all I kept thinking about was how I wanted to be deep inside you again."

His face so close to hers . . . his eyes so full of heat . . . made her feel deeply desired. Her insides stirred, longing for the same thing.

He kissed her again, his lips against hers making her melt inside.

Then he drew away.

"Unfortunately, I have to get going. I have to leave in a half hour."

"Are you flying home today?"

Disappointment washed through her and she realized she wanted to spend more time with him. To experience his potent sexuality again. God, the man was addictive.

But of course, now that he'd gotten what he wanted—sex and her help to win his client—there was no reason he'd want to keep being around her. A busy, wealthy man like him didn't need to keep the likes of her around. If he wanted a woman to warm his bed there were any number of Ritas or Charlenes available. Or for someone like Reid Jacobs, he could just whistle and women would fall at his feet.

His comment that he wanted her again was him simply being charming.

"No, I'll be in town a while longer, but I have meetings today. But relax," he said. "You can stay as long as you like. When does your shift start today?"

"Usually in the afternoon, but I'll drive you to your meeting."

"It's all right. I can call a cab."

She raised an eyebrow. "*I'm* a cabdriver, remember?"

She pushed back the covers and got out of bed, then suddenly felt self-conscious standing there totally naked. She grabbed her shirt from the floor.

With a grin, he grabbed her hand and tugged her to the bed again, then sat up and kissed her.

"I hate to argue with a beautiful, naked woman, but there are other cabdrivers, and I insist that you relax here until you have to go to work."

Then he got up and led her to the bathroom, right into the shower with him.

After an exhilarating ten minutes of scrubbing each other's body to gleaming cleanliness, she stared at herself in the mirror, dazed. She wanted him so badly right now, she could barely stand it. Her whole body ached for him.

But there was no time.

"What time is your meeting?" she asked.

"Eleven forty," he said as he stared at his reflection in the mirror behind her, combing his hair.

"Well, at this time of day, any cabdriver worth his salt can get you anywhere in the city in less than twenty minutes. That means that . . ."

His lips turned up in a sexy smile and he tossed the comb onto the counter. His hand glided along her shoulder, then untucked the towel wrapped around her body.

"I know exactly what that means," he said as the towel fell to the floor.

Stevie, wrapped in a towel again, walked him to the door. He kissed her soundly, then smiled as he stroked tendrils of hair from her face.

"I'd like you to come back here after your shift."

"You would?"

What she'd meant to say was that it wasn't a good idea. That they really had nothing in common and they should just leave it at a one-night stand. But something about this man had dug into her heart and settled there, making it ache at the thought of walking away from him. She'd never felt so close to a man before.

"Yes, very much."

Her heart pounded and the thought of spending another sensational night in Mr. Reid Jacobs' arms was too much for her to resist.

"It'll be late."

He smiled. "I'd wait an eternity."

God, the man was just so frigging charming.

Then his lips found hers and all thought melted away.

He pulled a card from his pocket and handed it to her. It wasn't a business card, like she'd expected. It was a keycard.

"Why are you giving me this?" she asked.

"It gives you access to the various facilities in the building if you'd like to use them. Like the pool, weight room, hot tub, et cetera. If you want something more extensive than the equipment I have here, of course."

She couldn't help grinning at the thought that the *equipment* she liked best, he was taking with him.

"And here's my business card, in case you need to get in touch with me." He handed her a soft gray card this time.

Then he leaned forward and kissed her, a light, sweet brush of lips. Then he went out the door, closing it behind him.

Stevie enjoyed the stunning view of the city through the large window as she worked out on the recumbent exercise cycle. Reid had a nice setup here. He had a whole mini gym in one corner of the vast apartment, with an elliptical machine and weights in addition to the cycle. There was even a half-bathroom with a shower only steps away.

Her cool-down period ended and she stood up, using the small towel she'd draped over the handlebar to wipe the sweat from her forehead. She opened the door to the bathroom and stepped inside. The glass-and-tile shower stall was spacious, with a selection of bath towels on a shelving unit.

After her shower, she stepped out of the stall and dried her hair, then wrapped a plush towel around her body. She ran a comb through her long, blonde hair. Exhilarated from the endorphin rush, she opened the door, feeling ready to face anything today.

"Who the hell are you?"

Chapter Six

Stevie's gaze shot to the source of the deep, masculine voice. There in the center of the room stood a man in tight jeans and black T-shirt, a leather jacket slung over his shoulder and a leather duffel bag by his feet. His right arm was inked with a thorny vine spiraling up from his wrist to his bulging biceps. His other arm had a scaly serpent—or maybe it was the body of a dragon—disappearing under the short sleeve. His face was angular with a square jaw tufted with coarse stubble, and his dark brown, wavy hair was tousled, as if he'd just pulled off a helmet.

She gripped the towel, ensuring it was secure.

"Who are you?" she countered.

He looked like a tough biker and she shivered at the sense of danger that emanated from him. She knew martial arts, but something told her that would hardly be effective with this man. She suspected he could easily subdue her if he chose to.

His midnight-blue eyes bored into her, assessing.

As silence hung between them, she realized it wasn't just

his startling presence that had her so unsettled. It was also because she found this situation extremely . . . exciting. A dangerous bad boy who could throw her down at any second, ripping away her scant covering, and have his way with her. She would be at his mercy as his hands and mouth explored her body, then as he drove his thick, hard erection into her. Deep and hard as she was helpless to stop him. Not *wanting* to stop him.

Her stomach somersaulted. Good heavens, she would never have thought there could be a second man who could trigger as strong a visceral reaction in her as Reid Jacobs had, yet this man, with his dark, rough persona, reeking of bad-boy danger, set her pulse pounding.

Which made her even more intensely aware that she was nearly naked, the towel around her just covering the tops of her breasts and barely brushing the tops of her thighs. One wrong move and . . .

He stepped toward her and she found herself stepping back, until she bumped against the wall.

As he moved closer, she realized he couldn't be a rogue biker who'd broken in. First, he never would have gotten past the security in this building. And second, she could tell that both his jacket and jeans were designer quality.

This man was obviously a friend of Reid's.

"I own this penthouse," he responded. "I don't know how you got in here, but I'm going to call the police and have you charged with breaking and entering." His eyebrow arched. "It will go better for you if you haven't stolen anything."

Her back stiffened. "I haven't broken anything and I certainly didn't steal anything."

She raised her chin. "And if I had, do you think I'd take the time to stop for a shower?"

"If you didn't think anyone was going to be here for a few days maybe."

Her eyes narrowed. "It's funny you say you own this place, because Reid told me it's his."

"You're saying you're here with Reid? Where is he?" The man's intimidating blue eyes were locked on her face.

She drew in a deep breath. "He had to go to a meeting."

His lips compressed. "That's convenient."

Dylan frowned. Reid's plan had been to fly back to Philadelphia last evening, which meant he wouldn't be able to take possession of the penthouse they had purchased for their trips to New York, since it wasn't available until late yesterday afternoon. Their business trips here would be much more frequent if they sewed up this contract with Raphael Allegro to design and build the new skyscraper he wanted to be the headquarters of a line of luxury designer stores he intended to set up countrywide. That's why Dylan had decided to make the trip to ensure everything was in order.

He'd expected to find the place well stocked, but didn't think that would include a beautiful woman. He stared at the blonde-haired beauty, with her wild tresses tumbling over her shoulders in waves. She was stunning. But she was also much taller—at about five feet ten—than the women

Reid usually consorted with. He usually preferred elegant redheads with petite frames and large breasts.

He glanced at the swell of soft flesh visible above the towel she clung to so desperately. She did have the fullness there Reid liked. In fact, she was well-filled out in all the right places. Slender but with enough curves to fill a man's hands nicely.

His groin tightened at the thought of cupping one of those delightful mounds right now.

"When did you meet him?"

She bit her lip. "Last night."

"You're telling me Reid picked you up last night, brought you here, then just let you stay?"

"Yes. We're seeing each other again tonight." She tipped up her head, her pretty blue eyes flashing. "If you don't believe me, I'll show you the keycard he gave me."

"Which you could have stolen."

She frowned. "Look, this can all be cleared up easily enough. You can just call him. I have . . ."

She patted the side of her towel, then bit her lip again and walked to the jeans hanging on the machine. She searched through the pocket with one hand while continuing to hold on tightly to the towel with the other. Finally, she pulled out a card. He recognized it as one of Reid's.

She walked toward him, holding it out to him. He took it and pulled out his cell. He already had the number programmed in his phone, so he selected it and listened to the rings. Voice mail picked up.

"Hi, it's me. Call. It's urgent." He hung up, then typed

in a text. If she was right and Reid was in a meeting, it could be a while before he checked his messages. The text he'd see right away.

"He's not there."

"Fine. I'll just be on my way. I'm sure he'll be in touch before I return tonight."

"Not so fast. You aren't going anywhere."

She glared at him. "Why? I haven't done anything wrong."

"I don't know that."

She frowned, her blue eyes flaring with irritation. "Look, I have to make a living and my shift starts in a half hour."

"And what do you do?"

"I drive a cab."

"I was wondering what a taxicab was doing sitting in the parking spot for the penthouse. The staff told me they noticed it there and had it towed."

Her eyes widened. "What? No!"

"Well, you might as well sit down and wait. Or would you rather I call the police and they'll hold you in a cell until we clear this up?"

She frowned, clearly wishing she could strangle him. "At least let me get dressed."

"You're not leaving my sight."

"Seriously?"

He could barely stop from chuckling as anger flashed across her sky-blue eyes. He wasn't callous to her feelings but he couldn't resist messing with her. She was just so damned sexy when she was mad.

"You have some clothes there." He gestured to the elliptical machine. "Go ahead and put those on. I'll turn my head."

Glaring, she strode to the machine and pulled the jeans free. He glanced away, but realized he could see her pulling on the pants in the reflection in the glass. He should turn away more but the sight of her unfastening the towel mesmerized him. She drew it open and dropped it to the floor, exposing her full, round breasts.

Fuck, his cock was swelling to a visible bulge. She pulled on a lacy white bra, then drew a sky-blue tank top over her head. She layered the bulky shirt over that.

But nothing could erase the memory of those lovely, full breasts from his mind's eye.

"I'm done," she said and walked to the couch then slumped down on it. "Now what?"

He sat down beside her. "Now we wait."

Reid stepped out of his meeting after receiving the text from Dylan. He was going to be tied up in there for at least another hour, so this short break was a welcome respite.

He dialed Dylan's number.

"What's up?" Reid said when he heard his friend's voice.

"Are you back in Philadelphia?" Dylan asked.

"No, I had to stay a little longer. Raphael invited me to a party last night and it was politic to attend. I rearranged my schedule and I'll be staying here another week or so. What's so urgent?"

"I just arrived in town, too. I'm at the penthouse and guess what I found?"

"Oh, shit. Did you walk in on Stevie? You didn't spook her, did you?"

"Maybe a little," Dylan admitted sheepishly.

"I take it she's there now. Put her on."

"Sure thing."

A second later, Stevie said, "Hello?"

The sound of her voice took him right back to the night they'd spent together. His groin tightened at the memory.

"Stevie. I'm really sorry about this awkwardness."

"Awkwardness?" she snapped. "First, this guy walks in on me and accuses me of breaking in, then he detains me until he can talk to you. Then when I tell him I have to go to work, he tells me they've *towed my cab!*"

"What? Damn it! Stevie, I'm really sorry. I promise I'll get this all straightened out and I'll compensate you for the lost income."

"I don't want your money," she snarled.

"Okay, we'll figure something out. Just please—"

"Reid?" It was Dylan's voice again. "She's stormed off to the bedroom."

"Look, do me a favor and convince her to stay, okay?"

"I'll do my best, buddy, but . . . why is this woman so important to you?"

He really didn't know quite how to explain that. Probably because he really didn't understand it himself.

"We just . . . hit it off. I enjoyed being with her and I'd like to see more of her."

"Man, I can't believe you picked up a cabdriver."

Reid gripped the phone tighter. "Don't tell me you're getting all snobbish on me."

Dylan just chuckled. "You know me better than that. I just think it's funny. And a bit confusing. She's not your usual type. Aside from the physical differences, she's pretty feisty. You always go for the sweet, shy type."

"There's just something about her I find refreshing."

"I get it. Women with a rebellious streak are hot. Makes you want to overcome that defiance. A real turn-on."

"And don't let her clothes fool you. She has a sensational body under that loose-fitting shirt and jeans."

"Yeah, I know."

His eyes narrowed. "What do you mean you know?"

"Oh, damn. I've got to go. She's halfway out the door with a suitcase."

"Wait!" Dylan caught up to the woman before she rolled her suitcase and garment bags all the way onto the elevator. He hooked his hand around the door so it wouldn't close. "Don't leave."

Her eyebrow quirked up. "Why?"

"Because I asked you not to."

The frown she sent him did nothing to diminish the prettiness of her face. Even though her sky-blue eyes were filled with annoyance, they were still wide and lovely.

"I'm not really feeling inclined to do you a favor," she said.

"It's not for me. It's for Reid."

Her eyebrow quirked up in that cute way again. "I've done enough favors for Mr. Jacobs. I'm sure he won't mind if I pass on this one."

Dylan's mind instantly bounced to the type of favors the

woman was hinting at and all he could think was that Reid was a lucky bastard.

Dylan stepped inside the elevator. "I bet you have," he said with a grin. "But he asked me not to let you get away."

Her eyes narrowed. "I'd like to see you try and stop me."

He grinned. "I'd love to. I'm sure Reid has a pair of handcuffs around the place."

Her eyes widened and Dylan wondered if it was his brazen flirtation that shocked her . . . or the mention of Reid's proclivities. Had Reid played the Dom last night?

"Okay, I want to leave here right now so let go of the door." Although her eyes had widened in alarm, now she pushed her shoulders back and stared at him defiantly.

He released the door and it closed behind him. The elevator began to move.

"I'm sorry. I didn't mean anything by that handcuff comment. I just thought . . ."

"I don't really want to know what you thought."

"Look, I'm sorry. We've gotten off to a bad start and I'd like to fix that." He offered his hand. "I'm Dylan Cole. Call me Dylan. Reid and I are business partners and old friends. I thought Reid had headed back to Philly yesterday so I took a quick trip here to check on things. I'm sorry I intruded on your privacy. Please forgive me and let me take you out to lunch."

She hesitated, then finally placed her small hand in his and they shook. The feel of her soft fingers wrapped around his did things to his hormonal system that shouldn't be allowed, especially with a woman who'd already been claimed by his best friend. Like heightening his senses, causing his heartbeat to race, and his groin to tighten.

But there it was. Fuck, he couldn't help wondering if Reid would consider sharing her.

Stevie released Dylan's hand, a little shaken at his effect on her. He was big and masculine and every bit as sexy as Mr. Reid Jacobs, but in a totally different way, with his dangerous, bad-boy vibe. She wasn't used to being thrown off so thoroughly by a man, yet two men in the space of twenty-four hours had her practically swooning at their feet.

And both were disgustingly rich.

Finally, he released her hand, she sensed a little reluctantly. Did she have the same effect on him? She wrapped her hand around the handle of her suitcase as he pressed the button for the lobby, then he pulled out his cell and tapped on the keys.

She should get straight over to the impound lot to get her cab back, but she had to eat and an hour wouldn't hurt. And it would be ungracious to turn down his peace offering.

The elevator stopped and she followed him into the large, elegant lobby. Dark wood-paneled walls, large plants, taupe leather chairs and couches forming sitting areas, and gleaming mahogany furniture topped with fine crystal vases of fresh-cut flowers.

Dylan led her out the front entrance and flagged down a cab. One pulled up in front of them and the driver got out. He took Stevie's bags and put them in the trunk, then opened the door for her. It was odd being on the other end of things.

She got into the car and Dylan got in beside her.

"I've got to admit, I half expected you to lead me to a big motorcycle."

He grinned. "I would have. I rode my Harley here. But you have luggage with you, so I thought this was a better choice. Speaking of which, how about I have the driver take it back to the penthouse for you?"

"Are you holding my luggage hostage so I'll come back?"

He shrugged. "If that's what it takes. You did say you were going to see Reid again tonight. I don't want to be the reason that doesn't happen."

She really did want to see Reid one more time.

"All right."

The driver pulled up to the curb and Dylan instructed him to take her bags back to the apartment building and ask the doorman to deliver them to the penthouse, then he gave him a big tip and guided her from the car and into the restaurant.

"So how did you meet Reid?" he asked after they'd settled into their table with a fabulous view of the park and drinks had been served.

"He got into my cab. He needed me to drive him a couple of places and . . ." She shrugged, embarrassed.

"Do you like driving a cab?"

She smiled. "I do. I like being behind the wheel, rather than in an office somewhere. I like the constantly changing view while I travel around the city, meeting new people, talking to them."

"Are your passengers usually friendly?"

Her back stiffened. "I don't sleep with most of them, if that's what you're insinuating."

"No, of course not. I just wouldn't think many people chatted with their cabdrivers."

She shrugged. "You're right. Most sink into their electronic media, or chat with each other, but some, especially tourists, ask about the city."

"I think you like the freedom more than anything else."

He was right. As much as she liked to connect with people, she also enjoyed observing the passengers from the outside. Overhearing their conversations, seeing where they were going. Where they were coming from. Piecing together stories in her head about what their lives must be like. Not actually talking to them and hearing the mundane details allowed her to imagine fascinating tales with infinite possibilities.

She even liked to write stories about them. Not that she'd ever told anyone about her writing. Or shown anyone her stories. She sometimes dreamed of one day getting them published, but for now it was just something she did to express herself. To try and tap into who she really was and where she was going in her life. To explore possibilities.

"You're perceptive," she said. "I do enjoy the freedom."

He shrugged. "I get it. I'm the same way. I'm an architect. I like to design things . . . be creative. I hate being stifled in a suit, or working a nine-to-five gig. I do the suits when I'm meeting clients, but on the whole I keep my own hours and wear what I like. And I love the open road. Taking off on my bike anytime I can."

The waitress set plates of hot food in front of them. Stevie squirted a bit of lemon on her salmon steak with dill sauce, then took a bite. It melted in her mouth in a delicate combination of flavors.

"I'm glad you joined me for lunch," Dylan said. "I'm especially happy for the opportunity to get to know you, since you're seeing my best friend."

She put down her fork. "Wait. I'm not *seeing* your best friend. He and I spent the night together, and I'll spend time with him again tonight, but I don't intend to see him after that."

He frowned. "I don't get it. You like Reid, don't you?"

"Yes, of course." She wouldn't have spent the night with him otherwise.

"And he's a great guy. Why won't you see him again?"

She shook her head. "It's just . . . complicated. I'm a cabdriver. He's a wealthy entrepreneur. We don't exactly have a lot in common."

His eyebrow arched. "Is that really it?"

She sighed. "Look, I don't sleep with my passengers. This was a one-time thing and I don't know what I was thinking. I was emotional after a bad breakup and finding my ass out on the street. I wasn't really thinking straight."

"Are you saying you regret it?"

"No. It's not that." She didn't want Reid to think that about the incredible night they'd shared. "I just don't think it's a good idea to pretend what we had is any more than it is."

"But what if it could be? Why not give it a chance?"

She frowned. "Look, I don't mean to be rude, but . . . I don't want to be involved with some self-absorbed billionaire type who thinks he can get whatever he wants by waving money or material things in my face. I slept with Mr. Jacobs because there was a mutual attraction, then I let him talk me into coming back again tonight. But that's the end of it."

"I see. You have an aversion to wealthy men." His midnight-blue gaze locked on her face. "I take it some bastard hurt you in the past."

If he only knew. But she said nothing and he nodded, clearly accepting her silence as confirmation.

Then his hand rested on hers, sending tingles dancing up her arm.

"We're not all bastards, you know."

Chapter Seven

Stevie could get lost in the blue depths of his eyes. Good God, she felt her barriers crumbling at the warm sincerity she saw there.

"Maybe, but let's just call this what it was. A hookup. Nothing more. I'm sure Mr. Jacobs will get over me. Now, if you don't mind, I'm going to go and get my cab."

With Dylan's help, Stevie was reunited with her cab in short order. He'd insisted on driving her to the lot and paying for the towing fee and fines. He was also able to speed up the process.

He opened the driver's door for her and she slid inside.

"Thank you for your help," she said. "And lunch."

He stood with his hand curled around the top of the door. "My pleasure. I hope I'll see you at the penthouse later." He smiled. "I'll make sure no one tows your cab this time."

"Good. Thank you. Now, if you'll let me get to work . . . The clock is ticking."

● ● ●

Stevie parked her cab in the underground spot in Reid's building and walked to the elevator. It had been a long shift and all she wanted to do was relax. Though the thought of a rousing round of lovemaking with Mr. Reid Jacobs was reviving her spirits.

She took the elevator up and stepped into the large penthouse, expecting to find Reid waiting for her, but instead she found a note telling her he was out for drinks with a client. She sighed and decided to take a nice, hot bath.

Forty minutes later, she sat relaxing by the fire in the bedroom, reading a book.

A thump in the other room jarred her and she realized she'd dozed off, the book laying closed on her lap. Was that Reid in the other room, or maybe Dylan? Or both of them.

Heat stirred inside her and she remembered she'd been having a hot, erotic dream starring the sexy Mr. Dylan Cole. Well, actually he'd co starred, along with big, dominating Reid Jacobs.

She shifted in her seat, her thoughts turning to last night when she'd been with Reid. The way he'd had her call him sir. And master. Her insides quivered.

Of course, Reid Jacobs was enough to keep any woman satisfied, but she sighed at the knowledge she would never be able to experience what it would be like to be in Dylan's arms. That simply was not an option. He and Reid were friends and she knew their bro-code would not allow it.

She stood up and walked to the bedroom door, tucking the silk robe she'd borrowed from Reid's closet snuggly around her.

She opened the door and waltzed out with a smile.

Reid stared at Stevie, who looked soft and feminine wrapped in his robe, wishing he had her wrapped in his arms right now.

"I'm sorry I wasn't here when you got in."

She shrugged. "You had business. I understand."

He smiled. "I'm glad you're here."

He walked toward her with a slow, purposeful stride. Dylan had told him that she didn't intend to see Reid again after tonight.

But all day, all he'd been able to think about was their wild encounter. And how sultry and sexy she was. He craved her like he'd never done with a woman before, the yearning sinking into his bones, encompassing his nervous system, until he could no more deny his need for her than he could give up air.

She might have decided that a one-night stand was all she wanted from him, but he found that unacceptable, so he intended to convince her otherwise. And once he set his mind to something, he never failed.

He took her hand and drew her close, gliding his arm around her waist. He kissed her palm, then pressed his lips to the pulse point on her wrist, noting with satisfaction the increase in her heart rate. He lowered his mouth to hers and she melted against him.

Stevie felt his hand at her waist, then the robe parted.

Oh, God, she could hardly wait to be in his bed again, their bodies joined in intimate delight. There was something magical about what Reid did to her. From the tingling in her body that swept from the tip of her toes to the top of her head—and all her most intimate places in between—to the way it just felt . . . *right* around him.

She may have been dreaming about Reid's friend, but now that Reid was in the room . . . touching her . . . she could barely remember his friend's name.

As his fingertips brushed lightly over the naked flesh of her stomach, she expected . . . *longed for* . . . his hand to cup her breast . . . but instead she felt the sash slide from around her waist. She felt the fabric curl around her wrist, then his other arm curl more tightly around her as he used both hands to tie a knot, securing her wrist.

"What are you doing?"

But he propelled her backward into the bedroom, their bodies still close together, like dancers. He guided her to a wide, deep, easy chair in the corner and pressed her back until she sank into it. She forgot to protest as she watched him lift the hanging plant above her from the ring suspending it from the ceiling. He set the plant on the dresser, then pulled a small remote from the drawer. At a humming sound, she glanced up to see the ring lowering, attached to a sturdy metal rod disappearing into the ceiling.

He threaded the sash through the ring, then grasped her other wrist and knotted the other end of the sash around it.

Another push of a button on the remote caused the thick ring to split in two as the rod separated in a Y, pulling the sash tight and drawing her arms apart.

As fascinating as all this was, she remembered that she had intended to resist Mr. Reid Jacobs.

"Wait, I don't want to—"

His lips stopped her words, his tongue pushing into her mouth, taking her breath away. Weak with need, she succumbed to the kiss. He was crouched in front of her, holding her against his solid body. When he drew his mouth away, she nearly cried.

She gazed up at him with wide eyes and he smiled.

"What was that you were saying? Would you like me to stop?"

"No, please don't stop," she said breathlessly. God, the man simply devastated her senses.

"Okay."

He pulled something from a pocket on the side of the chair and pressed it against her lips. A ball filled her mouth, attached to a strap he fastened behind her head.

He pulled her ankle to the side, then curled a strap around it. He quickly fastened another around her thigh, keeping it secured to the chair. The restraints were built right into the leather armchair, cleverly designed to look like ornamentation. He drew her unbound leg to the other side, opening her thighs, then restrained it the same way.

He leaned back and admired his handiwork, his focus on the straps around her legs. His gaze drifted up her thighs, held wide by the restraints, then slid up her robe—which had fallen open—coming to rest on the swell of her breasts.

Her nipples were still hidden by the satin fabric, but the way they hardened, pushing against the thin cloth, she was sure he could see every detail of the pebbled surface.

He smiled, with a purely predatory gleam, and his heated gaze leisurely drifted downward again, until it rested on her tiny, violet, lace panties. He stroked his finger along the lace adorning the top, sending quivers through her. Then his fingers tugged the fabric down, exposing a little more skin. Then a little more.

She wanted him to press his fingers against her skin, then glide down and cup her intimate flesh. She wanted him to stroke her, then glide his thick fingers into her slick opening.

But he drew his hand away. He watched her, surely seeing disappointment flicker in her eyes. Then he gathered long tresses of her wavy hair in his hand and brought it to his face. She watched his look of delight as he breathed in the scent of her herbal shampoo.

"I've missed you," he murmured.

The simple words warmed her heart and the desire in his eyes took her breath away.

Then he grasped the sides of her robe and parted them in a quick motion, like opening drapes. His hot gaze took in the sight of her full breasts, her nipples thrusting forward. Her insides melted, slickness dripping between her legs.

He cupped her breasts, lifting them, his gaze locked on them in awe.

"So beautiful."

Then his mouth was on her, his tongue lapping at her hard, aching nipple, his lips surrounding her in his warmth.

She moaned at the exquisite sensation, the ball in her mouth muffling the sound. He teased her other nipple with his fingertips, stroking it lightly, then he switched, covering it with his mouth, his fingers finding her damp nipple.

She arched, wanting to push deeper into his hot mouth. Then he suckled and she moaned again.

When his mouth drifted away, she whimpered, but his downward movement sent her heartbeat racing. His teeth dragged over the skin just above her panties, then she felt the panties drag downward. He was pulling them with his teeth. He gazed up at her, his cobalt-blue eyes shining. Then he pulled her panties down her hips. When he couldn't get them lower because of her bound, spread legs, he pulled something from his pocket. It was a pocketknife that he flicked open. Light gleamed on the shiny and very sharp blade as he pressed it against her belly. The flat of the metal blade was cold and goose bumps danced across her skin as he tugged on the elastic of the panties and slid the blade underneath. A quick motion toward him and he cut the delicate lace from top to leg opening. He then slashed the other side. He folded the blade and pushed it back in his pocket, then stared at her shredded panties. He lifted the center strip with a wide smile.

"There's the pretty pussy I remember."

His eyes blazed so hot she feared the panties would go up in flames.

She certainly was.

He leaned down and licked her, his tongue dragging over her slick folds. Then he tunneled into her wet opening, swirling inside her. Her muffled moan filled the room.

He found her clit and teased it a little, driving her wild. Then he stood up and took a step back.

She was disappointed . . . until he dropped his suit jacket to the floor and loosened his tie, then unbuttoned his crisp, white shirt. Her throat went dry at the sight of his muscular chest being slowly revealed. Once his shirt was tossed aside, he unfastened his belt, then the button of his pants. The raspy sound of the zipper pulling down set her nerve endings pulsing.

His pants fell to the floor with a thunk, then he pushed down his boxers.

Oh, God, his cock was so big and hard. She could see the veins pulsing along the side and the head was so purple she was sure it must hurt from the pressure.

He stepped close. Her fingers flexed, longing to wrap around him. He smiled and pressed his cock close to her bound hand, then guided her fingers to wrap around him. God, his flesh was as hot as a branding iron. And hard as marble.

She squeezed him and he glided his cock forward and back within her grip.

A pleased sound rumbled from him. "That feels so fine, sweetheart."

She squeezed, delighted at his moan of approval.

She gazed up at his cock gliding between her fingers, yearning for it in her mouth. He must have seen the depth of longing in her eyes because he stepped back.

"Sweetheart, I'm going to take off the gag, but only if you promise not to say a word. Do you promise?"

She nodded vigorously.

His fingers played along the back of her head, then she felt the gag loosen. He drew the ball from her mouth and she licked her lips, then swallowed the saliva that had pooled under her tongue. Then she opened her mouth, inviting him in.

He chuckled, then cupped her chin. His cock brushed her cheek, then he placed it on her upper lip. Instead of sliding his shaft inside her, he dragged the tip over her lips like a giant lipstick. Her tongue flickered out, tasting him as he glazed her with the clear fluid of his arousal.

Then he centered himself on her mouth and pressed forward. She widened, gladly taking him inside. He filled her slowly. Deeper and deeper. Giving her time to open her throat and take him all the way inside, despite his thick length.

He drew back again, dragging over her lips. He glided forward . . . and back . . . slowly. After several times, her heart racing at the feel of his big member filling her, he drew back and almost completely out of her mouth, sitting poised on her lips.

Then he surged forward, filling her throat. Then he drew back again. This time, his cockhead still stretching her mouth wide.

"Suck me, baby."

She obeyed, sucking his thick corona, her tongue swirling over the tip. She longed to cup his balls and stroke them. He moaned at her gentle suction, then she pulled deeper, increasing the rumbling murmur emanating from his throat. He pulsed into her a few times, then drew out of her mouth completely. She leaned forward, her gaze on his tight sacs. He smiled and held his erection close to his stomach and moved close so she could reach his testes with the tip of her tongue. She lapped at the shaven sacs, then opened her mouth, gazing up at him with pleading eyes.

He chuckled and moved closer still. She pressed her lips to his textured flesh and kissed, then opened and took him inside. First one ball. Then the second. His sacs were nestled in her mouth, all warm and cozy, as she stroked them with her tongue.

His fingers glided over her scalp, firmly, forking through her long hair.

"Oh, fuck, baby." He drew her to him, his hand holding her tight to his groin.

She suckled him softly.

"Ah, damn!" His straining jaw told her how much he was enjoying this.

He coiled his hand in her hair and tugged her head back, then pressed his cockhead to her lips and drove inside. She gasped at the invasion, then squeezed him as he pulsed in and out of her mouth.

"Fuck no," he exclaimed as he pulled his shaft free of her heat. "I want to be inside your pussy when I come."

He fell to his knees in front of her and ripped away the scrap of lace that used to be her panties, then buried his face in her. She moaned at the feel of his tongue pushing into her opening . . . swirling inside. His fingers dragged over her folds, then two thick digits slipped inside as his mouth found her clit.

"Oh, God!" She wrapped her fingers around the silk holding her hands bound, and squeezed tightly as his tongue lapped over her.

His fingers pulsed inside her canal, sending pleasure wafting through her. She arched and he pushed his fingers deeper inside her.

"Oh, yes. That's so good."

His mouth slipped away from her and his gaze locked on hers. His fingers, still inside her, stilled. She licked her lips, wanting his fingers moving again. Wanting his mouth between her legs. But his stare was unnerving.

Still, she couldn't help arching her hips, but he flattened his free hand on her belly and held her flat.

"What are you supposed to call me?" he asked.

"Uh . . . sir?"

"And?"

She bit her lip. She just wanted him to make her come.

But the word fluttered through her brain. The designation he had assigned himself that she was surprised she actually longed to call him.

"Master," she said in a hushed whisper. Oh, God, just saying it sent a thrill through her.

His lips turned up in a slow smile. "That's right."

He continued to watch her. She shifted a little, or tried to with his hand holding her firmly to the chair.

Why didn't he do something?

"I don't understand," she finally uttered. "What's happening?"

His eyes darkened to a midnight blue.

"Let me tell you a little about myself. I like to control

a woman. To command her. I want her to submit to me completely. It's her choice, but once she makes that choice"—his eyes flared with heat—"she is mine completely. Do you understand what I'm saying?"

She nodded, though she didn't know if she did truly understand. But his words filled her with an intense yearning so deep she ached with it.

Could she really be longing for him to control her? For him to make her surrender to his will? To become *his*?

All she knew for sure was that she wanted him to continue what they were doing. She wanted to experience that thrilling ride of exquisite pleasure again.

"But as much as I am in control, I love it when my sub asks for things." He smiled. "As long as she begs." His voice grew low and raspy. "I love it when a woman begs."

Part of her was shocked, knowing she would never want to beg a man for anything, but the stronger, more needy side of her quivered in excitement at the very thought.

He continued to watch her. The muscles in her vagina squeezed so tight she feared she would crush the bones of his fingers, her yearning to feel him move inside her was so great.

Her insides ached and her clit felt abandoned.

"Please?" was all she could manage with her senses so befuddled.

He dipped down his head and kissed her lips, then his face hovered close to hers.

"Please what, my love?"

"Please, sir?" At a flicker in his eyes, she added, "I mean, master?"

"Very good. But I mean what is it you want me to do? I want you to learn to ask for what you want. And nothing vague like, 'touch me down there.'"

"Oh. I . . . want you to move your fingers inside me . . ."

When his eyes flickered again, she corrected, "I want your fingers to move inside my . . . uh . . . pussy. In and out. And I want your mouth on my clit. Licking and sucking."

His eyes lit up with approval, but she knew she wasn't done yet.

"Please, master. I beg of you."

Saying those words sent a ripple of arousal through her.

He chuckled out loud, then she caught her breath as his fingers wiggled inside her. Then they pushed in deeper. At the same time, he grazed her nipple with his teeth, making her gasp, then he kissed down her belly. When his mouth found her clit again, her head fell back against the chair, her whole body trembling with need.

He lapped at the little button, sending heat fluttering across her nerve endings. He moved his fingers inside her, his fingertips stroking her tender passage. Pleasure rippled through her.

He raised his head, his cobalt gaze locked on hers.

"Do you like that?"

"Oh, yes, master." Calling him that made her shudder with need. Why did she like it so much?

His fingers thrust deeper as he suckled on her clit. Pleasure pummeled her senses.

"Ohhhh, yes."

The gliding touch of his fingertips inside her stimulated a deep craving that grew and grew, until it seemed it would consume her completely. His tongue flickering over her clit threw her senses into chaos. A storm coiled in her belly and swelled outward in a growing spiral.

She moaned, longing to grasp his head, her fingers forking through his dark waves of hair, and hold him tightly to her until she smothered him in her juices.

She arched, the tumultuous sensations expanding.

"Ohhh," she cried.

A sharp sensation lanced through her, prickling with delight and she gasped. He sucked harder and she moaned, her head tossing back and forth as she squeezed him tight inside her. An orgasm blasted through her, hurling her into the precipice as she wailed her release.

Hot liquid flooded her canal, then rushed from her opening.

Oh, God, she'd heard it was possible for a woman to ejaculate, but never in her wildest dreams had she thought it would happen to her. This man knew how to bring her to a fever pitch, driving her arousal higher than she'd ever experienced before. She stared at him with wide eyes as he lifted his head, his mouth glistening with her slickness, a big smile on his face.

"God damn, you are so fucking hot." He wiped his mouth then leaned in and kissed her.

She could taste a little of her salty dew on his lips. His tongue plunged deep inside her, thrusting and swirling, possessing her completely.

"Now I'm going to drive my thick, hard cock into you and fuck you until you scream my name." He kissed her ear, then nuzzled. "Which is 'master' to you."

Chapter Eight

Stevie felt his hot cockhead brush her tender, slick flesh. He pushed inside her, slow and sure, stretching her passage wide. She squeezed around him, needing him deeper.

"You want me, don't you, baby?"

"Yes, sir," she whimpered. She wanted him more than she'd ever thought it was possible to want a man.

His interminably long shaft kept on filling her.

"Oh, sir, please." The word dragged out long and needy. "Fill me all the way."

But instead he stopped.

Her eyes widened. "Please, I beg of you." Her whimpered words were laced with need.

His chuckle, rumbling from deep in his chest, thrilled her.

Then he surged forward. She gasped at the delightful invasion.

He had her pinned to the chair, his big body tight to hers, both of them panting for air. She pressed her mouth to his temple in a gentle kiss, loving the feel of his dark waves of hair against her lips. He shifted his head, capturing her mouth in a tender kiss.

Their gazes locked and she could feel a connection like she never had before with a man. Close. Intimate.

Revealing.

He wanted her. And for more than just a short fling. And he must see that same need in her. A need to be with this incredible man who seemed to see straight into her soul and understand what she wanted. What she *needed*.

Things she didn't even understand about herself.

Oh, God, but she didn't want it to be true. Not really. Not with him.

Confusion swirled through her. And panic.

Then he moved. His cock dragged along her inner passage, enthralling her with the delicate, yet immensely exciting sensations.

Then he surged forward again, filling her completely.

"Do you like me inside you?" he asked as he thrust again.

"Oh, yes. Thank you, sir."

He chuckled, a sound filled with satisfaction, as he continued to pump into her. His hard cock, thick and long, possessing her body.

He nuzzled her breast, then suckled lightly on her nipple. She arched her chest upward, then her pelvis, wanting more of him in every way.

He thrust hard. Faster. And deeper.

"I . . . Love . . . Fucking . . . You." He panted each word between thrusts.

Pleasure coiled tightly inside her, about to release at any second.

He thrust deep and swirled his hips.

An orgasm blasted through her, knocking her into the void, her senses pummeled with delightful ripples of bliss. She felt hot liquid fill her . . . his this time, and she moaned. She didn't care how loud she was. She just let the pleasure wash through her in rippling sounds of ecstasy.

"Oh, yes, master," she cried. "I'm coming."

He continued to pump, fast and steady. Every cell in her body seemed to explode in euphoria. The strokes of his cock inside her sent trembling pleasure rocking through every part of her. Her wails filled the room as she rode the ecstatic waves to paradise and beyond.

But still he pumped. Her throat ached from the continuous wash of pleasure buoying her on and on until she was a quivering mass of limpness.

Finally, he slowed and the incredible pleasure waned, leaving her spent and sated.

She felt one of her hands lower, in the sure grip of his fingers. She'd barely felt him untie the sash from her wrist. Then he released her other hand and scooped her up. It seemed he'd already unbound her legs. She rested her head against his solid chest, her hands curling around his neck, as he carried her to bed. She immediately fell asleep in the comfort of his arms, his heartbeat thumping against her ear.

Lips nuzzled Stevie's neck and she opened her eyes. She was still in Reid's arms, his masculine body wrapped around her, his leg hooked over hers. It was as if she was bound by his limbs.

And she could stay there forever.

Surrendering to her own need to be completely possessed by him.

His lips brushed her temple and she could feel his cock hard against her butt. They were still totally naked.

"I can't help thinking how lucky I am that you agreed to come with me to the party," he murmured. "Otherwise, I wouldn't have been able to talk you into staying here with me that night. Then you wouldn't be in my arms now."

He drew back on her shoulder, rolling her onto her back. She gazed into his vivid blue eyes, totally captivated as his face moved close to hers.

"And I wouldn't be able to do this right now."

His lips brushed hers in a light, tender gesture, then fluttered over hers like a butterfly's wings, in light, delicate kisses, then finally settled firmly. His tongue dipped inside, then slowly glided deeper, his lips coaxing hers to respond. The kiss deepened, filling with passion, until she clung to his shoulders, barely able to catch her breath.

Oh, God, she wanted this man.

He smiled at her, and seemed about to roll away, so she tugged him into another kiss, reveling in the feel of his lips on hers, his big body leaning into hers.

She stroked down his chest, then wrapped her fingers around his solid erection. God, it was so hard it could be made of marble. Her intimate muscles contracted at the thought of it gliding inside her and suddenly she needed to feel that more than she needed to breathe.

"I want you to fuck me," she said in a low, bold voice. "And don't even start that shit about sir or master. I just want you to do it."

The smile that spread across his face lit his eyes.

"Whatever you say, my love."

She widened her legs as he prowled over her, opening herself to him. Wanting to feel his hard member in her depths. He wrapped his hand around his cock then she felt it brush her intimate folds. At the same time, he stroked her hair from her forehead, then his hand cupped her head as he gazed at her.

He teased her, stroking her with his tip. Coating his cockhead with her slickness. When it neared her opening, she arched forward, but instead of slipping it inside, he glided it away again.

"Fuck me," she demanded.

He glided his cockhead to her opening again, but kept it poised there, watching her.

"Please," she whimpered, needing him so badly she thought she'd die.

He laughed and thrust forward, filling her in one stroke. She moaned at the feel of her body stretched around him, his big member deep inside her. She squeezed him and it was his turn to moan.

She tightened her grip around his shoulders, then tipped her head up and nibbled lightly on his earlobe.

"Please fuck me," she whispered against his ear.

He turned his head and kissed her, his face pressing her head back to the pillow. Then he began to move. His big body drew back, then surged forward, his thick cock spearing into her again. He moved in a steady rhythm, stroking her insides again and again.

"Oh, yes," she murmured against his ear, holding him tight to her.

It felt so good having his cock inside her. Better than anything she'd ever experienced before. Definitely better than any man she'd been with.

How could she give this up? How could she walk away from something so special?

He drove deep. Her consciousness flickered, the pleasure so great she thought she might black out.

He rode her, filling her with his rock-hard cock. Effervescent sensations bubbled through her, raising her pleasure higher and higher until her moans turned to wails. Her body, coiled tight as a spring, released in a burst of joyful bliss.

She moaned, loud and long, riding the surging wave of ecstasy until she was clinging to him, gasping for air. He plunged deep, then exploded in her depths, filling her with his heat.

They collapsed on the bed, her arms tight around him.

Once they caught their breath, he kissed her, then led her to the shower. He must have felt she was a really dirty girl because he washed every inch of her with thorough attention to detail. When they stepped from the shower, she felt sparkling clean.

He insisted on preparing breakfast for her, so she sat at the kitchen table gazing out the window at the gorgeous view of the city as she sipped her coffee. The aroma of coffee was joined by onions and herbs as he cooked the omelets.

He set a plate in front of her with a perfect half-moon-shaped omelet, tomato slices fanned out, and garnished with a sprig of parsley.

"It looks great," she complimented.

He sat across from her and they ate. He really was a good cook. Most billionaires would've had staff to prepare meals, or had something delivered.

"I was wondering if you might like to stay here with me for a week or two. I'd love to spend more time with you, and Raphael has been hinting that he'd like me to attend another event, and he'll want me to bring you along. He was quite taken by you."

"I don't have to stay here with you just because we'll be going to a party together."

He chuckled. "I know. I'd just really like to spend more time with you. When you're not driving, of course." He smiled. "Unless you'd like me to ride around in your cab all day doing sightseeing. That could be fun."

"Well, I could take a day off." Except she still had bills to pay, and driving a cab was a seven-day-a-week proposition in order to make ends meet.

"You really won't let me pay for your time, even if it's to do what you do anyway? Your friends must love you if you're giving them free cab rides all the time." At the flair of annoyance in her eyes, he smiled. "Or am I special?"

He certainly was special, but a bit of a pain, too.

"Look, I don't know why you've decided that you and I should have some sort of relationship, even if it's just something casual, but that's not what I signed on for. We had a one-night stand—"

"Two now, actually."

She sent him a loaded stare. "The sex is great between us. I get it. But there is no way a relationship of any kind will work for us. We're just too different. And I'm not about to be your casual hookup anytime you come into the city."

"I don't think we're all that different. We're both entrepreneurs, running our own businesses. Keeping our own hours, within logical constraints. We're both independent, know what we want, and aren't afraid to go after it."

"And you live in a luxurious penthouse," she said gesturing at the room around them, "and—"

"And none of that is important."

His cobalt-blue eyes were unsettling as he stared into her soul.

Finally, he sat back. "But you know, I don't think our differences are what you're really worried about. I think at some point you were hurt by some jerk who had a lot of money and that's left you cautious."

She narrowed her eyes. Dylan had made the same observation. Was she so transparent, or were they both just that good at reading people?

"There's nothing wrong with a little caution."

"True." His hand moved over hers and he held it, his big fingers enveloping hers. "But I want to keep seeing you and I'll do whatever I can to convince you."

She drew her hand away. "Not going to happen."

"Give me one good reason. And I don't want it to be because we're from different worlds. I know we can get past that."

She frowned and sipped her coffee. "There's more than the issue of wealth between us."

He raised an eyebrow. "Oh? Do you want to expand on that?"

"Okay, how about the fact that you order me around in the bedroom?"

He sipped his coffee. "What about it?"

"Last night you tied me up," she said, eyebrows arching.

He smiled, his eyes glowing with way too much self-satisfaction. "Yes, I did."

"I don't like that kind of thing."

"Really? Because you seemed to be enjoying it immensely last night."

"That's just because . . . uh . . ." Damn, it's not like she could deny that he had a powerful effect on her sexually.

"Because my natural dominance combined with my suave and charming manner overwhelmed your better judgment?"

Her lips quirked up despite herself. "You think a lot of yourself, don't you?"

She drew in a breath, deciding to tackle this head-on.

"The thing is, you had me happily begging for sex last night. And again this morning." She shook her head. "I don't know who that woman is and it disturbs me that I can be so . . . subservient."

Last night, she'd convinced herself they'd made a real connection. That her arousal at his dominance was because he was satisfying something deep inside her that she'd been missing.

But in the light of day, she knew it was just that the man was an experienced and persuasive lover. An *incredible* lover who could arouse her with an expert touch, making her crave whatever he offered.

"Okay, if you really don't like the dominance and submission, I can curtail that, but—"

"I don't believe you. It's part of your nature."

His eyes grew serious and he drew her hand to his mouth. The play of his lips on her skin sent need shimmering through her.

"Sweetheart, I can control my nature as easily as I can control you, and I'll do whatever it takes to keep you in my bed."

She froze, disturbed by the intensity and determination in his eyes.

She glanced at the clock on the wall. "I have to get to work." She stood up, but he continued to hold her hand.

"Stevie, please come back tonight so we can continue this conversation."

"I don't want to continue it."

"How about you come back tonight or"—he grinned—"I'll call your company and tell them I want to hire you and your cab for the day, then you'll have to drive me around and listen to my arguments all day long."

She narrowed her eyes. "So it's come to blackmail, has it?"

He shrugged. "Only because I want to see you again so badly, and you've given me no other choice."

She drew in a deep breath. God, the man threw her so off kilter she could barely think straight around him, let alone deny his request. He wanted to see her again and she couldn't deny she wanted to see him again, too.

"All right. I'll come back here and we'll talk."

He kissed her hand with a satisfied smile. "Good."

She drew her hand away, tremors quivering through her, and hurried to the bedroom to change.

Ten minutes later, she exited the bedroom and strode down the hall. Dylan was sitting in the living room, coffee mug in hand, talking to Reid. It was odd seeing the two of them together. Reid in his well-tailored designer suit, Dylan in his jeans and faded T-shirt.

A wide smile, enhancing his bad-boy good looks, claimed Dylan's lips when he saw her.

"Good morning, Stevie," he said.

"Good morning." She couldn't help returning his warm smile in kind. "I'm sorry I can't stay. I'm on my way to work."

"I understand. Maybe we can see each other again later." He glanced at Reid. "The three of us could grab dinner."

Reid watched the whole exchange between them, his demeanor seeming to darken at their casual yet warm friendliness.

"I'm sorry, I'll be working pretty late," she responded as she started toward the foyer.

"Another time then," Dylan said graciously.

She was sure she saw a flicker of jealousy in Reid's eyes.

She pulled on her coat and raced out the door.

All day as she was driving, she pondered how she would successfully discourage Reid from pursuing her. He wanted her in his bed and he was clearly determined. He had already agreed to dispense with the domination, if that's what she wanted, but . . . it's not like she didn't enjoy it—in fact, it was totally hot—but she was disturbed by the way she fell so easily into submitting to him.

And begging him.

Even now she craved his touch. And wanted him to command her. She could imagine stripping naked in front of him and kneeling down, then gladly begging for his touch. Oh, God, the need pulsed through her.

But she was an independent woman. She wasn't willing to give that up. And she certainly didn't want to become his slave, willing or otherwise.

So what would she do when she finished her shift tonight? He'd be expecting her to come back. And if she did, she'd share his bed, feel his touch driving her wild, and probably grovel for him to drive his cock into her.

Her head spun with a swirl of erotic images, every one with her as his willing slave.

She could try to find somewhere else to stay tonight— she knew she could knock on Jon and Derrick's door anytime—but the truth was, she wanted to go back to Reid Jacobs' arms. Wanted to fall prey to his compelling brand of seduction.

Every day she stayed with him would make it harder to pull away. Somehow she had to force him to realize that he didn't really want to be with her. With the strong mutual attraction between them, it wouldn't be easy, but . . . if it was a relationship he was looking for, and she got the impression it was . . . Maybe she could scare him off. Make him understand she was not relationship material.

•   •   •

Reid glanced up from the news article he was reading on his tablet when Stevie walked in. She'd been gone over twelve hours and he'd wondered if she'd chosen to avoid him and stay somewhere else tonight. But here she was.

She looked tired.

He smiled. "Tough evening?"

"No, not really." She slumped on the couch beside him. "Just the usual."

She worked long hours, seven days a week it seemed.

He wished he could do something to lighten her load, but she was proud and independent. No matter what he offered, he was sure she'd turn it down. It was frustrating that it would be nothing for him to pay for a nice apartment for her so she could have some breathing space and be able to afford to take some time off, but he knew she wouldn't accept it. She'd barely accepted his offer to stay here temporarily and he was worried she would bolt at any time.

If he could convince her to stay here, that would help her financially. And he'd ensure he was in town a lot. She was smart and hardworking, so he hoped he'd be able to encourage her to get a better job. He could certainly offer her something at his company, or with any number of companies with friends or clients. One word from him and he knew several executives who would hire her on the spot.

She drew her legs close to her chest and wrapped her arms around them.

"You said you wanted to talk, so here I am," she said.

He nodded and took her hand, his warm fingers surrounding hers.

"I can't believe you want to give up what we've found with each other," he said.

"Honestly, where do you see this going?"

"I don't know. But I'd like to explore the options."

She drew her hand from his and settled back on the couch.

"Look, you and I met and had a brief fling," she said. "I don't see anything more serious between us and I don't want to lead you on."

He shrugged. "So we don't worry about how serious it is."

Her eyebrow arched. "You're okay with it being a casual fling? No strings?"

"If that's what you want."

She tipped her head, her eyes gleaming. "If I tell you what I really want, will you get mad?"

"Of course not," he answered, intrigued.

"Seriously? I won't tell you unless you promise not to get mad at me. Or Dylan."

His stomach tightened. "What does Dylan have to do with this?"

"Promise first."

"Of course I promise."

A smile spread across her face. "I don't want a serious relationship with you. And I'm concerned about the domination stuff. But if you agree to back off on those, then I'll agree to keep seeing you. On one condition."

"And that is?"

"Well, as I said, I don't want to get into a relationship right now—not just with you, but with anyone—especially not something exclusive."

"I get it. You've just gone through a difficult breakup."

"That's right." She shrugged. "And I don't see this thing between us going anywhere in the long run anyway. We just aren't right for each other."

He wasn't going to argue with her, even though he didn't agree. If she needed time, he'd give it to her. Because he was confident that he'd eventually be able to convince her how right they were together.

"So you'd have to agree to us not being exclusive," she said.

"That sounds like a workable arrangement."

"But that's not all. I want to let you know right up front that I find your friend Dylan very sexy, and"—she watched his face intently—"I'd like to start seeing him, too. I don't know if he's interested, but I'm sure he'd only agree if he knew it was all right with you, so I'd like you to give him the go ahead."

He had to stop his jaw from dropping. Was she really so brashly asking for him to set her up with his best friend? So she could go out with him at the same time as she was seeing Reid?

The thought of her in Dylan's arms—in Dylan's *bed*—sent jealousy burning through him. But if he had to share her with anyone, Dylan would be his choice.

Sharing her.

The idea of a different kind of sharing quivered through

him. The three of them together. Him watching her with
Dylan. Seeing Dylan's big cock pumping into her. And
thrusting his own cock into her at the same time. Excitement shot through him at the mere thought.

In fact, it would bring a different fantasy to life for
him, too. He liked being adventurous in the bedroom and
the thought of sharing a woman with Dylan had been something he'd often fantasized about.

"I see." He kept his expression unreadable.

"I'm sorry. I see this is upsetting you," she said. "I get
it that I'm asking too much, so I think it's better if we just
forget the whole thing."

Her expression was innocent, but he could sense something behind it.

*Damn, she's just doing this to push me away. Assuming her
suggestion of pursuing Dylan, too, will scare me off.*

Well, he could play at that game, too.

He shook his head. "I'm not upset. You're trying to find
a solution and I appreciate that. I do think Dylan will have
trouble with this, though. He's my best friend and he knows
I'm interested in you, so I don't think he'll agree to go out
with you even if I suggest it."

She nodded and he was sure he saw relief flash in her
eyes. But he also caught a glimpse of disappointment,
which encouraged him.

"But I have another idea."

She gazed at him, curiosity glowing in her lovely blue
eyes.

"Have you ever had a threesome before?" he asked.

Her eyes widened. "Excuse me?"

"You seem like the adventurous type. Have you ever fantasized about being with two men at the same time?"

She shifted in her chair.

"Are you suggesting that you and me . . . *and* Dylan . . . ?"

"That's exactly what I'm suggesting. You want to be with both of us. Why not at the same time?"

Her eyes flickered with uncertainty.

At her hesitation, he took her hand in his and kissed the inside of her wrist, his gaze never leaving hers.

"It would be incredibly hot to watch you with Dylan. To touch you at the same time as he's touching you. To be *inside* you at the same time as he is."

He could feel her tremble and her eyes shimmered with excitement. He pressed her palm to his lips, watching her barriers slip away.

"It . . . has been a secret fantasy of mine." She licked her lips. "Do you think he'd agree?"

He let a slow smile spread across his face.

"I think I'll be able to convince him."

Chapter Nine

Reid sat back in his chair, the steaming mug of coffee in his hand, a smile spreading across his face. Last night had been fucking sensational. After he'd suggested the idea of a threesome, Stevie had been like a wildcat in bed. Passionate and animated. Fuck, she'd been all over him.

At one point, she'd sunk to her knees in front of him and stroked her fingers over his engorged cock—still confined in his pants—and told him she'd changed her mind about the domination and submission. The way she'd gazed up at him, her eyes glittering, the tip of her tongue gliding over her lips, he could tell that she'd wanted him to command her right then, so he ordered her to suck his cock.

Clearly, she was still figuring out what she wanted in the bedroom and he was happy he was the one who'd opened this very satisfying door for her.

He glanced at Dylan who was reading the paper, his empty breakfast plate pushed to the side.

Reid leaned forward, resting his arms on the table.

"What do you think of Stevie?"

Dylan lowered the paper, peering over it at Reid. "What do I think of her?" He folded the newspaper and set it down. "What are we talking about here? You want me to tell you how sexy she is and what a lucky bastard you are?"

Reid smiled. "For a start. So you find her sexy?"

"I've got a dick, don't I?" Dylan grinned. "And last night . . . what the fuck were you two doing in there? I was hard half the night hearing the sounds coming out of your room."

Dylan sipped his coffee and his gaze flickered to Reid's, distance in his midnight-blue eyes.

"Are we going to get into something now?" Dylan asked. "I've sensed your jealousy when I've paid her any kind of attention. You've got to know that I wouldn't let anything—even a sexy treat like Stevie—get in the way of our friendship."

"Of course. I appreciate that. And, yeah, I admit it. She's different than the other women I've been with. Special."

"You're falling for her."

Reid nodded. "You might be right. But she's insistent that there can be nothing long-term between us." He leaned back again. "I have convinced her to keep seeing me for a while, though. And hopefully during that time, I'll be able to win her over. But I'll need your help."

"Anything. What do you want me to do?"

A slow smiled spread across Reid's face. "I want you to fuck her."

Dylan's jaw dropped open. "What the hell are you talking about?"

"Well, it seems our little lady cabdriver is excited at the

idea of being with two men. And we're the lucky bastards who have the opportunity to bring that dream to life." Reid sipped his coffee. "So, are you in?"

"Are you fucking kidding me?" Dylan said. "Of course I'm in."

Reid smiled, but a part of him was still a little disconcerted with the thought of another man—even his best friend, Dylan—fucking Stevie. But the thought of Dylan gliding his cock into her and making her whimper in pleasure was a powerful aphrodisiac.

"Okay," Reid said, "so I was thinking we'd get started tonight after Stevie gets back from her shift. Now, let's set some ground rules."

Stevie pulled up to the apartment building, anxious to drop off this last fare of the night. It was a couple she'd picked up outside a club downtown and she didn't know if they'd hooked up at the club or if they were already dating, but there were obviously sparks flying between them. Their amorous activity in the backseat made Stevie long to be back at Reid's place.

Reid had texted her earlier that he thought they should take a step forward with their threesome plans that night. She didn't exactly know what he meant by taking steps forward, but excitement had coursed through her all evening.

The whole idea of the threesome set her a bit on edge. The thought was wildly sexy and when Reid had suggested it, she'd become . . . uh . . . a bit maniacal with lust. She'd practically forced herself on him, diving onto his hard cock

and riding him until he groaned his release. And her . . .
she'd wailed so loudly she could have woken the dead.

But the thought of actually going through with it . . .
of returning to the penthouse and facing the men, both of
them knowing what was going to happen . . . anticipating
her stripping off her clothes and getting naked . . .

Her stomach clenched. Would she really be able to go
through with it?

The couple got out, tossing some money her way, then
held hands as they hurried to the front entrance. Stevie
pulled away and headed toward the posh neighborhood
where Reid's apartment was.

Soon she was riding the elevator up to the penthouse,
her nerves fraying. She'd texted Reid as soon as she'd
parked the cab. The elevator door opened and both men
stood smiling at her, Reid in an impeccable suit, Dylan in
his usual tight jeans, but wearing a casual button-down
shirt, the long sleeves hiding the tattoos she knew were
under there.

She stepped into the foyer, her stomach tightening.

Reid stepped forward, but instead of taking her in his
arms and kissing her, as she half expected, he walked past
her and into the elevator.

"I'm heading out," he said. "I won't be back until tomorrow."

"Wait. But I thought . . ." Confusion simmered through
her. They couldn't exactly have a threesome without three
people.

Reid grinned. "Don't worry. Dylan will explain." Then
the doors whooshed closed.

She stared at the elevator, slowly drawing in a deep breath. Then she turned around.

"Want something to eat?" Dylan asked.

"No, thanks. I had a burger earlier." She followed him into the living room.

There was a bottle of white wine on the table and two stemmed glasses. He poured a glass and handed it to her then sat down on the couch.

"Join me," he invited with a smile.

Oh, God, he was so sexy sitting there with his broad shoulders and twinkling blue eyes. The top few buttons of his shirt were undone and she could see the edges of a tattoo on his chest.

But she wasn't here to have sex with Dylan. Well, yes, she was, but as part of a threesome. She wouldn't feel right doing it with just him. It would be like she was cheating on Reid.

"So why did Reid leave?" she asked as she sat down beside Dylan on the couch, leaving a good foot between them.

"Reid told me about your fantasy, and how you'll only continue seeing him if it's part of a three-way relationship that includes me."

She nodded, feeling more than a little embarrassed. But she sucked in a breath to say what had to be said.

"I need to be clear. It's not a relationship I'm looking for."

He nodded. "Of course. Nothing long-term. No commitment. I get it." He smiled. "I have to say, I'm very flattered you chose to include me."

Her gaze drifted to his. "Um . . . well, you know you're very attractive."

"As are you." He put down his glass and leaned a little closer. "And I'm very excited about getting started."

"But Reid isn't here." The words came out slightly panicked and she mentally kicked herself.

"Don't worry. I'm not trying to make a move on you. The reason Reid went out is because he wanted to give us some time to get to know each other a bit better. To spend some alone time together and get used to the idea of becoming intimate with each other so we'll all be more comfortable when we move forward with the three of us."

"So we're going to sit and chat?"

"Yes . . . and no."

Her gaze flicked to his and her stomach tensed. "What do you mean?"

"What Reid suggested was that we should go in the hot tub and talk."

She calmed a little. "That sounds relaxing."

"He suggests we go in naked."

Every muscle in her body tensed. "Oh."

"You don't have to if you don't want to, but he thinks— and I agree—that it'll give you a chance to get used to us being naked together while removing the pressure of us being intimate right away. What do you think?"

What he said made sense. If the three of them just started into it, she would be uncomfortable undressing in front of Dylan and it would make the whole experience awkward. Why not get over that awkwardness now? And once she was in the water, he wouldn't really see her anymore with the bubbles going, so she wouldn't feel on display.

"Okay, so are we going to do that now?"

He smiled. "If you feel ready."

She nodded. "I'll just go take a quick shower and meet you out there."

There was a large, private terrace as part of the penthouse and the hot tub was just outside the mini gym. She stood up and he picked up the wine and two glasses. He followed her, then continued out the patio doors.

She stepped into the gym bathroom and shed her clothes, then coiled her hair on top of her head and used a large hair clip to hold it in place. She didn't want wet, straggly hair while she was sitting with Dylan—her soon-to-be new lover. The thought sent a quiver through her.

She stepped into the shower stall and soaped herself up, then rinsed off. She dried herself, then grabbed a fresh towel and wrapped it around her body. She stepped out of the bathroom, feeling a little self-conscious with just the towel covering her nakedness, then remembered this is how Dylan had seen her the first time they met, when he thought she was an intruder.

She opened the patio door and stepped into the night air. It was a cool night and she looked forward to getting into the hot water of the tub. The terrace was lit with tiny white lights and the full moon shone down with a soft glow. Dylan had already lifted the cover off the tub. A waterfall spilled from one side and LEDs lit the tub from within. As she watched, the color changed from blue to purple. Soft music played and she realized there was a sound system built into the tub.

Dylan was still wearing his jeans and shirt, though he was barefoot.

She clung to the towel, ensuring it didn't slip away.

"You still have your clothes on."

He smiled. "I thought you might find it disconcerting if you came out and I was standing here naked."

"Point taken." She stood by the hot tub now, which was sunken into the deck. She stared at the water, then at him. "I guess I'll just get in now."

He nodded, but she felt frozen to the spot.

"I can look away if you want . . ." he said.

"Uh . . . no. That would defeat the purpose, right? I mean, we're going to see each other naked and so I should just . . ."

She was babbling like an idiot. She sucked in a breath, then tugged the corner of the towel free and slowly unwrapped it, staring at the water rather than Dylan's face. The cool air surrounded her naked skin and her nipples hardened. She stepped into the tub then lowered herself into the water.

The jets weren't on yet, so the water was calm and clear, leaving her exposed. She couldn't help wrapping one arm over her breasts and resting the other over her lower region, even though he would have seen everything as she'd stepped into the water.

She gazed up at Dylan and the heat in his midnight-blue eyes was unmistakable.

"Your turn," she said simply.

"Yeah, of course."

She watched, enthralled, as he unbuttoned his shirt, slowly revealing his muscular chest. A dramatic tattoo of an angel sitting atop a building gazing down on the street below adorned the left side of his chest. He shed his shirt, then unzipped his jeans. A quiver raced down her spine at the raspy sound. Then he unbuttoned and dropped his jeans to the ground. She watched, her breath locked in her lungs, as he slid his fingers under the waistband of his boxers, then pushed them down to his ankles. When he stood up, her gaze locked on his rock-hard, pointing-to-the-sky erection.

Clearly, seeing her naked body had had an arousing effect on him. And that made her feel unsettled . . . and intensely turned on.

He stepped forward and lowered himself into the water, sitting kitty-corner to her. He reached for the two glasses of wine that were sitting on the deck and handed her one.

She had to move an arm to take the glass, so opted to reveal her breasts.

"Thank you. Are you going to turn on the jets?" she asked.

A smile spread across his face. "If you insist."

Then he pressed a button and bubbles surged into the tub. Soon nothing could be seen below the burbling water.

"So where are you from?" Dylan asked. "Are you a native New Yorker?"

"No, I grew up in Chicago." She settled back in the contoured seat, beginning to relax now that she was submerged in the bubbling water.

"Any brothers or sisters?"

"No. Just me. My parents divorced when I was still fairly young. I have a stepsister and a cousin who are about the same age as me."

"Are you close to them?"

"No. I don't have much in common with them. Nor my parents for that matter. They all have a very different way of viewing the world and the people around them."

They saw people as merely pawns to be manipulated in the game of building a powerful financial empire. That included their own family members.

That included her.

"Except my great-aunt. She and I were a lot alike. I loved spending time with her. She made me feel special and important."

"You're both of those things."

She glanced at him, almost forgetting she'd been talking to him. "Thank you. But you don't even know me."

"I know enough. I've seen enough of the kind of person you are."

Her cheeks flushed. She wasn't used to someone talking to her as if she mattered. Other than her friends Jon and Derrick, of course. But they were friends.

This man . . . who she was intensely aware was going to bring one of her most erotic fantasies to life . . . the way he was looking at her . . . the way he made her feel . . . It was unsettling.

"Why don't you tell me about your family and where you grew up?" she suggested.

"Okay. I grew up in Philadelphia, where I still live. I have two brothers and my family gets together for Sunday dinner every other week. My brothers both take after our dad whereas I'm more like our mom. And she and I are really close. I'm close to Dad, too, but Mom and I have a special bond."

"That sounds sweet. All of you getting together. Still having such a close relationship."

"Yeah, we're a pretty happy family." He sipped his wine and set it down on the deck again. "So how long have you been driving a cab?"

"About five years." Her cares were drifting away as the water massaged her body. "When my great-aunt died—the one I told you about—she left me a sizable amount of money, wanting me to use it to follow my dream. I used it to move to New York and buy my cab medallion."

Dylan's eyebrows arched. "Really? From what I understand, a medallion in this city would have cost upward of about three quarters of a million dollars. You could have lived quite well on that money. Maybe bought a nice condominium and worked an easier job that doesn't require so many hours."

Her back stiffened and she straightened in the seat. "I don't mind working hard and I don't like answering to anyone. And if by an easier job, you mean a typical nine-to-five gig, no thanks. Not for me."

"But wouldn't it be easier? And what about the stress? Doesn't it worry you that the medallions have dropped to less than half their value since Uber and other ride-share companies have popped up?"

Her stomach knotted. Of course she worried about that. Did he have to rub it in?

But as she lifted her gaze to his, she realized he wasn't taunting her as her family would have done. There was very real concern in his midnight eyes.

But she steeled her expression, unwilling to let him see any vulnerability.

"I'm all right."

He nodded, and she feared he saw more than she wanted him to.

"I didn't mean to upset you, Stevie. And I know you enjoy the freedom. You told me that before."

"I do, and there are so many different story ideas, so that's another benefit of the job."

"Story ideas?"

She shrugged, trying to hide her embarrassment that she'd let that slip.

"Are you a writer then? That makes a lot of sense. I can tell you're the creative type."

"You can?"

"You strike me as having an artistic soul."

"I wouldn't go that far. It's just a hobby. I make up different stories about the people who get in and out of my cab, think about them while I'm driving and then I come home and write them down. But it's not something I do seriously."

It was her way of connecting to the world. Of distancing herself from her background. It helped make her feel more like a regular person.

And the fact that she hoped that someday she might actually publish them . . . well, that was her little secret.

"Why not? Maybe I could help. I know a few people in

the publishing world. Maybe I could get someone to look at your work."

"I said I'm fine," she said in a tight voice, then picked up her half–full wineglass and drained it. "Look, I appreciate what you're trying to do but I like my life just fine and don't need someone rushing in and trying to change it for me."

She twisted her body to reach the bottle on the deck and fill her wineglass. When his eyes jolted to water level, she realized her jostling exposed a good portion of the swell of her breasts. She sat back down, her hand gripping the stemmed glass as she took another sip.

"Maybe we should talk about something a little racier than careers. This conversation is killing the mood."

"Yeah, okay," he said with a smile. "Racy, eh? Well, here's one. Have you ever been with a woman?"

She pursed her lips. *Well, I did ask for it.*

"When I was a teenager, I had this one friend. She was pretty curious about sex and she talked me into . . . uh . . . trying a few things."

She saw how his eyes lit up and she took another sip of her wine.

"What kind of things?"

Aw, damn. "Well, there was some touching. I'm sure you can imagine."

A grin split his face. "Oh, yeah. I'm imagining it now. Did you kiss?"

She nodded, remembering the soft lips on her mouth. Then moving down her shoulder. Finding her nipple.

"Let's just say we did *lots* of things, but I'm *not* going to give you details."

"You're a cruel woman, Stevie."

She looked at him, watching her with his wicked eyes and she couldn't help laughing. Which caused her to spill some wine.

But it was such good wine. She took another sip.

"Okay, so tell me. Have you ever been with a man?"

"Wait, before we move onto that question, at least tell me . . . Did you enjoy it?"

"Yes, of course. But if you're asking if I ever considered staying with women sexual partners instead of men, the answer is no."

"If you liked it, then why not?"

She grinned. "Because I like the feel of a big cock inside me, that's why." Her words shocked her a little bit. She didn't usually talk so frankly about sex. "But that doesn't mean if I was in a threesome with a man and another woman that I wouldn't interact with the other woman." Her grin broadened. "Especially since I know how much it would turn the guy on."

His jaw dropped open. "Really?"

"Well, it would, wouldn't it? Of course I'd want to do something that would excite my partner that much."

"Are you sure we can't ditch Reid and carry on with you and me and some other sexy woman?"

She laughed. "You are such a bad boy."

He grinned. "And you are a dirty girl."

Their interchange was stirring something inside her. She felt heat simmer through her that had nothing to do with the bubbling hot water surrounding her.

"So stop stalling," she said. "Back to my question. Have you ever been with a man?"

He shook his head. "I'm sorry to disappoint you, but . . . no, I haven't. I have, however, had thoughts of sharing a woman with Reid for a long time now. I just never mentioned it to him."

"Because you want to be with him?"

He laughed. "No, because he has great taste in women and I wanted in on the bounty."

Her cheeks heated at his compliment.

"Yeah, I'm sure you attract more than your share of beautiful women," she said.

He shrugged. "Yeah, okay. I like doing things with Reid and sharing something that intimate with him— watching him fuck a woman . . . bring her to orgasm . . ." His blue eyes glittered. "I find that exciting."

The thought of him watching her while Reid drove his big cock into her had her heart stuttering. Even more, the thought of him touching Reid of seeing his big masculine hands moving over Reid's muscular body sent dampness pooling in her core.

Chapter Ten

"So will you interact with Reid while the three of us are together?" Stevie's voice had deepened to a throaty whisper.

His gaze sharpened on hers. "I hadn't really thought about it."

She gazed at him intensely. "So think about it."

His hot gaze bored through her. "Does the thought turn you on?"

Her breathing was shallow, desire flickering through her, and she nodded.

"Intensely," she said.

"Then I will *seriously* think about it."

The timer went off on the bubbles and they dissipated, leaving her body visible in the clear water. Her nipples were hard and distended, her aureoles pebbled. And she made no move to cover them. In fact, her gaze dropped unashamedly to his cock, which was standing at full mast in the hot water.

. . .

Dylan's cock twitched at her obvious scrutiny. And the sight of her delightful breasts.

Damn, she was so sexy.

"I know that we're only supposed to be talking right now . . ." she said as she leaned toward him.

Then she glided through the water, her breasts swaying in the clear water, until she was in front of him, her knees resting on the bottom. Her warm hands slid over his shoulders.

"But . . ."

He dragged her into his arms and onto his lap, his mouth covering hers, unable to stand another second without touching her.

Fuck, the sweetness of her lips on his was insanely delightful, and the feel of her soft breasts crushed against his chest drove his already rock-hard cock to a painful state. His tongue glided into her mouth and swirled inside.

Her thighs cradled his hips and his cock pressed hard against her soft belly.

The need in her eyes was palpable. With the two of them still locked in a passionate kiss, she glided her body up and down. Just a little at first . . . then more . . . stroking his cock with her body.

Then he felt her slick folds move over him and he nearly choked.

She kept gliding as he tore his lips away. Their gazes locked as she kept moving . . . stroking . . . up and down . . . driving him insane with need.

Then she slid a little higher and he felt his cockhead against her slickness.

He sucked in a breath when he felt his cock sliding in-side her.

Her eyes widened, as if it had caught her by surprise, too. But she kept moving down his shaft. Taking him into the incredible warmth of her body. She whimpered a little as she neared his root.

Then he was all the way inside her.

She stared at him, her eyes wide, as if startled by find-ing herself in this position.

He cupped her face and kissed her. Her tiny mewing sound made his cock pulse with need, in turn making her whimper.

When he ended the kiss, they stared at each other.

"I guess we're pretty comfortable with each other intimately now," he murmured.

She bit her lip. "Maybe too comfortable."

Her intimate muscles squeezed him and he groaned. From the look in her eye, she hadn't intended it.

"What do you mean by too comfortable?" he asked, waging a losing battle to stay focused on anything other than their joined bodies.

"You said that . . . uh . . . Reid just wanted us to talk."

Then it dawned on him. "You feel like you're cheating on him?"

She bit her lip and nodded, looking troubled.

He didn't want to point out to her that she was the one insisting that she didn't want a relationship with Reid. That she would only continue what they did have if he agreed to a non-exclusive relationship.

Yet she was treating this as if they were exclusive and

she was being with Dylan with Reid's permission, rather than her being a free agent.

But she didn't pull away. With his cock still fully immersed inside her, she rested her head against his shoulder.

And he liked the feel of it there.

He stroked her hair.

"I don't think Reid would have any problem with us having sex right now," he said.

With one arm still snugly around her, he slid his hand between them and found her clit, then stroked it. She quivered in his arms. He teased it more aggressively and her trembling increased.

A moment later, she convulsed against his body, squeezing his cock tightly with her intimate muscles. He pivoted his hips, driving his cock deeper into her. Pulsing rapidly inside her.

She began to moan, her face glowing. Her features blossomed in shimmering joy as an orgasm claimed her.

He pumped deeper and his groin tightened, then heat flooded through him, erupting into her. She clutched his shoulders tightly as her moan transformed to a deep, reedy song of ecstasy. He kept rocking his hips, his finger still gliding over her clit, keeping her in a state of bliss.

Finally, she sucked in a breath and collapsed against him.

"God, that was incredible." She sucked in a breath, her eyes shimmering with pleasure. "But . . ."

He leaned back, holding her against him.

"I don't want to hear any buts."

"No, I don't mean . . . There are no buts about how

great it was. I just . . . I don't feel right about doing this without Reid here."

He kissed the top of her head.

"I got that. But I promise you. It'll be fine."

She's left for work.

Reid read the text from Dylan and pushed his phone into his pocket, then finished his coffee. He'd been waiting at the café on the corner near the apartment building. He paid his bill and stepped from the restaurant to the sunny street outside.

Ten minutes later, the elevator doors opened on the penthouse. One of the many things he shared with his partner and friend, Dylan.

And soon Stevie would be another.

Dylan was sitting on the couch with a cup of coffee. Sunlight streamed across the glossy, dark cherry hardwood floors.

"So how did it go last night?" Reid asked as he sat down across from Dylan.

Dylan smiled at him. A smile that was so full of satisfaction that he wondered if he actually wanted to know the answer.

"It went amazingly well."

"So you two are pretty comfortable with each other now?"

"Oh, yeah."

"Okay, so you seem a little more pleased with yourself than I would expect from a man who'd spent time in a hot tub with a beautiful naked woman and didn't get any."

"Yeah, about that . . ."

"You two fucked?" Reid's stomach tensed but he knew he was being an idiot.

He'd agreed to share her with Dylan. But the thought of the two of them being that intimate with each other . . . without him there . . . unnerved him. Fuck, he knew he was falling for the woman.

Hell, he'd already fallen. Hard.

"I didn't make a move on her," Dylan said. "I promise. It just . . . happened. We talked about family and her driving a cab. She got defensive about it and suggested we change topics . . . and we wound up talking about her being with another woman. And we were naked in the hot tub."

"What the fuck? Really?"

The thought of Stevie with another woman . . . the other woman's hands gliding over Stevie's naked body . . . pleasuring her . . . Stevie running her hands over the other woman's breasts . . . licking her nipples . . . Stevie whimpering in pleasure as the other woman buried her mouth in her pussy . . .

"Fuck!" Reid's cock ached as it strained against his pants.

Dylan nodded, his eyes twinkling. "Oh, yeah. It was hot. Then she asked if I'd ever been with a guy. Man, you should have been here. She got this hot, hungry look in her eyes."

"Are you saying that Stevie was turned on by the idea of two men having sex with each other?"

"Are you kidding? I think if I'd hinted that you and I

would be willing to just touch each other, let alone more,
she'd have come on the spot."

"So you're saying she jumped you?"

Dylan held up his hands, palms toward Reid. "Before
this conversation goes any further, I need you to understand
that Stevie was very turned on, but she was really worried
about doing anything with me while you weren't there."

"Really?" The thought made Reid smile.

Dylan nodded. "So am I right to assume that you want
more than just a short-term fling with this woman? Are you
hoping for something long term?"

He nodded. "I am."

Dylan grinned. "That's good news then, because it was
as if she was worried about cheating on you."

Reid laughed. That was the best news he'd heard in a
long time, and given how well things had been going lately,
that was saying a lot.

And they were only going to get better. He could hardly
wait for their threesome.

"So, I have to ask," Reid said. "If the idea of watching
two men together turns her on so much . . . would you be
willing?"

Dylan's eyes widened. "You're really asking what I think
you're asking?"

Reid held up his hands. "Hey, if I've gone too far, I'm
sorry. I just thought . . ."

"Yeah, I'd be willing," Dylan said decisively.

Now it was Reid's turn to be surprised. "I thought
you'd want some time to think about it."

"I have thought about it. Many times. I mean, I'm totally into women, but that doesn't mean I haven't been curious about being with a guy. But I didn't want to mention it because I didn't want to do anything that would make things awkward between us. Now that this opportunity has presented itself . . ." Dylan shrugged.

Reid smiled broadly. "Well, I'm good with it, too. I think the three of us will be amazing together."

Reid sat in the living room waiting for Stevie to return after her shift. She'd texted him that she'd be up in a few minutes.

The elevator whooshed open and Stevie stepped into the entrance.

"Good evening," Reid said, keeping his voice cool and indifferent.

She gazed at him uncertainly as she took off her sneakers.

"Hi." She plunked her bag inside the closet, then stepped into the living room.

He stood up as she approached and she stopped, watching him uneasily.

"I'd like to talk to you about what happened last night," he said.

She nodded, her gaze dropping to the floor. Fuck, it looked like she felt incredibly guilty.

"Dylan's in the other room, so let's go to the bedroom where it's more private," Reid said.

He led the way, with Stevie close behind him. Once she stepped inside, he closed the door.

Then he turned to her.

His eyebrow quirked up. "Anything you want to tell me?"

She bit her lip, her eyes filled with anguish. He almost felt guilty putting her through this.

Almost.

But he loved that she was so unnerved by having had sex with Dylan without Reid being there. Because it showed that she really cared about Reid and their relationship.

"I . . . uh . . ." she said slowly, her gaze dropping from him to her hands. "I had sex with Dylan last night."

He said nothing and she lifted her gaze, searching his face for a reaction, but he gave her none.

After a long pause, he drew in a deep breath.

"You had sex with Dylan," he finally echoed, a stern expression on his face.

Stevie nodded, looking repentant.

He could barely keep the grin from spreading across his face. When Dylan had told him what had happened . . . at first he'd felt jealous, possessive. But after hearing that she hadn't wanted to cheat on Reid . . . Fuck, he'd been delighted.

Because that meant she really did see what they had as a relationship, even if that logical brain of hers refused to acknowledge the fact.

"Do you feel bad about doing it?" he demanded.

She stared at the floor. "Of course. I know we agreed to it, but it felt like cheating somehow. I'm really sorry."

"Well, that's not enough. You need to be punished."

Her gaze shot to his and her eyes widened as she saw the burning desire in his eyes.

"Are you angry?" she asked.

He raised an eyebrow. "What do you think?"

He knew that would feed into her frenzy of uncertainty and keep her off kilter.

She bit her lip again.

When she didn't answer, he grabbed her hand and tugged her with him to the bed.

"As I said, you need to be punished."

He pressed her over the bed until her torso rested on the surface and her ass was in the air.

"Drop your pants," he commanded.

Staying put, she unfastened her jeans and pushed them to her hips. He grasped them and pulled them down her legs and lifted each ankle to pull the pants free. Then he stood up and slid the hem of her flannel shirt up her back, exposing her round ass, still covered by skimpy lace undies.

He tugged on the lace garment and slowly rolled it over her rounded buttocks, then down her legs. When he tossed it aside, he stood up, his gaze locked on her naked derriere.

"Open your legs. I want to see you."

She obeyed, widening her stance until he could see her pussy lips, the delicate petals between them glistening with moisture. Unable to help himself, he ran his fingers over her slickness.

"Aw, fuck," he said, then took his damp fingers into his mouth and sucked, tasting her musky feminine essence.

He cupped her round ass in his hands and squeezed, then gave a small, sharp slap across one cheek.

"Tell me why I'm punishing you."

"Because I had sex with Dylan."

"Because you *fucked* my best friend. Say it."

"Yes, sir. Because I fucked your best friend."

He slapped her ass again, harder this time. Her cheek glowed a lovely rosy pink.

"Did you enjoy it? Did you *like* feeling his cock inside you?"

"Yes, sir."

He spanked her again, the sharp sound ringing through the room.

"Did he enjoy it, too?"

She hesitated for a second. "Yes, sir."

"Stay exactly as you are. Don't move a muscle. I'll be back in a minute."

Chapter Eleven

Stevie stood perfectly still, barely breathing, as she waited for Reid to return. She couldn't tell how mad he was. He insisted on punishing her, but there was no anger in his touch. On the contrary, the way he touched her—with calm authority—was intensely arousing.

She heard the bedroom door open and waited for Reid to speak again.

But she sensed he wasn't alone.

"You've apologized to me," Reid said. "Now you need to apologize to Dylan."

Oh, God, Dylan was standing behind her. Seeing everything on display. She wanted to close her legs and stand up. To cover herself.

But Reid had told her not to move.

And, in fact, knowing that both men were staring at her most private parts . . . was making her wetter.

"I'm sorry, Dylan, for . . . putting you in a difficult position."

"Very good," Reid said, and she could hear the smile in his voice. "Now go ahead and punish her, Dylan."

She jumped at the feel of a big, masculine hand stroking over her ass. The fingertips gliding over her skin, then the large palm cupping her.

Then the hand lifted and . . .

Smack!

Her ass burned where he'd slapped her. Then he cupped both her cheeks and opened them wide, exposing even more of her intimate folds.

"Isn't that the most beautiful pussy you've ever seen?" Reid asked.

"Fuck, yeah, man."

Fingertips stroked over her and she knew it had to be Reid, since both of Dylan's hands were on her ass.

"She's incredibly wet," Reid said. "You should feel."

Dylan's hands released her ass and she expected that he would run his fingers over her, too, but then she felt his hot, hard cockhead brush against her. Gliding the length of her slit.

"Ah, fuck man," Reid groaned. "I really want to see your cock slide into her."

At that, the cock gliding over her slickness centered, then slowly pushed inside her. She drew in a long breath, feeling dizzy at the wild swirl of sensual delight spiraling through her.

He moved deeper and deeper. Filling her with his thickness. Gliding inside her passage.

She silenced her murmurs by pressing her face against

the plush comforter, not wanting to draw a punishment . . . which would mean that beautiful cock disappearing from inside her.

"What does it feel like inside her?" Reid asked.

"It feels incredible," said Dylan. "So hot and velvety."

Reid coiled his hand in her hair and lifted her face a little. "And what about you, Stevie? What does it feel like to have Dylan's hard cock inside you?"

"It's thick and long. It's stretching me." She was careful not to say anything about how much she was enjoying it.

"So you don't like it?"

"I do. I want him to . . . move inside me."

Reid tightened his hold on her hair, tugging on her scalp.

"So you want him to fuck you?"

Oh, God, she couldn't lie.

"Yes, sir. Please let him fuck me."

He chuckled. "In good time, my love."

Dylan moved back a little, then swooshed in deep again, taking her breath away. Sparks danced across her nerve endings, promising delightful things to come.

But then Dylan drew back, and his cock pulled from her body. She had to bite her lip to stop herself from protesting out loud.

Then she felt Reid's cock surge inside her, filling her all the way, and she actually felt herself teetering on the edge. But then he pulled out, too.

He leaned over her and pressed his lips to her ear. "As

enticing as your sweet body is, my love, we are not going to fuck you now. I think you need to lie there and think about what you've done." He stood up. "Come on, Dylan. Let's go have a drink."

Oh, God, no. They couldn't leave her like this.

She lifted her head and glanced over her shoulder, seeing them approaching the door. They were both naked and their stiff cocks pushed straight forward.

"Please, Reid." Her words sounded desperate.

Reid stopped and turned back to her, Dylan standing behind him in the doorway.

"Please what, baby?"

"Please come back . . . please finish this."

He smiled. "I told you. You have to wait to have Dylan fuck you."

Her inner passage clenched, needing a cock so bad.

"Right now," Reid continued, "just lie still and think—"

"Please, Reid," she cried desperately. "I need you inside me. Right now. I beg of you. Come and fuck me."

The teasing glint in his eyes vanished as his blue eyes darkened and he strode toward the bed. She dropped her head back to the bed and opened her legs wider. As soon as his hands cupped her hips, she moaned, knowing what was to come.

The burning tip of his cock brushed her ass, then glided over her slick flesh.

"Oh, yes, Reid. Please . . . drive inside me."

He surged forward, his cock spearing into her in a sudden thrust. Filling her deeply.

She moaned.

He drew back, then thrust fast again. Sparks flared inside her as pleasure quivered through every cell in her body. Static electricity flashed across her nerve endings at his third thrust, and she sucked in, air on his fourth.

She saw Dylan move beside the bed, watching. He glanced to her face, then watched his friend's cock now steadily impaling her.

"Oh, God." Her words came out as almost a squeak as he drove into her again and again.

Pleasure coiled inside her, tighter and tighter as she squeezed his big cock, causing even more exciting friction.

"Aw, fuck, baby. You are so fucking hot!"

Then Reid drove even deeper and grunted as heat filled her insides. She gasped, then the tightness in her belly exploded in a vibrant, mind-numbing orgasm, the pleasure wafting through her in tumultuous waves. The air seemed to thin and she sucked it in, floating in a blissful state of oblivion.

Until Reid collapsed on top of her, the heat and weight of his body a welcome reminder of what they'd just shared. His arms tightened around her and he kissed her neck.

"I told you I love it when a woman begs. That was fucking fantastic."

Stevie woke up beside Reid, snuggled cozily in his arms. She blinked against the morning light and she realized he was awake and watching her.

"Good morning," he said. His hand stroked over her

shoulder to her face and she realized she was still wearing her shirt from last night.

She remembered. After the punishment sex last night— God, she'd take punishment like that from Reid anytime— he'd kissed and cuddled her, then rolled her over. Both men had been naked and she'd still worn her bra and flannel shirt, but she'd been sure they were going to move on to their threesome. She'd been delighted and anxious and definitely warmed up.

But Reid had insisted they take a break and sit together in the living room. In no time, she'd fallen asleep. He must have carried her to bed.

His lips brushed hers in a sweet kiss.

"You were tired last night."

"I didn't mean for the evening to end so soon. Poor Dylan . . ."

"Is fine. He completely understood."

Dylan's cock had been hard as a rock—she remembered how long and stiff it had been while he'd watched Reid fuck her last night—so she wasn't sure how fine he really was. He was probably very tense and frustrated.

She'd find a way to make it up to him.

"So tonight for sure?" she asked.

Reid grinned. "I love your enthusiasm." He kissed her again, but this time he lingered.

She wrapped her arms around him and held him close, returning the kiss with all she had, her tongue sweeping into his mouth. She rolled onto her back and he rolled over her. Her hands glided over his shoulders. She felt his cock rising and she arched against him.

He groaned and rolled away. "Baby, if you keep doing that, I'm going to take you on the spot, but I want you to keep up your strength for tonight."

She stroked his cheek, gazing into his cheery, cobalt-blue eyes.

"I have lots of strength," she said as she pulled him in for another kiss.

His lips moved on hers, then his tongue thrust deep into her. His cock was solid now, ready to fill her full to bursting.

He wrapped his fingers around her wrists and drew her hands away.

"I know you do, baby, but take pity on me. I have to hold my own against Dylan tonight."

She wrapped her hand around his thick cock and squeezed, then stroked gently and laughed.

"All right, I'll wait." She rolled away and stood up.

She faced him as she pulled her shirt over her head, ignoring the buttons, then stripped off her bra. Her gaze locked with his as she cupped her naked breasts and lifted

"But remember, it was your idea to wait." Then she stroked her nipples until they blossomed into hard buds. "Maybe I'll just go and"—she stroked down her stomach and glided her fingertips over her slick folds—"take care of a few things in the shower."

She turned and walked toward the en suite.

"Ah, fuck!"

She grinned as he strode after her.

Stevie sat in the cab with her coffee, taking a well-deserved break. She exchanged a few texts with her friend Jon, who was questioning her about this sexy man she was spending so much time with. She did *not* tell him about the impending threesome. Not that he'd disapprove. On the contrary, he'd cheer her on, twisting her arm if she had second thoughts.

He'd also want all the details afterward.

She smiled. He was her friend, so she'd definitely tell him about it.

Eventually.

She sat back and sipped her coffee. She pulled her notebook out of her bag and glanced over the notes she'd jotted down over the last few days. Usually when she got home from a shift, she'd start turning her notes into a story. Building characters and situations from things she'd heard and seen, but she'd been so busy spending time with Reid and Dylan, she hadn't really had the time.

And, damn, considering the experiences she was having with them, she was more interested in writing about a very naughty cabbie who was having sexual adventures with a very sexy fare she'd picked up one rainy day.

Her cell bleeped with another text and she picked it up.

Been invited to an overnight event starting this Saturday. Can you take the time off? Allegro asked after you specifically.

It was from Reid.

She bristled a little. He wanted her there because it would help him with his client? Although she wanted to avoid a relationship with Reid, it bothered her that he just considered her a business asset . . . and a sexual partner.

God, she was screwed up. She didn't want anything

more than a sexual relationship with him yet here she was getting upset because that's all he wanted from her.

She sighed. If it was an overnight event it would probably be at Allegro's summer house a couple of hours from the city. She'd seen an article about his posh place with the stunning pool with natural rock around it and a beautiful waterfall feeding into it. He had acres of land around the house, a stable with horses, and a huge house with guest rooms galore.

There was bound to be a fancy party in the evening. She'd barely gotten the chance to enjoy the last party Reid had invited her to and she had loved getting all dressed up again. Dancing and drinking champagne. Remembering a life long past . . . a life that, at least in this respect, hadn't been all bad.

Then she frowned. Not that she'd ever go back.

But partaking one more time . . . there was no harm in that.

She had been working long hours, seven days a week, but not having to pay rent right now afforded her some leeway for this month.

You're on. She tapped the SEND button.

Stevie drove to her apartment—her *ex*-apartment. She'd texted Hank to let him know she'd be dropping by to pick up some things while he was at work.

She walked into the place and her heart constricted.

She'd been so happy here. Happy in her blissful ignorance.

She'd been ignorant of Hank's wandering eye. Of his ungrateful nature. Of his totally uncaring attitude at taking advantage of hers—and anyone else's—generosity.

Her ignorance was because she had so wanted to have a real relationship. Not like what she'd had in the past. People who merely used each other.

After her experience with Hank, she realized that it wasn't just wealthy people who used and manipulated others for their own ends.

She glanced around at the furniture they'd picked out together, the colors of the walls they'd finally agreed on after countless arguments—complete with make-up sex afterward—over other colors they'd each wanted.

She had thought she'd been happy with Hank, but she realized now that she'd merely been clinging to a dream . . . of having a normal life with a normal guy. Both of them working for a living, facing each day together.

But that had all been a lie.

Hank had stayed with her long enough to help him get his business off the ground, then had allowed his roving eye to destroy everything.

She marched through the bedroom to the walk-in closet and grabbed the clothes she'd come for, glad to see Hank hadn't sold them.

She got out of there as quickly as she could, suitcase in tow, glad to be back in her cab. The one thing she could truly depend on.

Pulling into traffic, she smiled, looking forward to getting to the penthouse and enjoying the adventure to come with Reid and Dylan.

. . .

The elevator doors opened and Stevie rolled the suitcase into the penthouse entryway and set it upright as she took off her shoes. Reid closed his laptop and stood up from the couch then walked toward her with a grin.

He wore a dark gray button-down shirt with black stripes and black dress pants. The fitted line of the shirt accentuated his trim waist and broad chest. The sight of him sent her hormones fluttering.

"Are you moving in?" he asked teasingly.

She quirked an eyebrow. "I can take it back to the cab if it's an imposition."

She reached for the handle, but he grabbed hold of it and rolled it into the penthouse.

"On the contrary. I'm delighted."

Dylan walked out of the kitchen carrying a sandwich on a plate. He wore comfortable, threadbare jeans and the top several buttons of his casual shirt were open, revealing enough of his solid chest to make her long to run her hands over it. To feel the sculpted muscles. To run her fingertips over his hard-as-beads nipples.

"Did I hear that Stevie's moving in?"

"Her suitcase is right here," Reid said as he continued to the bedroom.

"That's great," Dylan said, following them.

"I'm *not* moving in," she said.

Reid lifted her suitcase onto the couch, laying it flat.

"You're protesting a lot," Reid said, "but you already had a suitcase here, and now you've brought another." He smiled. "You know you're welcome to move in."

"We'd love for you to stay here," Dylan said.

She shook her head, glancing from one to the other. "You hardly know me. And you don't even live in this city."

"That's why it's so perfect," Dylan said. "You don't have an apartment right now and we have this one that will sit empty a lot of the time, so you might as well use it."

"And when we are in town," Reid said, "we can visit."

She raised an eyebrow. "*Visit?* Is that what you call what we've been doing?"

Reid walked toward her with a smile and wrapped his arm around her waist, then nuzzled her neck. Electricity crackled along her nerve endings.

"Don't you like how we *visit*?" he murmured against her neck.

She laughed and slid out of his hold. "I do, in fact. But I won't be moving in here."

She heard the raspy sound of a zipper unfastening and glanced at Dylan, who was opening her suitcase. She raced over and pushed the lid down before he peered inside.

"I just thought we could help you unpack," Dylan said.

"I can manage."

Reid came over and opened the case before she could stop him. Lingerie formed a frothy topping of lace and frills, since she'd thrown it in last.

Dylan lifted a burgundy satin brocade basque with black lace edging and whistled.

"Very nice."

Reid eyed the contents and held up a black lace bra and matching thong.

"I want to see you in this." His voice was a low growl, the heat in his eyes melting through her.

She felt her heart quivering in her chest.

"I mean right now," he insisted, his voice holding that note of authority she'd learned to respond to instantly.

Her hands automatically moved to the top button of her shirt to unfasten it.

He dropped the tiny garments on the bed and grabbed Dylan's arm, then led him from the room.

"In the living room in five minutes, Stevie. Got it?"

"Yes, sir," she responded, her shirt already half undone.

Chapter Twelve

The door closed behind them and heat vibrated through Stevie as she stripped off her shirt, then her jeans. She shed her panties and sat down on the bed, then pulled off her socks. Her bra went next, then she donned the black, sexy bra. It was cut low, and lifted her breasts high. She stood up and pulled on the thong.

She caught sight of herself in the mirror and sucked in a breath.

She looked like a sexy stranger as she walked toward the dresser, pulling off the covered elastic that held her hair captured in a ponytail. The long locks flowed freely around her shoulders. She picked up a brush from the dresser and ran it through her honey-gold hair until it gleamed.

Then she pushed her shoulders back. Her breasts thrust proudly forward.

She turned and walked toward the door. It was time to experience the adventure of a lifetime.

To be fucked by two incredibly sexy billionaires.

.   .   .

Stevie walked into the living room, a sway to her hips. Both men sat on the couch watching her, their eyes glowing like hot embers.

She felt so . . . attractive. So . . . desirable.

Her gaze drifted over them. Both were still fully clothed and it felt wicked standing in front of them in her barely-there black lace outfit while their hot gazes warmed her tingling skin.

The fact that these two incredibly handsome men wanted her, made her glow with delight.

There was a bottle of white wine on the table and three filled stemmed glasses.

Reid rose and handed her a glass, then gestured for her to sit in the armchair across from the couch. She sat down and took a sip.

"We're anxious to get started," Reid said.

"Me, too," she said, her voice gravelly, longing for the two of them to touch her.

He smiled. "But first, since you have been so good to us, we want to give you a special surprise."

"What is it?" Her gaze flickered from Reid's smiling face to Dylan's, then back again.

Reid set down his glass. "Well, it's become clear to us that this fantasy of yours . . . to be with both of us . . . to have us touch you . . . and"—he smiled—"*fuck* you . . . has a little more to it."

She quivered. "And what's that?" But she knew what he meant.

"You fantasize about watching the two of us together. Isn't that right?"

As images wafted through her mind of these two sexy men touching each other . . . *stroking* each other in intimate places . . . her heart pounded.

"Yes," she murmured. "I think that would be"—she had to suck in a breath—"incredibly sexy to watch."

Reid's smile widened. "So you'd like to see me run my hand over Dylan's chest?"

Her breath caught as Dylan unbuttoned his shirt and took it off. The two men were less than a foot away from each other on the couch.

"For me to run my hands down his chest . . ." Reid continued. "Over his stomach and . . ." He grinned. "Lower?" His cobalt-blue eyes were locked on her.

She was sure he could see the need sparking in her eyes. She nodded, wishing they would just go ahead and do it. To satisfy the hunger growing in her.

Reid unbuttoned his shirt, too, and dropped it from his shoulders, then tossed it aside.

"Would you like to see Dylan's hands stroke my chest? Maybe play with my nipples?"

Heat simmered through her and her breathing tightened. She nodded.

"What else would you like to see?" Dylan asked.

"I'd like to see you"—she drew in a breath—"kiss each other. And touch each other in"—she licked her lips—"intimate places."

Dylan rested his hand on Reid's chest and glided it downward. Her breath caught as his hand approached the huge bulge in Reid's pants. But then Dylan's hand stopped, inches from the tip of Reid's confined cock . . . and stayed poised there.

"So you'd like me to unzip Reid's pants and touch his cock?"

She nodded, her eyes wide.

"Then you'd like me to reach inside his boxers," Dylan continued, "and pull it out, then stroke it?"

She nodded more vigorously.

"And then," Reid said, "would you like him to suck it?"

She felt faint, electricity crackling over her nerve endings.

"I'd like that very much," she said in a throaty whisper.

Both men chuckled.

"You are a dirty girl," Dylan said, his lips curling up in a grin.

"And we do love dirty girls," Reid said.

She licked her lips again, her body trembling with the need these two men had built up in her with their teasing.

"Look how anxious she is," Reid said.

"You know, sweetheart, we want to give you what you want, but we need a little encouragement first."

Excitement quivered through her at the thought of seeing these two men touching each other in such an intimate way.

"What kind of encouragement?"

"Well, maybe you do something, then we'll do something."

"Oh."

She wrapped her arms around herself and glided her

hands down her arms and over her hips. They watched her aptly as she dragged her fingertips up her stomach, then traced the bottom of her skimpy bra.

They stared at her fingers, practically drooling. She cupped the bottoms of her breasts and lifted.

"This kind of encouragement?" she asked with a coquettish smile.

"It's a damn good start," Reid said, his heated gaze gliding from her hands to the swell of her soft mounds spilling from the top of the sheer lace bra.

Her nipples hardened, straining against the fabric.

She smiled. "I'll give you a little more, but then you give me something."

She unfastened her bra, then peeled it away and dropped it to the floor.

She could see both their cocks straining against their pants.

Reid grinned. "Baby, you need to learn to negotiate better. Set your terms *before* you give it away."

Both men's gazes were locked on her hardened nipples.

She laughed. "Okay, fair enough. How about this? I'll touch my *naked* breasts . . ." She narrowed her eyes, wondering what to ask for first. "If you two kiss."

Dylan glanced to Reid, who returned his look. She couldn't read their expressions.

"What do you mean by *touching* them?" Reid asked.

She smiled, knowing she had them.

"I'll stroke them." She raised her hand and held it an inch from her breast, as if she was about to cup it. "And, depending on how much I like your kiss, maybe I'll tease the nipples."

She moved her fingers in the air as if she was toying with the hard beads.

"Even pull on them a little."

When she mimicked that movement, she was amazed flames didn't shoot from their eyes, they were blazing with such heat.

"Deal," Reid said.

He turned to Dylan and leaned toward him. Dylan closed the distance and their lips touched.

She couldn't help herself. Her hands cupped her breasts and she stroked them. Heat washed through her.

Dylan slid his hand around Reid's head and pulled him closer. She could see their lips moving on each other's.

Their mouths parted and they turned toward her. She was still stroking her soft mounds.

"That was hot," she said huskily.

Reid pulled Dylan close again, until their mouths were a half inch apart, then . . . oh, God, her heart stuttered as his tongue glided out and stroked Dylan's lips. Dylan opened and Reid slid between his lips, then pulled him closer. Their mouths moved on each other's hungrily and she had trouble catching her breath.

Then they drew back and watched her expectantly.

As promised, she teased her nipples, stroking them with her fingertips. Feeling the dusky pink flesh surrounding them pebble.

"I think we deserve the full treatment after that," Dylan said.

She pinched her nipples tightly between her fingertips then pulled on them.

Dylan groaned. Then he stood up, unzipped his jeans, and dropped them to the floor. His cock stretched his blue boxers. Reid stood up and shed his dress pants, too. His charcoal boxers couldn't even contain his stiff cock. The mushroom-shaped head peered out over the waistband.

"I like that," she said in a husky voice. "But I'd like to see you get rid of those boxers."

"We will if you do," Reid said, his cobalt-blue eyes twinkling.

She rose and slowly glided her tiny thong down her thighs, over her calves, to her ankles. Then she stood up and stepped out of them. The men's gazes locked on her pussy as they surged to their feet and stripped away their underwear.

She knelt on the floor, as they sat down again. She rested her elbows on the glass coffee table, unable to drag her gaze from the sight of their two rigid, twitching cocks. Cocks that would all too soon be inside her.

"I want you to touch each other's cocks." Her words came out a mere whisper.

"In exchange for what?" Reid's eyes twinkled with his smile.

"I promise I'll reward you. Just trust me."

"Good enough for me." Dylan reached over and wrapped his hand around Reid's cock.

Reid reached for Dylan and grasped his tall cock, too. Stevie sucked in a deep, calming breath.

She eased herself onto the armchair again, settling back

into it. With her feet flat on the floor, she widened her legs, exposing her naked folds to their sight. Then she grazed her inner thighs with her fingertips, stopping barely a breath from her intimate flesh.

"If you stroke each other, I'll touch myself."

"Where, Stevie?" Dylan asked. "Where will you touch yourself?" His voice was hoarse with need.

She smiled. "I'll touch my pussy."

"Will you tell us how wet it is?" Reid asked.

She nodded.

Each of their hands began to move. Each long, hard shaft grew even longer as the other man's big, masculine fingers moved up and down.

She found it hard to breathe, the sight was so . . . incredibly erotic.

She stroked over her slick petals, the glaze coating her fingertips.

"I'm sopping wet," she volunteered. "So wet," she murmured, "I would probably come on the spot if one of your cocks thrust into me right now."

"Ah, fuck, baby." Reid's gaze, locked on her slick folds, blazed with heat.

"What will you do if I suck Reid's cock?" Dylan asked huskily.

Her breath caught. Oh, God, that would be something to see.

"What do you want me to do?"

Dylan crouched down in front of Reid, watching Stevie.

"I want to see your fingers buried deep inside that hot pussy of yours. I want to watch you finger fuck yourself."

She opened her legs wider, stroking her slick flesh faster. Then she pushed her fingers inside her slit.

Both men watched her—at least, her hands—their eyes filled with primal need. She glided her fingers out, then in again.

Then she stopped, waiting.

Her breath held as Dylan leaned forward. The sight of his lips wrapping around Reid's big cockhead . . . of his masculine mouth gliding down the thick shaft . . . had her gasping for air. The memory of her own mouth moving on Reid like that intensified her excitement. She had to force herself not to continue stroking herself, saving it for when Dylan could watch her.

Dylan's head moved up and down on Reid, his gaze still locked on her fingers. Reid watched her, too, but his cheeks flushed and his eyes were glazing with the pleasure Dylan was giving him.

"Keep going, baby," Reid insisted. "Dylan can still see you."

Dylan nodded.

The sight of Reid's thick cock gliding between Dylan's lips was driving her wild. Her fingers drove inside herself again and she almost cried out. She thrust in again and again as heat thrummed through her.

"Oh, God, it's so hot watching you two." She thrust in deeper. "Reid, are you going to come in Dylan's mouth?" She thrust faster. "Because if you do, I swear, I'll come on the spot." She could already feel the orgasm pulsing inside her like a flower ready to blossom.

"Aw, fuck, baby!" Then Reid groaned, his body convulsing against Dylan's mouth.

"Ohhhhh!" she moaned as the orgasm swelled within her, expanding to quivering bliss.

Her eyes fell closed, but she heard them moving toward her.

"God, I need to be inside you, sweetheart," Dylan said and she felt his cock brush against her opening.

She pulled away her fingers, still shuddering her release. He drove deep inside her and she gasped. He began to thrust and she spiraled off to bliss yet again. With each thrust of his cock, her pleasure rose . . . higher and higher . . . until she was clinging to him. Begging him for more.

"Oh, yeah. Please. Deeper."

He thrust deeper into her, increasing his speed. She clung to his shoulders and quivered as he groaned. Then she felt the heat of him releasing inside her.

Too soon he pulled out, but Reid took his place and his big cock drove inside her.

"Oh, God," she practically squealed.

"Too much, baby?" Reid asked, concern in his cobalt eyes.

"No. More," she begged.

He smiled and thrust again. She wrapped her legs around him and his cock drove deeper still, filling her with incredible bliss. His arms around her . . . his body tight to hers . . . his thick cock pumping into her . . . sent her head spinning in a vortex of exhilarating sensations.

Pleasure swamped her senses and with each stroke of his

cock, she felt her hold on the here and now fray . . . until she was hanging on by a thread, and . . .

He drove deep into her and the thread broke.

She wailed, clinging to him but feeling she was in free-fall. Floating on the edge of ecstasy.

Then she tumbled over.

"Stevie . . . Stevie . . . *Stevie* . . ."

She kept hearing someone call her name. More and more insistently.

Her eyelids fluttered open and she saw Reid's face right in front of her, his eyes filled with concern. Dylan was right beside him, staring down at her.

Both were naked.

She felt a little disoriented, but she reached out for Reid and wrapped her arms around him. Her lips found his and she kissed him, her tongue gliding into his mouth, sweeping inside and tasting the delightful white wine they'd drank earlier.

"Oh, please, Reid. Fuck me. I beg you."

"Fuck, baby, it shouldn't even be possible for me to do it again, but . . ."

She felt his hard cockhead stroke over her slick slit. She groaned as he slowly slid his big member inside her.

He guided her legs around his waist and lifted her up.

"But this time, we're both going to be inside you. Okay?"

The thought of Dylan filling her with his big cock right along with Reid's made her heart thunder.

"Yes. Oh, please."

He chuckled as he sat down on the couch.

Dylan grabbed some lube from the side table and slathered it over his cock, then knelt behind her. He stroked her hair to one side and his lips nuzzled her neck, sending quivers down her spine. Then she felt his slick cockhead press against her back opening.

She rested her head against Reid's shoulder, trying to relax.

"Oh, God, I can't believe this is happening."

Reid kissed her temple. "We want you to enjoy it, baby." He smiled against her skin. "I know *we're* going to."

Dylan pressed a little harder against her. Her tight opening stretched around his big cockhead as he pushed forward. Just a little at a time. It was strange and sexy and unnerving.

And unbelievably exciting.

Her fingers curled around Reid's shoulders as the big cock pressed deeper. He stroked her back, his fingertips gliding over her spine.

"It's all right," he murmured against her ear. "Dylan will go slow and easy. And if you want to slow down . . . or stop . . . just tell us."

She nodded. Dylan kept pushing into her, almost to the widest part of his corona.

"There's no way I'll tell you to stop," she said breathlessly.

Then his cockhead was all the way inside her. Dylan paused and she sucked in a breath.

She pressed her lips to Reid's skin in a soft kiss.

"Keep going, Dylan," she whispered, barely able to find her voice.

"Whatever you say, sweetheart." Dylan pushed forward and her tight canal was stretched impossibly wide by his thick shaft.

And she loved it.

"Oh, yes," she cooed as Dylan pushed deeper. "You feel so good inside me."

Dylan continued his slow pace forward, but finally he leaned against her back, his hot, hard chest tight against her. His big cock fully immersed in her.

Reid's cock twitched.

"Oh, God, I can't believe you're both inside me." She sighed, delighting in the heat coiled deep in her belly.

Dylan's lips fluttered along her neck in light kisses.

"Do you like it, sweetheart?"

She nodded, then turned her head. Dylan's lips captured hers and he kissed her passionately. His cock twitched inside her and she moaned inside his mouth. Her intimate muscles tightened and Reid groaned.

"Oh, fuck, baby. That feels so good," Reid murmured.

"I want you both to fuck me now. I want to feel your cocks moving inside me."

Dylan drew back slowly, then glided forward. As he kept up his slow assault on her senses, Reid pivoted his hips, pushing his cock deeper into her.

"Oh, yes." She clung to Reid's shoulders as the two cocks continued to fill her. Stretching her. Stroking her inside.

"You're both so big. So hard."

Her needy words urged them on. They moved faster, thrusting now. Filling her deeply. Heat quivered inside her belly, then curled outward in an ever-widening spiral. The world seemed to blur around her as pleasure swelled from deep inside her. Spreading out in waves. Her whole world becoming a sea of bliss.

Her moans filled the room, rising as the cocks drove into her in unison.

"Baby, I love hearing you come." Reid's words were strained. He was holding back.

"Fuck!" Dylan surged deep, then his cock blasted inside her. The heat of him filling her was incredible.

Then Reid groaned, his cock driving deep and exploding inside her.

She wailed even louder, her orgasm igniting to a new level. She rode the wave as the men kept filling her, her body ablaze with ecstasy.

Then she crumpled, limp between them.

"Stevie?" Reid said, his voice filled with concern. "Are you okay?" He gazed at Dylan. "Fainting twice so close together can't be good for her."

She giggled. "I didn't faint." She pressed her lips to his chest and kissed the hot, damp flesh. Then she lifted her head and gazed up at him. "But if you like, we could try it again. I might faint then."

Both men laughed. Dylan stood up and drew her to her feet. The feel of the two cocks sliding from her body left her feeling like something was missing.

"I think what you need right now is some rest."

She laughed, but when she tried to take a step, her legs were wobbly.

"Well, maybe a little rest, then we can try again. Right?"

Dylan kissed behind her ear. "I guess we don't have to ask if you enjoyed it."

She turned and smiled at Dylan. "Did *you* enjoy it?"

She was totally unprepared for the intensity of his solemn expression, his midnight eyes filled with deep longing.

"Sweetheart, I don't think I'll ever get enough of you."

Chapter Thirteen

Stevie awoke to the shimmer of sunlight on her closed eyelids and the warmth of two hard, masculine bodies snuggled against her. She opened her eyes to see Reid's face close to hers on the pillow.

So that meant it was Dylan spooning her, his cock hard and thick against her back. Reid was still asleep. Dylan might be, too, but his cock was definitely awake and ready to go. She pressed her behind tighter against him and wiggled a little.

"Mmm," Dylan murmured softly, then nuzzled her ear.

She felt his hand move between their bodies then the hot head nudge against her thighs. She opened enough to let him glide between them. He eased forward, his rigid shaft stroking over her intimate flesh . . . which was already slick with need.

He moved forward and back a few times, then he adjusted his cock to push against her opening. She pivoted her hips to give him a better angle of entry. She exhaled a soft moan as he slid inside her, his big cock filling her.

She trembled in Dylan's arms as she watched Reid's sleeping face. She felt like she was cheating on Reid, right here in front of him, even though she knew she wasn't. Reid was totally okay with Dylan fucking her. In fact, it turned him on. But she still didn't feel right about doing it when he wasn't present, and not being conscious . . .

Dylan glided deeper.

"I should wake up Reid," she said.

"Don't worry. Your moans will wake him when you start to come," Dylan said.

"But . . ."

His kiss behind her ear, his breath stirring small tendrils of her hair, took her breath away.

"He'll love waking up to see you coming."

He glided in deeper and she sucked in a breath, her eyelids falling closed as his cock drove her need higher. This was so wildly erotic.

"Are you sure?" she whispered.

"He's sure."

Her eyelids popped open to see Reid looking at her.

"Reid, I—"

But Dylan's cock surged into her again and she lost coherent thought.

"It's okay, Stevie. Dylan was right. I'd love to wake up to see you coming."

His gaze drifted over her face. She was sure her cheeks were flushed and her hair was a mess around her face.

Reid grinned. "But since you're not there yet, I'll help."

He pulled the covers away and cupped her breasts. He

caressed them gently. Dylan had paused, his cock immersed inside her. Reid stroked her nipples, then he captured one in his mouth and suckled. She arched toward him, which tilted her hips, causing the angle of the hard shaft inside her to change. Shivers danced through her, sparking delight in every cell.

"Start fucking her again, Dylan."

Dylan's thick cock glided along her passage, exiting her. Then he surged forward in a slow, smooth stroke. Reid suckled her other nipple, which was hard and distended. He teased it with his tongue and she curled her fingers through the dark waves of his hair, holding him tight to her bosom.

Dylan slid back and glided deep again. Another deep suck, then Reid escaped her hands and slid lower, his lips trailing kisses down her stomach.

Dylan thrust just as Reid stroked her folds. He drew them apart, then—

"Ohhhh . . ." Pleasure surged through her at the feel of Reid's tongue teasing her clit, amplified by Dylan's cock caressing her insides with his now steady thrusts.

She cupped Reid's head as he licked her and suckled. Teasing and cajoling her bud while Dylan thrust deep and hard.

"Ohhh," she whimpered. "I'm so close."

"Fuck, so am I, sweetheart."

Dylan surged deep and she pulled Reid tighter to her as he suckled on her clit.

Then an orgasm exploded inside her and she moaned.

Still both men pleasured her. Dylan's big cock moving inside her. Reid's mouth moving on her.

"Ohhh, Dylan. Reid." Her insides quivered in bliss. "You're making me come."

The pleasure surged higher, propelling her to pure ecstasy. She hovered in the delightful state, then as she slowly drifted back to earth, Dylan moaned and his cock erupted inside her. She moaned in ecstasy once again.

Reid licked her clit, then kissed up her belly. He drew her into his arms and held her close as Dylan lay panting behind her.

"Fuck, that was hot," Reid said with a smile.

"What about you?" Stevie asked.

Dylan shifted behind her, his cock pulling free.

"You relax," he said. "I'm happy to do the heavy lifting this morning."

With that he crawled over her and pushed Reid onto his back. Dylan crouched on the other side of him and grasped Reid's tall, throbbing cock in his hand. Dylan leaned down and wrapped his lips around Reid's cockhead.

Heat surged through her as the big, bulbous tip disappeared into Dylan's mouth. As she watched Dylan glide up and down, taking the cock deep into his throat, her insides quivered with desperate desire. She crawled down the bed and leaned in close to watch Dylan.

As Dylan moved up, exposing Reid's shaft, she leaned in and wrapped her lips around it. When Dylan glided back down, she slipped away, then nuzzled Dylan's neck as he held Reid deep inside him. She dragged her teeth over his raspy jaw, then nipped the tender skin under his chin.

He glided up again. She lifted Reid's sacs and licked one, loving his moan of appreciation. Then she took it into her mouth and cradled it gently against her tongue as Dylan continued to bob up and down. She suckled Reid's soft flesh as Dylan sucked his cock like a big, meaty Popsicle.

Reid groaned.

Dylan smiled at her as he slid off the top of Reid's cock, then wrapped his lips around the side of the shaft like it was an ear of corn. She returned his smile and wrapped her lips around the other side. Together they glided up and down the enormous shaft.

After several times, with Reid's breathing turning to pants, Dylan's lips met hers at the top and they kissed, then they both covered Reid's tip, half of the big cockhead in each of their mouths. Dylan wrapped his hand around Reid's shaft and pumped up and down. They both licked and suckled the tip. Then they took turns, her taking the cockhead fully inside her mouth and sucking, then Dylan. He stroked the thick shaft with his hand while she cradled Reid's balls in hers, caressing gently.

"Oh, fuck, you two. I'm going to come any minute."

Dylan, who had the tip in his mouth, opened, exposing Reid's cockhead, his lower lip still resting on the hot flesh. Stevie moved close, pressing her upper lip to Dylan's, her lower lip anchored under the ridge of Reid's cockhead. Dylan still pumped and Reid groaned. Hot liquid erupted from Reid's cock, shooting against their joined lips. She glided her tongue over the tip, bumping against Dylan's doing the same thing.

When the stream stopped, she closed over his cock and sucked lovingly. Dylan cupped her head and dragged her into a kiss. His tongue swept inside her mouth and stole away some of the salty semen for himself. Then their tongues tangled in a deep, passionate kiss.

When their lips parted, they smiled, then moved up the bed. Dylan dropped back on the bed while Stevie glided close to Reid's body, then nuzzled his neck. He captured her lips, kissing her passionately, his tongue filling her with deep thrusts. Then he stroked her cheeks and gazed at her with his serious cobalt-blue eyes.

"Don't ever worry about starting without me, baby."

Stevie took the hand Reid offered to help her from the limousine. Raphael had sent the car to drive them to his country house. She stepped onto the interlock driveway and Dylan followed her from the car.

As the chauffeur gathered their luggage from the trunk, she walked up the steps with Reid and Dylan. The place was stunning. A tall, central A-frame in stained cedar with windows from the ground to the roof and two wings extending from each side. The glass of the windows reflected the trees surrounding the building, which was situated in a clearing in the woods off a small, private lake.

The door opened and a butler welcomed them into the large, bright foyer.

"Ah, there you are." Raphael and his girlfriend, Francesca, appeared with smiling faces. "How good to see you," he said as he shook Reid's hand, then Dylan's. "And you, my dear, Stefani. I'm so glad you could accompany Reid and Dylan. It's a delight to see you again." He lifted her hand and kissed it.

"Thank you, Raphael."

Francesca shook each of their hands. "I'm glad you're here. Henry will show you to your room." She gestured to the butler.

"A moment," Raphael said. He glanced into Stevie's eyes and she felt stripped bare, as if he'd read all her secrets. Then he glanced to Dylan and then to Reid.

He turned to the butler. "Henry, put them in the large suite in the east wing." He smiled. "There are two large bedrooms and a living room, so you can discuss business if you're so inclined."

"Thank you. That's quite considerate," Reid responded.

"Of course. Take your time settling in," Raphael said. "You can join us on the terrace for cocktails whenever you're ready." He smiled. "There's no rush."

An uneasiness prickled along Stevie's spine as she glanced around the large, elegant room filled with people in suits and evening dresses, partaking in the abundant supply of champagne and hors d'oeuvres waiters carried on trays around the room.

Reid and Dylan had gone off with Raphael to discuss business and Stevie was chatting with Francesca and a couple of her friends.

As they talked, Stevie spotted a man entering the room and her gaze locked on his face.

Oh, God. It's Sean.

This was the second time she'd been in the same place as her ex-fiancé in as many weeks. It made sense that he would travel in the same circle as Reid and Dylan—in fact, he was obviously here at the invitation of Raphael—but why was he in New York? Was he after the same contract as Reid and Dylan?

She noticed that Sean was looking her way. She did *not* want to talk to him, so she glanced around for an escape.

"Stefani, my dear." Francesca leaned in close. "Come. There's someone I want you to meet."

"Yes, of course, Francesca," Stevie said, "but first I need to go fix my lipstick."

"Nonsense. You look perfect."

"I'm sorry. I really must go." She saw that Sean was heading toward them through the crowd. "I'll be back. I promise."

She hurried away, wishing she could head toward the suite, but Sean was between her and that escape route.

She seemed to lose him and she grabbed a glass of white wine from a passing waiter's tray and sipped it. She sighed, wondering how she could stay out of Sean's sight. Maybe on the patio . . .

"There you are, Stefani," Francesca said from behind her. "I told you I have someone for you to meet."

Stevie turned around . . . then stopped cold.

"Hello, Stefani." Sean's gaze locked on her.

Chapter Fourteen

Stevie could tell Sean was worried she would fly off into the crowd again. And she would if she thought she could get away with it.

"I thought this would be a delightful surprise for you," Francesca said with a big smile. "Sean here tells me you two are old friends and you haven't seen each other for several years. In fact, you just missed him at the party in the city that Reid brought you to."

"I saw you," Sean said, "but as I was coming over to talk to you, you disappeared. Francesca told me you had to leave suddenly. When I explained we knew each other in Chicago, she graciously invited me here for the weekend so we could reconnect."

"That is very kind of you, Francesca."

Francesca beamed, clearly totally lacking the ability to read people, in contrast to Raphael's exceptional ability to do so. If Raphael were here, Stevie was certain he would have sensed her total panic and desire to flee.

"Now, Sean, I insist you ask Stefani to dance. Raphael is keeping her date, Reid, busy and poor Stefani should be having fun." Francesca smiled. "It'll give you a chance to talk undisturbed so you can get reacquainted."

"It would be my pleasure." Sean offered his hand.

Stevie took only a split second to realize there was no polite way out, so she rested her hand in his and allowed him to lead her onto the dance floor. His arm swept around her back and he guided her around the floor.

It was strange being in his arms again. Feeling the same traitorous attraction she had five years ago. But it wouldn't sway her.

"You're dating Reid Jacobs? Is it serious?"

"That's none of your business," she answered tightly.

He watched her as he spun her around the floor. He was a good dancer. It was one of the things she'd loved about him. As well as his great taste in music and clothes, and how he'd always been able to make her laugh. He had excelled at Princeton, finishing top of his class. Since then he'd taken the reins of one of the major companies in his father's empire and even just a few years out of college, had shown great promise.

He was everything her parents should have wanted for her . . . and had wanted. For all intents and purposes, they had been a perfect match.

Yet, their parents had put an end to their five-month engagement, snuffing it out like a discarded cigarette.

And Sean hadn't even fought back. He'd simply conceded to their wishes.

"Look, Stef, I know I hurt you, and I apologize for that

from the bottom of my heart. I was a total idiot. I know that now and I wish I had done things differently."

She wished she had more distance between them. Being so close to the man who'd torn out her heart and tossed it away, then thought a few words of apology would fix it, had her chest so tight she could hardly breathe.

"That's easy to say now that Mitzi and Todd have divorced," she grated. "If they were still together, you wouldn't be saying that."

"That's not true," he responded a little too loudly, his eyes flaring. Several couples on the floor glanced over at them. His mouth compressed and he took a deep breath. "I'm sorry, Stef. I really want to talk to you about this. Can we go somewhere quieter? Maybe to the terrace?"

She pursed her lips, but nodded. Now that they'd started the conversation, they might as well finish it. She followed him through the room to the French doors leading outside, then into the night air. She breathed in the sweet scent of lilacs.

The spring evening was a little cool and her bare shoulders pebbled in goose bumps. He led her to a quiet spot against the elegant stone railing overlooking the lake. Moonlight glittered on the water's surface as she gazed over it.

"You're cold," he observed and took off his jacket.

He wrapped it around her shoulders and the warmth of his body settled around her. Along with his scent. Warm and musky. Reminding her of sultry nights in his arms. That summer they'd spent together after college had been magical. A fairy-tale romance where everything was perfect.

Her parents and his had been thrilled with the match.

When they'd gotten engaged, both families were behind them. Her parents loved him. His parents loved her. Everything had progressed like a dream until the engagement party when the two sets of parents met.

"It's a beautiful spot." Sean moved close to her side and leaned against the railing. "It reminds me of Jeremy's lake house where we met." He laughed, a soft chuckle. "The first time I saw you, I couldn't take my eyes off you. I wangled an introduction from Jeremy then talked your ear off all afternoon."

He smiled as he gazed at her.

God, she'd memorized every detail of his warm hazel eyes. The dark brown ring around the pupils. The underlying glow of amber. The green flecks that darkened when he looked at her. Just like now.

Those eyes had haunted her dreams for far too long.

"But you didn't seem to mind." His devastating smile curled her toes. "Then that evening . . . do you remember what happened?"

"No," she said curtly, turning her gaze to the lake.

"I think you do." His soft, raspy voice reminded her of intimate, passion-filled moments spent in his arms. "We went out for a walk to get away from the noise and the people. Just you and I holding hands and walking along the beach. I remember the beautiful sunset over the water." His eyes glittered as he watched her. "But it didn't come close to rivaling your beauty."

"Sean . . ." She wanted him to stop. The memories were too painful.

"Then the rain came down. A sudden downpour and

we ran for cover. We found that little wooden shed and waited there for the rain to stop."

She remembered the drumming of the rain on the roof. The flood of water turning the sand to mud. The two of them huddling in the cramped structure.

But she hadn't minded. The thrill of meeting this new, exciting man . . . of the possibilities that lay ahead . . . had filled her with delight.

She knew she should stop his reminiscing, but his re-telling of this, her most cherished memory, mesmerized her. She'd tried so hard to forget it, but it had burned through her on those lonely nights after he'd abandoned her, along with thoughts of what might have been.

"Then do you remember what happened?" he asked, his husky murmur sending shivers through her.

She shook her head, unable to utter the lie out loud.

"We kissed for the first time."

His words shimmered through her, triggering a mé-lange of emotions. Her heart stuttered.

He stroked her hair from her face, the effect of his gen-tle touch threatening to topple her barriers.

Dear God, she'd missed him.

As if sensing her weakness, he leaned in closer and she knew he intended to kiss her. She steeled herself to the memories of how she'd longed for him after things had fallen apart, and focused on the pain he'd caused her.

She turned from the railing and took a step away, put-ting a little distance between them.

"Sean, you said you wanted to talk to me. If it's just to reminisce, then we're done here," she said bluntly.

"No, I wanted to say that I was an idiot to let Mitzi and Todd influence our relationship in any way."

"I'm not going to argue with that," she said flatly.

There was no reason she should make this easy on him. Especially after the devastating pain he'd caused her. The man she'd loved . . . who had told her he loved her and asked her to marry him . . . had walked away without a backward glance. Shattering her whole world.

"It was unfair of them to ask what they did," he continued.

"They didn't ask. They ordered." Anger sizzled through her at the memory. "And you just . . . obeyed. Like a puppet."

"For the good of both our families."

Anger blazed through her and she thrust his jacket back at him as she gritted her teeth and pushed past him. Clearly, his apology was all a lie.

He grabbed her arm gently.

"No, Stefani. Please don't go. I didn't mean to justify what I did. I told you I know I was wrong. But back then . . . I was still so young . . . I didn't know how to stand up to them."

"And you do now?"

"It's not easy to stand up to an empire, but if that's what it takes to win you back, I'll do it."

Her blood ran cold and spots flashed before her eyes.

"You want me back?" Of course that's the only reason he'd chase her like he had. This wasn't just about an apology.

Oh, God, she had always wanted him to regret his decision. She'd wanted him to suffer the loss of losing her as much as she'd suffered at his rejection. Because she wanted to know that he'd longed for her as much as she had longed for him.

And him saying he wanted her back . . . she'd always thought that would somehow ease the pain just a little.

"Why?" she demanded.

"Because I've never forgotten you. Or forgiven myself for letting things fall apart between us. After I lost you, my life became so empty. I distracted myself with work, and cars, and women, but none of it filled the void." He wrapped his hands around her arms, his hazel eyes glowing with warmth. "Because, Stef, I've never stopped loving you."

The depth of longing in his eyes held her mesmerized, even as he drew closer. This time she couldn't force herself to pull away. His lips brushed hers, then his arms swept around her and he deepened the kiss. Forgetting herself, she leaned into his body, responding to his tender touch. His familiar lips.

She felt lost. She'd wanted this for so long but at the same time . . . she didn't.

She thought she heard someone behind her and she started, then found the presence of mind to pull away. In a daze she glanced around in time to see the French doors to the house closing as someone disappeared back into the house.

Chapter Fifteen

Stevie's stomach clenched.

Oh, God, what was she doing kissing her ex-fiancé on the terrace? What if someone saw her and told Reid or Dylan?

She couldn't let that happen.

"Please, Stefani," Sean said. "Tell me. Do I have a chance with you?" He gazed at her with hope in his hazel eyes.

"I don't want to continue this here. Are you an overnight guest?" she asked.

"Yes."

"Good." She took his hand. "Let's go to your room."

Reid watched Dylan step in from the terrace, stride to a waiter and grab a glass of wine, then down it. Reid walked to him.

"Did you find Stevie?" Reid asked.

When they'd returned from their talk in the den with Raphael, solidifying some of the terms of the contract, one

of the staff told them they saw Stevie go outside. Dylan had
gone out to see if he could find her while Reid had perused
the room for her.

"Uh . . . yeah, I did." Dylan's face was pale and his eyes
haunted.

"What the hell's wrong, man? You look like you've seen
a ghost."

A waiter passed by and Dylan grabbed another glass of
wine and took a sip, but Reid was distracted by a flash of
emerald-green satin. Stevie's dress. She was hurrying across
the room with a man following her and . . .

"What the hell?" He watched as the two of them disappeared through a side door that he knew led to the guest
rooms in the west wing. "Where is Stevie going with that
guy?"

"If I had to guess," Dylan said, "she's going to his room."

Reid's eyes narrowed. "Why do you say that?"

"Because . . ." Dylan's gaze locked with Reid's. "I just
saw the two of them kissing on the terrace."

Stevie stepped into the guest room Sean was staying in and
Sean closed the door behind them. It was a beautiful room.
Not as big as the master bedroom in the suite she shared
with Reid and Dylan, but still a generous size. The curtains
were open, displaying a lovely view of the moonlit lake. A
plush love seat faced the window and a few feet over was a
very large bed.

Oh, God, what would Reid think if he knew she was
in a bedroom with another man? A man she had history
with. A man she'd had *sex* with.

Guilt washed through her. But it wasn't like she intended for anything to happen between her and Sean. She was here to set him straight.

Sean strode toward her and rested his hands on her arms and started to draw her into a kiss, but she backed away.

"That's not why I'm here, Sean."

"Stefani, you know we're right together. Everything about us—our families, our upbringing, our interests— we're perfect for each other."

She frowned. "Sean, do you know what I've been doing in New York the past five years?"

"I don't know. Socializing, charity work, maybe starting your own business venture? Obviously you've done some excellent networking, associating with people like Raphael Allegro and Reid Jacobs."

"Yes, well . . . I have started my own business venture. I bought a taxi medallion and I drive a cab for a living."

Sean laughed.

"I'm not kidding," she said.

Sean's chuckle faded and his eyes widened.

"Seriously? You drive a taxicab?"

She nodded.

"Why would you do that?" Then he smiled. "Of course. It's a lark. You drive a cab to see how the other half lives. Then when you tire of it, you'll go back to living the way you should."

Her eyebrow arched. "The way I should? You mean like my parents did? Spending every waking moment of their lives adding to their obscenely large pool of family wealth? Or perhaps I should treat people ruthlessly, the way they did. You realize that my parents' company polluted numerous lakes and rivers, crushed small businesses that stood in their way, and laid off employees indiscriminately in order to improve their bottom line?"

"There's nothing wrong with being powerful, Stef. And if you marry me, you can do whatever makes you happy."

"I'm already doing what makes me happy. I'd like to work a little less, maybe, and pursue my hobbies a little more. But I'd never be happy going back to the life I grew up in."

Her writing was more than a hobby for her, but she wouldn't tell him about that.

He stepped closer, his eyes beseeching. "But Stef . . ." He took her hands, his big fingers enveloping hers. "The way I feel about you . . ." He drew her close, his warm brown eyes oozing desire. "I love you."

Then he pulled her into a kiss. His lips moved on hers gently, as his arms tightened around her. The sizzling chemistry that she felt every time he took her in his arms rose inside her again and instead of pulling away when he deepened the kiss, she melted into it.

When he released her, he smiled, gazing down at her as he stroked her cheek.

"There's still the same magic between us. You felt it, too, didn't you?"

She gazed deep into his eyes and rested her hand on his cheek.

"Yes, I did. But I'm afraid . . ." She drew in a deep breath, not wanting to hurt him, despite the pain he'd caused her. But she had to say it. "It's nothing compared to what I feel with Reid."

•   •   •

Stevie walked to the door, desperate to get away from Sean and the devastating pain in his eyes. He wasn't a bad man. And she knew now that she couldn't really blame him for the pain he'd caused her. He'd been a product of his upbringing, never learning to question his family. It had been too much to expect him to fight for their love back then.

Now, deep in her heart she knew . . .

What she felt when she was in Reid's arms . . . the magic that pulsed through her . . . it wasn't just desire for the intensely pleasurable sex between them.

What she felt with Sean—which she'd believed to be undying love for a true soul mate—paled in comparison. But when she'd thought she loved him, she'd had no idea what real love felt like.

Reid's touch ignited a need deep inside her. A yearning to be in his arms forever. And that scared her so much, she'd convinced herself it was just lust.

But now she couldn't run from the truth.

She was deeply and hopelessly in love with Reid Jacobs.

Reid strode down the hall, Dylan following close behind.

"What are you going to do?" Dylan asked. "She has every right to—"

Anger flared inside Reid. "She has no right to hook up with another guy while she's here with me."

Dylan caught up and fell into stride beside him. "You mean us, which has a certain irony that you're upset she might have sex with another guy, but I really doubt she's hooking up with him. She had trouble being with me without feeling like she was cheating on you, even with your explicit permission."

A couple exited their room behind them and headed toward the party. After Reid and Dylan had put a bit more distance between them and the couple, Reid turned his head toward Dylan as they walked.

"*You're* the one who saw them kissing," Reid growled under his breath. "And suggested she was going to his room."

"Okay, I was a bit in shock. But I didn't say she was going to have sex with him. I don't believe Stevie would do that. There's some other explanation."

After a few more steps, Dylan said, "Do you even know which room they're in?"

Chapter Sixteen

Reid stopped. Fuck, he didn't know what the hell he was doing. He just knew he had to stop Stevie from slipping away from him. He raked his hand through his hair.

"We could go back and ask the staff if they know," Reid suggested.

But as he started to turn, a door opened. He held his breath when he saw Stevie step into the hallway, smoothing down her dress. Her hair was disheveled and her lipstick smeared. Jealousy surged through him.

She turned and her eyes widened when she saw him facing her in the hallway.

She drew in a deep breath and started to stride forward, quickly closing the dozen or so feet between them. But before she could dodge past him, he stepped in front of her.

"We need to talk," he said in a tight voice.

"Yes, I agree, but"—she gazed over her shoulder at the closed door she'd just exited—"let's get away from here."

A sudden surge of protectiveness knocked him off balance. What exactly had happened in that room? Had the man forced himself on her? Was she hurt?

She grabbed his hand and towed him along with her.

"Dylan, is there a way to our suite without going through the party?" she asked.

"We'll find a way," Dylan said.

Dylan found a sliding glass door to the backyard where guests could go out and enjoy the patio. They passed a few guests enjoying the view of the lake, but most were inside at the party. When they reached the other side of the grand house they found another glass door leading inside.

Once they were back in the suite, Dylan closed the door behind them.

"Are you all right?" Reid asked, his concern more for Stevie and her well-being than thoughts of jealousy.

"What were we running away from?" Dylan asked.

She shook her head and sank onto the couch, resting her face in her hands. Reid's chest constricted, worried about what she'd say. She still hadn't answered his question.

"Just an awkward situation," she mumbled.

He drew in a breath.

"Dylan told me he saw you kissing a man on the patio earlier. Then we saw you leave the party to go to his room."

Stevie lifted her head and sighed, then stared at her folded hands resting in her lap.

"He's a man from my past. In fact . . . I was engaged to him."

"He's the reason you don't want anything to do with rich men." Dylan observed. "He's the one who hurt you."

"When he decided not to go forward with our marriage, it did hurt. We were young and had so much in common . . . and I was so in love with him. It tore me apart that he could walk away from what we had so easily."

Dylan sat down beside her and took her hand. "I'm sure it was very difficult for you," he said in a soothing voice.

"So he was rich and he jilted you? That's why you reject a relationship with any wealthy man?" Reid asked.

"It's not just that. It's everything I'd seen about the wealthy. Sean isn't a bad guy. He just did what his family wanted. Because they felt it was better for the family if we didn't get married, he did as he was told and broke up with me."

"Because you didn't come from a rich family?" Dylan asked.

"No. That wasn't it. In fact, I do come from money. If I had been willing to be the good daughter, I'd have quite a healthy bank account right now. I'd never have to work a day in my life. I could even take on a branch of the family business, or start a venture of my own, financed by the family. But, to me, the cost was too high."

"So you walked away from it all for a simpler life," Reid said, nodding in understanding.

"Yes, that's how I came to be a cabdriver. After our families broke us up . . . or rather, when Sean decided to follow their order to break up with me . . ." She frowned. "Well, that was the last straw. I refused to be manipulated for the good of the family." Her heart contracted. "I mean, it's not that I didn't love my family. And I would do whatever I could to help any of them emotionally. But with them, money and power were the driving forces and that went beyond anyone's feelings." Pain lanced through her. "Their business sense was incredible, but ruthless. What they wanted . . . in love and in business . . . always came first."

Reid sat down beside her and took her other hand. "So why did he break up with you?"

She drew in a breath. "Because when our parents met . . . it was a big weekend away at his father's country house so that the two families could get to know each other. . . . Well, my mother and his father, who were both divorced . . . hit it off. They got to know each other quite well that weekend and over the course of about a month, had a fling. But it turned serious and they decided to marry."

"That's crazy. So why did that affect your engagement?" Dylan asked.

"They didn't want any hint of a scandal because, of course, one they got married, Sean and I would be step-siblings."

"So your ex-fiancé is your stepbrother?" Reid asked.

She shrugged. "I don't know. Are we still considered steps now that our parents are divorced?"

"So what you're saying," Reid said as he squeezed her hand, "is that your mother put her happiness ahead of yours. Then she used her money and power to control you, driving you away from everything you held dear."

Stevie's gaze shot to Reid's. That's exactly what it meant. Reid had pushed right through the crap and gotten to the heart of it. She'd never thought of it in just that way, but now the sense of betrayal overwhelmed her.

She choked up and tears flooded from her eyes.

Reid's heart constricted at the sight of Stevie's tears. He enveloped her in his arms and held her close. Her soft face rested against his chest and he could feel dampness on his shirt, but he didn't care about that.

He stroked her soft hair, still nicely coiled behind her head, and murmured, "It's okay, baby."

Which was insane. It wasn't okay that her mother had treated her that way.

His heart ached. He wished there was some way he could fix it.

Dylan retrieved a box of tissues from the bathroom and set them on the coffee table while Stevie sobbed against Reid's chest.

But soon, she drew back and snatched a tissue from the box, then wiped her eyes. She glanced at Reid.

"I'm sorry, I didn't mean to . . ." She waved her hands, wiping her eyes again.

"No need to be sorry. You must know I'm always here for you," Reid said. "Dylan is, too."

She nodded, blowing her nose.

"Thank you. I'm fine. It was just hard seeing him again." Her lips pursed. "Dealing with all of this again."

Reid stroked her cheek, running his fingers through the soft wisps of hair around her face.

"You don't have to deal with it alone," Reid said, gazing into her eyes. "We're both here for you. Whatever you want . . ."

She stroked his face, her soft hand gliding over his raspy jaw.

"Thank you."

Reid slid his arm around her and drew her close to his side.

"Hey," Dylan said, "why don't we all curl up together and watch a feel-good movie?"

"If we're going to do that, I'm going to change," Stevie said and headed to the bedroom.

After changing into her pajamas, she went into the en suite to let down her hair and brush it out, then take off her makeup. When she returned to the living room, the men were both in casual pants and T-shirts. She sat down on the couch between them.

Dylan had located a list of movies using the on screen menu.

"Maybe a classic black-and-white romance? How about this one with Cary Grant and Deborah Kerr?"

He clicked on one of the movies on the list.

Reid glanced up at Dylan, his eyebrow arching.

"*You* like old romance movies?"

Dylan shrugged. "I think Stevie'll like it. My mom used to cry through the last half of this one." He glanced at Stevie. "But not in a bad way. You'll love the ending."

Stevie laughed. "I think it's a great choice. I like to watch old classics. I think that's what first got me interested in writing."

"Okay, good," Dylan said. "I'll go round us up a bottle of wine and some snacks from the staff."

Dylan disappeared out the door and Reid tightened his arm around Stevie, loving the feel of her snuggled against him.

"You know, I think writing is more than a hobby for you. I know you don't want help getting published. Dylan told me he already offered that. And I get it. You want to succeed on your own. But I would love to read some of your stories sometime." He stroked her hair from her face. "I know it takes a lot of trust to share something so close to your heart with someone." He cupped her cheek. "And I really want you to trust me that much."

"I . . ." She seemed mesmerized as she stared into his eyes. "I'll think about it."

He smiled. "That's all I can ask."

The door opened and Dylan returned with a bottle of wine and bags of chips and pretzels in one hand, and three stemmed glasses in the other.

"They didn't have any popcorn, but these should do nicely." He dropped the bags on the coffee table, then set the glasses down. "You two look cozy. May I join you?"

Stevie smiled invitingly. "Of course."

Dylan sat down and she eased away from Reid and leaned into Dylan, then kissed his cheek.

"Thank you for bringing the goodies."

Dylan laughed. "Anytime, sweetheart."

He opened the bottle and filled the glasses, then handed her one.

Reid grabbed his glass and started the movie. Then

Dylan leaned in closer, so Stevie was pressed close between them.

The movie was fun and romantic, then tragic, then heart-wrenchingly fulfilling. She found herself crying at the end, her heart swelling for the characters. Dylan handed her a tissue to wipe her eyes, and she couldn't help herself. She wrapped her arms around him and hugged him tight. Reid stroked her back and she turned to him and hugged him, too.

"I think you liked the movie," Dylan said.

She nodded. "I'm a sucker for a happily-ever-after. Especially after so much strife."

Reid cupped her cheek. "And I'm a sucker for you." He kissed her, his lips coaxing.

She laughed. "If you're trying to get me into bed, you don't have to worry. Where you two are concerned, I'm a pushover."

She stood up and grasped the hem of her pajama top and raised it a little, watching their eager faces, then turned and started toward the bedroom. The men stood and followed her, so she raced ahead, laughing. She pulled the top off and tossed it in Dylan's face. Reid tackled her as she reached the bed and she fell across it, giggling. He rolled her over and his simmering blue gaze locked on her face. Then shifted to her naked breasts.

He grabbed the waistband of her pajama bottoms and pulled them off her. At the foot of the bed, Dylan was stripping off his clothes. Reid stood up and began to shed his own clothes while Dylan prowled over her. His hard, hot cock was ready to go.

And so was she.

She grabbed it and pressed it to her.

"Do it, Dylan," she said eagerly. "Fuck me."

His midnight eyes glittered and he thrust forward. The feel of him stretching her made her gasp.

"Oh, God, yes."

He pumped into her and she clung to his shoulders, riding the rising wave of passion. Within moments, she was moaning her release, arching against him as he erupted inside her. He kissed her and pulled away, then Reid took his place, his thick cock sliding deep into her body.

Reid grinned. "Now that I know old movies make you horny, I'll get a whole library of them."

He began to move inside her and pleasure surged through her.

"Oh, God, I'm going to come again."

"Yeah, baby. I want to see you come in my arms."

Reid pounded into her and she wailed as she shot off to ecstasy again. Within seconds, he lurched deep, then groaned his release.

Stevie woke up snuggled between two hot, hard bodies. Her cheek was resting against Dylan's tattooed back and Reid was behind her, his muscled arms tucked around her waist. She sighed at the delightful warmth of being here.

Their breathing was slow and deep and she didn't want to wake them, so she carefully turned in Reid's arms until she was facing him, then rested her head against his chest, listening to his heartbeat.

She loved him.

And she loved being with both of them.

The question was, how long could she keep this casual, erotic sexual fling going with both of them? Without giving Reid hope it could lead to more? Without hurting him?

Or could she actually try a relationship with him? See where it might go?

His hand glided from her waist to her cheek and he stroked, his fingers tangling in her long hair, then cupping her head. As he held her tightly to his chest, his lips nuzzled the crown of her head.

She gazed up at him and . . .

Oh, God, his cobalt eyes shimmered with love as he gazed back at her.

"Good morning," he murmured in his sleep-roughened voice.

Chapter Seventeen

"Good morning," Stevie said almost timidly, shaken by her reaction to his loving gaze, which was an overwhelming need to burrow into his arms and stay there forever.

Their gazes locked and his lips curled up in a slow smile.

She quivered, knowing he saw it in her eyes. The way she felt about him. She couldn't hide the love shining there.

He leaned in and captured her mouth, his lips coaxing hers. She couldn't help herself. She wrapped her arms around him and held on tight as she deepened the kiss. Giving herself to him completely.

She felt Dylan stir behind her. He sat up.

"Well, since you have the woman well in hand, I'll go take a shower." Dylan grinned. "If you need a second cock, you know where to find me."

As soon as Dylan left the bed, Reid rolled Stevie onto her back, his body on top of her. She felt his big cock fall across her belly and she sucked in a breath. It was so thick and heavy.

And rock hard.

He grasped it and pressed it to her opening. As it pushed inside her in a slow, smooth stroke, her body quivered, every cell lighting up with need.

He drew back and glided forward again. Her eyelids fell closed as she murmured her need. She squeezed him, wanting to pull him so deep into her he could never escape.

He chuckled and kissed her neck, then along her shoulder. She stroked his chest, her fingertips gliding over the sculpted muscles as his hips pivoted, keeping his cock moving inside her. She opened her eyes to see him staring at her, a smile of delight on his lips. She couldn't drag her gaze from his, getting lost in the shimmering depths of blue.

He moved faster, pumping deeper, bringing her to the brink so quickly it took her breath away. As she clung to his shoulders, pleasure swamping her senses, she knew only a few more strokes would send her over the edge.

She squeezed him inside her, and murmured sweet nonsense. That encouraged him and he thrust deeper, filling her with lightning fast strokes. Blissful joy spiraled through her and her insides coiled tighter and tighter until . . .

"Oh, my God . . ." Her words turned into a long, sweet wail of ecstasy as her body shuddered in release.

He pumped a few more times, groaning, then drove deep one more time, filling her with heat.

He sucked in a breath of air, then rolled her onto her side and into his embrace, his leg tucking around hers, his cock still buried deep inside her. She felt cocooned in his masculine warmth.

"I love you," he whispered against her ear, and she stiffened.

His fingers threaded through her hair and he drew back to gaze down at her, concern in his vivid blue eyes.

"Are you two finished fucking yet?" Dylan said as he walked into the room, a towel slung around his hips as he dried his hair with another. Then he tossed it over the back of a chair and grinned. "Because I can join you if you like."

At the distraction, Stevie rolled away from Reid and his disturbing gaze, then sat up.

"I'm done for now," she said as she pushed aside the sheets and stood up. "But you can carry on with Reid if you like."

He smiled at the sight of her naked body. "But that's no fun if you're not here to watch."

"Sorry," she said as she hurried off to the bathroom, praying Reid didn't follow her.

Reid sat up, watching Stevie scurry away.

"Well, you look like shit," Dylan said. "Which is odd given you just finished fucking the sexiest woman alive."

"I fucking told her I love her and she couldn't escape fast enough."

Dyan dropped his towel and pulled on a pair of clean boxers.

"That was a bold move. Maybe you should have waited."

"You think?"

"Hey, don't get mad at me. She's still reeling from running into the guy who scared her off rich guys like you. What did you expect?"

"I guess I thought if she knew how much I care about her, she'd get past those things."

Dylan chuckled. "Yeah? How'd that work for you?"

Reid gritted his teeth. He knew Dylan wasn't being insensitive to his feelings. As always, he was forcing Reid to see things as they were, not as he wanted them to be.

"Yeah, so I screwed up," Reid said. "But you know, I'm not giving up on her. I'm going to convince her she's meant to be with me."

Dylan pulled on his socks. "I wouldn't expect anything less."

When Stevie returned to the bedroom, to her relief, both Reid and Dylan were gone. She could hear them talking in the living room.

The sun was shining outside and the large backyard thermometer said it was seventy-eight degrees out so she dressed in a nice floral dress with a halter-style top and sandals. Then she drew in a deep breath and opened the bedroom door.

Both men glanced up as she walked into the room.

"Coffee coming up," Dylan said as he rose to walk to a coffeemaker in the kitchenette in the corner.

Reid had a coffee cup in his hand and Dylan's sat on the coffee table, still steaming.

"No, thanks," she said. "I'll get some when we go down to eat." The plan had been to join Raphael and his other guests for brunch this morning.

"Actually, Stevie," Reid said, "I was wondering if you wanted to skip it and just head straight back to the city."

"No, of course not. It wouldn't look good if you and Dylan slipped away early. Raphael may be offended."

"Not if I explain to him."

She raised an eyebrow. "I take it this is so I can avoid seeing Sean again? Don't worry about me. I'm a big girl. If Sean's uncomfortable, he can keep his distance, but as for me, I'm capable of making polite conversation with an ex."

"I just wanted to avoid putting you in an awkward situation."

"I appreciate that, but there's no need to concern yourself."

Dylan, who'd been watching them from the kitchenette, stepped behind her and curled his arms around her waist, then kissed the back of her neck. Delightful shivers raced along her spine.

"That's what I love about you," Dylan said. "So feisty."

She leaned back against him. "Yeah, well, you're pretty lovable yourself."

With Dylan she was comfortable bandying about the word "love," but with Reid it was a different matter. Because with Reid the emotion was deeper. More impactful.

Her gaze locked on Reid and the tight line of his lips told her he wasn't happy.

"By the way, you look lovely," Dylan said, lifting her hand and turning her around in a slow spin so he could see her at every angle. His smile broadened. "I especially love the bare back and shoulders. Sexy."

"Yes, you do look lovely in that dress," Reid said, but she got the idea that he wished she'd worn something different. Something that didn't showcase her curves as well as this did.

He was worried about her and Sean.

Reid stood up. "Well, we might as well get going then."

Dylan drew his hand from hers and grabbed his cup of coffee, taking a final swig. She turned and walked to the door, the two men following her.

Reid followed Raphael out the patio doors from the study into the sunny afternoon, Dylan by his side.

After finishing brunch, Raphael had asked them to join him so they could discuss a few final points and so the lawyers could finalize the contract the next day.

"I'm sorry to have kept you from your lovely Stefani," Raphael said as they walked across the stone patio to the grass beyond, "but it looks like her old friend . . . Sean Benedict I believe his name is . . . has been keeping her occupied."

Reid's gaze shot to the dock jutting out on the lake. Stevie was sitting on the wood, her sandals beside her and her feet dangling in the water. Beside her sat Sean, her ex-fiancé. The two of them were talking, Stevie with a big smile on her face. The sunlight glittered on the water, also dancing across her soft, golden locks of hair, and she flicked it over her shoulder and laughed melodically at something Sean said.

Jealousy surged through him, so intense he could barely keep it from shadowing his features.

He did his best, but Dylan knew.

Dylan turned to Raphael. "Thank you for your hospitality this weekend. We all enjoyed ourselves immensely." He shook Raphael's hand. "We look forward to working with you."

"Yes, very much." Reid also offered his hand and Raphael smiled.

"My pleasure, gentlemen. Now I must go to my Francesca and make up for the time I have spent away from her. Give your Stefani my love."

More love for Stevie. Reid fumed as he walked across the grass toward the water. And she would accept Raphael's as easily as she'd accepted Dylan's.

And, it seemed, Sean Benedict's.

But not Reid's.

Stevie felt Reid's presence even before she glanced up to see him approaching, a sour glint in his cobalt-blue eyes.

"There's Reid and Dylan," she said to Sean.

"So it's time for you to go. I'm sure they won't want you anywhere near your ex-fiancé."

"I'm glad we had this time to talk," she said.

Sean was coming to terms with the fact she was not going to go back to him. He said he wanted to be friends and she appreciated that he was trying. He clearly loved her and to his credit, he seemed more concerned with her happiness than getting what he wanted.

She'd found herself opening up to him this afternoon. She'd even told him about her writing, which was a big step for her.

"So tell me," Sean said. "How serious are you about this guy?"

"Reid?" She shook her head. "No, it's just a fling. Nothing long term."

Even if she was starting to have second thoughts about keeping Reid at bay, she wasn't going to tell Sean. Or anyone else.

"Come on. After what you said last night when I kissed you, it's clear as day you're in love with him."

She stiffened. "I'm not in love with him. And even if I was, I've had enough of rich bastards, thank you."

"Ouch." He leaned in close. "Stevie, look, I get that you're not in love with me, and I'm sorry that what happened between us caused you so much pain. I just hope you won't let it get in the way of finding the happiness you deserve. Because if you are in love with this guy and you walk away, you'll live to regret it. Take it from me."

She gazed at him, her heart breaking at the pain in his eyes.

Reid and Dylan were almost at the dock now. Sean stood up and offered his hand, then helped her to her feet.

The wood of the dock was warm against her wet feet.

"Stefani, the car's waiting for us," Reid said, his gaze hard on Sean.

"Of course." She turned to Sean and held out her hand. "It was nice seeing you again."

He took her hand, but instead of shaking it, he drew her into a hug. "I'm glad we connected again." He squeezed her hand. "And if you ever need anything, you know you can call on me."

Reid watched them with a stormy expression.

"Thank you, Sean. Good-bye."

She slipped on her sandals and stepped from the dock

to the grass. She followed Dylan and Reid to find Raphael and Francesca, then all too soon, they were in the limousine on their way back to the penthouse.

Reid sat silently in the car, remembering how very comfortable Stevie had looked with her ex-fiancé. They'd been laughing and talking together like old friends, which they were, but they had also been in love. And as much as Stevie might deny her feelings for the man, that could just be because of his rejection of her. Now that they had resolved that and she had clearly gotten over her anger about it, maybe she would realize she *did* still have feelings for the man.

If Stevie only had issues being with a wealthy man because of that rejection and she had now resolved that issue, that could be good news for Reid. He was intensely aware, however, that the rich man she chose to be with could well be Sean over him.

The very thought tore at his heart.

There was only one thing he could do.

He had to convince her that he was a more enticing option than a man she'd known and loved for years.

And there was only one way he knew how to do that.

Chapter Eighteen

Stevie grabbed a coffee at a Starbucks, then picked up a newspaper from a box on her way back to the cab. She got into the car and pulled onto a side street, then opened to the want ads. It was time she found a place to stay. She picked up a pen from her caddy and started circling apartments to check out.

A few hours later, she stared at the tiny, grubby place as the superintendent waited at the door. Ugh, she'd definitely rather sleep in her cab than live here. And this was the best of the three she'd seen this morning.

She walked down the several flights of stairs, relieved to breathe in the fresh air when she finally reached the front door and opened it.

She glanced at her watch and realized it was time to go meet Jon and Derrick for lunch. She drove to the small bistro where she was meeting them and parked the cab in a spot conveniently right outside the place. Not that she would have minded walking a block or two, but there was something satisfying about finding the perfect parking spot. And it improved her whole mood.

She smiled as she locked the cab and walked to the door of the restaurant. As soon as she stepped into the trendy bistro with its colorful plants and light, airy artwork on the walls, she saw Jon waving to her from a table by the window. His hand rested on Derrick's sleeve, the two of them sitting side by side, Derrick probably cringing from the public show of affection.

The two men were quite a contrast. Jon in his royal-blue shirt and well-fitting jeans, tumultuous blond waves tumbling over his forehead, his smile bright and his green eyes glittering. Derrick in his impeccable charcoal suit, burgundy shirt, and a patterned tie sporting both colors. His hair was short, dark brown, and immaculately styled, unlike Jon's carefree hairstyle. His brown eyes and smile were more reserved than Jon's, but every bit as warm and welcoming.

"So, I want to hear all about this new guy you've been seeing," Jon said as soon as she sat down.

She knew Jon would ask about Reid, and she thought she'd been prepared, but thoughts of Reid telling her he loved her . . . of knowing she'd have to walk away, even though her heart longed for him . . . made it much harder than she thought it would be.

"Give her a minute to breathe," Derrick said.

She loved these two men. They were her best friends. Any advice she wanted, she knew they would give her a considered opinion, keeping her well-being at the forefront.

And not by assuming they knew what was best for her, like her family always had.

But she wouldn't ask their counsel about Reid. She'd already made up her mind.

The waitress came by to take their order. Stevie took a quick look through the menu while the men ordered, then she chose one of the specials. A fancy wrap with chicken and avocado, and a salad.

"So where have you been staying since you broke up with Hank?" Derrick asked.

Her breakup with Hank seemed a lifetime ago. In the short time since that had happened, she'd come to realize that Hank had never really loved her . . . that she'd never really loved him . . . that the same was true with her ex-fiancé Sean . . . and that what she felt for Reid really was love, but she still wasn't sure how to handle it.

She grabbed a celery stalk from the glass serving plate that had already been on the table when she arrived and dropped the tip into the white dip, trying to forget about that for now.

"I've been staying at a place just off Claremont Avenue."

"What's the address?" Derrick was a real estate agent, specializing in high-end properties.

"It's 724 Lalonde Boulevard."

"That's Lalonde Terrace," Derrick remarked.

"That's one of the most exclusive buildings in the city." Jon's smile lit up like a sun gone nova. "So your new guy is rich. Tell us about him."

Of course, Jon would assume she was staying with Reid. And she really couldn't deny it.

"Stevie, you've been staying with a man you just met?" Derrick's cautious tone, filled with concern, warmed her. "That's a bit dangerous."

She grinned. "Well, I guess I shouldn't tell you about having sex with him in a dark alleyway two blocks from Hotel Maison the day we met."

She knew she shouldn't tease Derrick like this—he was only expressing his concern for her.

"OMG, you are so bad," Jon said, his face beaming. "Where did you meet him?"

"He conveniently stepped into my cab just as you were telling me to screw my next fare." She shrugged. "So I did."

The look of shock on Jon's face was comical. He covered his mouth. "You're kidding. I didn't think you'd actually do it." He leaned forward. "So tell me all about him. Is he sexy?"

She laughed. "Sexy doesn't even begin to describe him. Just a glance at Reid Jacobs is enough to fill your mind with steamy, toe-curling sexual fantasies."

Her heart clenched, even though she kept a smile on her face. How could she possibly give up what she had with Reid? And Dylan? She'd never experienced anything so erotically intense and satisfying in her life.

"Reid Jacobs?" Derrick asked, tapping into his phone.

Jon stared at Derrick's phone display, then his eyes widened. "Wow! I'd definitely do him."

Derrick raised an eyebrow, but nodded.

The waitress stopped beside the table and set a plate in

front of Stevie, then Derrick and Jon. She continued on her way.

Stevie gazed at the green wrap on her plate, with dashes of red tomato in the filling offering a nice contrast of color. She picked it up and took a bite. After she took a sip of water, she turned to Derrick, knowing she had to get on with her request.

"Derrick, I was hoping you could help me with something."

"Of course. What can I do?"

"I've started looking for an apartment, but even once I find a place, it'll be a few weeks before I can move in, so I was hoping you might know of somewhere I can stay until then."

Because she couldn't keep staying with Reid and Dylan. She had to start putting some distance between them to get some perspective.

"You can stay with us," Derrick said.

"Thank you, but I wouldn't want to do that for more than a few days." She patted his hand. "I value our friendship too much to put that kind of strain on it."

"What about Reid?" Jon said. "Aren't you happy staying with him?"

She frowned. "Sure, it's been fun. But I need to put a little space between us to get my feelings sorted out. This relationship has dredged up major issues for me and it hasn't been easy."

"Good relationships never are," Derrick said.

She took another bite of her sandwich.

"What happened?" Jon asked.

"He's been extremely serious from the start and I'm not sure I'm ready for how quickly everything is moving."

"I know you've been burned before, sweetie. I understand why falling for him might scare the hell out of you. But don't let your past mess up your future."

Jon took Derrick's hands, and in that moment, Stevie hoped she could one day have the deep bond they shared.

"I think it would be crazy to let this guy go," Jon said. "A sexy, rich guy who's not afraid of commitment? God, that's a dream come true."

Stevie dropped off her passenger at the trendy nightclub in the Village. It had started raining about two hours ago, so the number of fares had picked up. Ordinarily, she'd knock off in about a half hour, but with the extra business, she might work longer.

Except that Reid had texted earlier asking her to eat light because he and Dylan had planned a nice dinner for the three of them that evening. She'd decided instead of having a snack when she usually ate her meal at about six, that she'd skip it and wait for dinner with them. But that meant she was hungry now . . . and she didn't want to make them wait too long for her.

Too bad because she could use the extra cash.

Her phone bleeped so she pulled it from her pocket.

When are you done with your shift? I'm at a meeting and could use a ride home.

It was from Dylan.

A man got into the cab and gave her an address.

One more fare. About 20 min. Let me know where and I'll text when ready.

A few minutes later she heard her phone. When she dropped her passenger off, she pulled it from her pocket and checked the address, then texted Dylan she was on her way.

She drove to the office tower, then pulled up in front. Dylan strode out the door and over to her cab.

"Hey, thanks for picking me up," Dylan said with a smile as he got in the back of the cab.

She gazed at him in the rearview mirror and smiled. "It's what I do."

He laughed. "Yes, well, I appreciate it. It's murder getting a cab on a wet night like this." He pulled off his damp suit jacket and lay it down beside him.

"So where to, sir?" she asked with a grin.

"Well, I have this great penthouse. How about you take me there and we both go up and I'll show you the fabulous view?"

She caught his gaze in the mirror. "I might be persuaded."

He opened his briefcase and pulled out a shopping bag from a designer store. "Would it help if I gave you a gift?"

She grinned. "I don't know. Depends on what it is."

She pulled off the main road and down a quiet street, then pulled over. She turned and took the bag he offered and peeked inside. She pulled out the tissue and found a lovely white shirred dress. It was very elegant, but at the same time, sexy, since the slinky fabric would cling to her every curve.

She gazed at him questioningly.

"We thought we'd dress for dinner."

"Should I be insulted?" she teased. "My plaid flannel shirt isn't good enough for you fancy penthouse dwellers?"

He chuckled. "Personally, I love your plaid flannel. It's so"—he grinned—"soft to the touch. Especially with you inside it."

The thought of him touching her shirt . . . stroking over the fabric . . . cupping her breast . . . sent her hormones spinning.

"The fact that you gave this to me now rather than when we reach the apartment . . . I assume that means you want me to put it on now?"

He nodded. "That way from the time you park the cab and we start upstairs, it's like we've started a date."

She smiled. "A date with two men. I could go for that." She pulled away from the curb. "I'll take us somewhere I can change."

Dylan was looking forward to this evening. He and Reid had put their heads together to plan the perfect evening to convince Stevie that what Reid could offer her surpassed anything she could get from being with her ex-fiancé, in case she was having second thoughts. Reid felt his biggest weapon was Dylan—a second man to ramp up the excitement.

Dylan was thrilled to be a part of it.

Stevie turned down a quiet street, then into a dark alley. She pulled over and stopped the cab.

"What are we doing here?" he asked, glancing around.

She tossed the shopping bag into his lap, then she got out of the car and opened the back door and climbed into the backseat beside him. Then she started unbuttoning her shirt.

"You're changing here?" he asked, his eyes widening as she slipped off her shirt, then tugged her navy tank top over her head, revealing her black lace bra.

"Sure. Why not?"

"I . . . uh . . . guess."

She'd kicked off her shoes and was already slipping off her jeans, pushing them to the floor of the car. At the sight of her in her tiny bra and panties, his groin tightened. She held up the dress.

"Hmm. It's off the shoulder, and I definitely don't want a black bra underneath."

She dropped the dress and reached behind her. His cock swelled as she peeled away her bra and dropped it on the seat. She grinned at him, clearly aware of the effect her perfect, round, naked breasts were having on him.

She pulled the dress over her head and let the slinky garment glide down her body. She pulled it into place, smoothing it down. It lovingly hugged every curve. And he couldn't help noticing that her hard nipples were clearly visible through the thin fabric.

She pushed herself up on her knees. "Do you like it?" she asked, swiveling a little to give him different views.

"Oh, yeah." His gravelly voice made it clear how much.

She smiled. "Can you see my black undies through the white fabric? Because I wouldn't want that."

His gaze jerked to her groin.

"I . . . uh . . ." *Just say yes,* a little voice shouted in his head.

"Better not to take any chances." She tugged the hem up a little and slid her hands under the dress, then began to wiggle.

"What are you doing?" But he knew damned well exactly what she was doing.

Chapter Nineteen

Dylan almost salivated as Stevie sat down again, then glided her panties down her shapely calves and slipped them off her feet.

"Any shoes?" she asked. "My sneakers will just ruin the look."

"Uh . . . yeah. In the bag."

God, she was totally naked under that dress. His cock swelled some more.

She pulled out the shoes—white satin stilettos with rhinestone trim—and slipped them on.

"Nice." She smiled at him and pushed herself onto her knees again, but this time she pulled up the hem of the dress enough to straddle his legs.

Her fingertips moved down his chest and he realized she was unfastening the buttons of his shirt. She pushed it open and smiled as she stroked his naked flesh.

"Thank you for the pretty gift."

"It was from Reid, too," he said absently, mesmerized by the glitter in her eyes.

She rested her hand so her palm cupped his nipple, keeping it warm, then she teased his other nipple with her fingertips.

"I'll thank him later."

He drew in a breath as she stroked over his hard cock, then she quickly unzipped him and wrapped her warm fingers around it.

"We should probably get going." Fuck, that's the last thing he wanted to do, but he was supposed to be helping Reid win her, not fucking her in the back of her cab.

But she took his hand and pulled it under her dress. Then he felt the slickness between her folds as she pressed his fingers to her opening.

"This'll only take a minute," she murmured against his ear. "I promise."

Then she lowered herself down, pressing his cock to her, and slid onto him.

He sucked in a breath as his hard cock glided deep into her body. She held him close, her lips nuzzling his temple.

"You feel so good inside me." Her voice was thick with desire.

Then she began to move.

Fuck, he couldn't believe he was sitting in a dark alley with a beautiful cabdriver fucking him in the backseat of her cab.

"Ohhh," she moaned softly, her head falling back.

Her long, blonde waves streamed down her back, gliding over his hands as he guided her up and down. His cock ached, his groin tightening with each thrust as she drove him into her body again and again.

"Oh, fuck, Stevie, I'm going to come any minute."

"Good, because I'm so close, I . . . ah . . ."

He pivoted up to meet her, then pressed his hand to her stomach and found her clit with his thumb. He stroked over it, again and again. She sucked in a breath, then started riding him faster, her hot, velvety passage squeezing tightly around him.

His body vibrated with intense need as he held back, waiting for her to come. He tweaked her clit and stroked over it faster.

She gasped, then moaned, her fingers clutching his shoulders as her face blossomed in orgasm.

Fuck, it was such a beautiful sight. The potent need coiled tightly in his groin released in a wash of intense pleasure. He erupted inside her, his whole body in spasm as he rode the wave of ecstasy.

She collapsed against him, her head resting on his shoulder. Then he realized she was giggling.

She lifted her head, her glowing, rosy-cheeked face smiling and a twinkle dancing in her eyes. "Well, that was fun."

"Yes, it was," he said, a little shaken by her potent effect on him.

Stevie held Dylan's hand as they went up the elevator. She knew he was intensely aware of the fact she still wore no panties under her dress. Or bra. Even though they'd just had sex, she could see that his cock was hardening again already.

The doors opened and she and Dylan stepped into the entryway of the penthouse. Reid walked toward them, taking in the sight of her, his admiring gaze gliding from her head to her toes.

"You look beautiful, Stevie."

She smiled. "I've already thanked Dylan for the dress and shoes." She sent him a dazzling smile as she released Dylan's hand and stepped toward Reid. "Now it's time to thank you."

She rested her hand on his cheek and tipped her face up. He closed the distance, finding her lips and kissing her with a sweet passion. She leaned in closer, pressing her breasts tightly to his body. She grasped his hand and pressed it to her breast and squeezed it around her. Heat flooded her senses.

He tipped his head back and smiled. "You're not wearing a bra."

"That's not the only thing she's not wearing," Dylan said.

A slow smile spread across Reid's lips.

"Oh, yeah?" His eyes glittered.

She just smiled, then stepped back. "I'm starving. You promised me dinner."

"Yes, of course." Reid took her hand and led her to the dining room, then pulled out the chair for her.

The table was set with fine china and delicate crystal stemware. Tall slender candles, flames softly flickering, stood in glass holders alongside an arrangement of flowers adorning the center of the table, and soft music filled the room.

"Hmm. It seems you gentlemen may be trying to seduce me."

"Don't worry, we wouldn't seduce a beautiful woman without feeding her first," Reid said.

At that comment, she glanced at Dylan, who was sitting down in the chair next to her, and giggled.

Reid gazed from one to the other. "What's going on?"

"Well, your partner was really quite . . . excited by my lack of lingerie."

"You're saying Dylan already seduced you?"

"To be fair, it was really me who did the seducing."

"Really?" Reid smiled broadly.

"I told you, I thanked him for the dress and shoes. And I haven't really given you as thorough a thank-you. I am hungry, but if you'd like me to do that before dinner"— she smiled—"I can wait."

"Oh, no. Please." He gestured to the salad that had already been served on her plate. Fresh greens with bright red cherry tomatoes and pine nuts, tossed in a vinaigrette dressing.

Reid filled her stemmed glass with white wine, then filled the other two.

Stevie picked up her salad fork and spiked it through some of the greens, then put them into her mouth. The tangy flavor was delightful. Next, she stabbed a cherry tomato and popped it into her mouth, then bit into it. It was juicy and a bit dribbled from her lips. When she swallowed, she swirled out her tongue to lap up the liquid dripping from her mouth.

She reached for her wineglass and realized both men were watching her intently.

She sipped her wine, then picked up a carrot stick from the plate of crudités beside the wine bottle. She dipped it into the creamy dip, then licked the length of the carrot, gathering the white dressing on her tongue, then lapped it over the tip. Intensely aware that both men's gazes were locked on her, she swirled her tongue over the tip of the carrot, then pushed the orange cylinder between her lips. She couldn't resist drawing it forward and back a couple of times before finally pushing it all the way into her mouth.

When she finished chewing it, she sipped her wine and smiled at Reid.

"Are you sure you don't want me to thank you now?" Her voice was deep and throaty.

She knew her little performance had had quite an effect on the men, but she hadn't realized how much it had turned her on. Thinking of gliding her tongue over Reid's cock . . . of feeling it push into her mouth.

He grinned. "You go ahead and eat. I'll accept your gratitude in a different way." Then he lifted the tablecloth and disappeared under the table.

She felt his hands on her calves, gliding up and down. She took another bite of salad as he slipped off one of her shoes, then the other. His big hands wrapped around her foot and he massaged. It felt glorious.

She ate another cherry tomato. Her eyelids fluttered at the delightful feel of Reid's hands moving on her foot. Then he switched to the other one and she sighed softly.

"You must be enjoying what he's doing," Dylan said, his eyes filled with heat.

"He's rubbing my feet," she said in a daze, but then Reid's hand moved up her ankle.

He continued massaging her skin, drifting up first one calf, then the other. She leaned back in the chair, enjoying his attention. Her legs were so relaxed at his touch, and tension faded from her whole body . . . until his hands continued up past her knee.

Both his big hands massaged her thigh, continuing under her dress. Dampness pooled between her legs, but he stopped inches short of that part of her, then moved on to her other leg.

"Is he still massaging your feet?" Dylan asked, his gaze glued to her face.

"No, he's just . . ."

His hand continued up her thigh . . .

"Massaging my . . ."

Under her skirt . . .

"Legs." She sucked in a breath as his fingertip brushed her intimate flesh.

Dylan grinned. "I bet that's not all he's massaging now."

Reid stroked over her slick flesh.

"Where is he touching you, sweetheart?" Dylan asked.

Reid pressed her thighs apart and she could tell he was staring at her folds. He glided his fingers over them again.

"He's . . . oh . . ."

Reid's finger brushed over her clit.

"He's touching my pussy."

She heard the sound of Dylan's zipper opening and she knew he was pulling out his stiff cock.

Reid's tongue pressed against her and she moaned softly.

"What's he doing now?" Dylan's voice was deep and raspy.

"He's licking my pussy."

His tongue pushed deep into her and she whimpered.

Then he licked her clit. His fingers stroked her soft petals, then dipped into her dampness.

She slumped on the chair, opening wider to him.

Dylan stood up, his big cock poking out of his suit and pointing toward the ceiling. He stepped behind her and cupped her breasts, stroking them as Reid drove his fingers deeper into her. His tongue continued to move on her clit as Dylan tweaked her nipples. Need shot through her, pleasure pooling deep in her belly.

"Oh, yes." She reached under the table and tangled her fingers in Reid's hair, pulling him tighter to her.

His fingers drove faster into her as he teased her clit. Dylan slid his hands under the top of her dress, cupping her naked breasts. She arched against Reid, moaning. Dylan squeezed her nipples and Reid began to suckle her clit as he fucked her with his fingers.

"Oh, God."

She gasped at the intensity of the sensations, then heat flared in her belly and the tightly coiled pleasure spiraled outward, consuming her. Tossing her onto a giant swell of tumultuous bliss.

She rode the wave, the pleasure augmented by Reid's thrusting and licking, and Dylan's fingers teasing her nipples, until finally her world exploded in a cataclysmic burst of ecstasy.

She collapsed in the chair, sucking in air.

Dylan leaned down and kissed her, his hands gliding from under her dress while beneath the table Reid continued to nuzzle her damp flesh, his tongue stroking her softly. Dylan arranged the top of her dress back into position and sat down, then he tucked his still rock-hard cock into his pants and zipped up.

Reid kissed and licked her a little longer, then appeared from under the table again. He grabbed his napkin and wiped his face, smiling.

"I hope you're enjoying your appetizer as much as I enjoyed mine," he said.

She gazed at him, certain he could see the satisfaction—yet yearning for more—gleaming in her eyes.

She took another bite of salad. Reid picked up his fork and began eating his.

For the next few minutes, the only sound in the room was the clinking of forks on plates over the soft background music . . . and the pounding of her heart. After she took her last bite, Dylan stood up and took her plate then removed Reid's and his own. She could see the outline of his still-swollen cock in his pants as he carried the plates into the kitchen.

He returned moments later carrying a platter with a silver cover. He set it on the table and lifted off the lid, revealing scallops wrapped in bacon and firm tips of glazed asparagus.

"Mmm, it smells delicious," she said as he placed a healthy portion of each on her plate.

Dylan served Reid, then himself.

She couldn't help watching the men as they ate, their lips moving as they chewed. Reid's tongue glided around his mouth as he finished one succulent scallop and she longed to push her tongue inside his mouth and taste what he tasted.

She took a bite of her own scallop, which was delicious, but it didn't satisfy the craving.

She watched as Dylan speared an asparagus tip and nibbled on the end, then sucked the rest of it into his mouth.

Before she knew it, her plate was empty and her insides were melting with need.

"We have dessert," Reid said. "Would you like me to bring it out?"

"I do feel like dessert," she murmured, "but not what you have in the kitchen."

Reid chuckled and stood up. "We can defer dessert for a little while," he said as he stepped to her chair. "I wouldn't mind doing a little dancing right now."

He took her hand and drew her to her feet, then led her to the living room. He curled his arm around her waist and drew her close to his body. Dylan followed them and he moved behind her, his body pressed to hers, his hands wrapping around her waist. The three of them moved to the music together, Reid leading.

Both their cocks were hard and pressed tightly to her, sending heat thundering through her.

Dylan's lips nuzzled her temple, sending shivers down her spine. Reid nuzzled her other temple and her whole body quivered. As Dylan's hands slid up her body and cupped her breasts, Reid's hands cupped her bottom. Which she was fully aware meant the backs of his hands were pressed against Dylan's hard cock.

She wished they would guide her into the bedroom, then strip off her dress and ravage her naked body. But at the same time, she didn't want this mélange of delightful sensations to end.

Reid captured her lips, his tongue gliding inside her mouth in a tender caress, kissing her with a rising passion until she was breathless. Then he released her lips and . . .

Her heart thundered as he pressed his lips to Dylan's. The two men kissed over her shoulder, the three of them still moving to the music and her heart rate accelerated as desire surged through her.

Then their lips parted and they continued to dance. She arched against Dylan's warm palms against her breasts. Reid tightened his hold on her ass, stroking insistently.

When she thought she couldn't stand any more, Reid stopped and stared down at her. He took her lips in a passionate kiss, driving her need higher, then as soon as he released her mouth, turned her to face Dylan. Dylan's sky-blue eyes were gleaming with heat and he met her lips with an equally passionate kiss.

Then Reid took her hand and led her to the sliding doors leading to the terrace. As he opened them, she glanced over her shoulder to see Dylan disappear down the hall.

"What about Dylan?"

He drew her outside into the warm spring evening. The water in the pool was lit with the soft glow of lavender-and-blue lights along with the gleaming moonlight on its glassy-smooth surface. His arms slid around her and he drew her close to his body.

"Don't worry, my love. We'll be joining him shortly."

My love.

Oh, God, she loved hearing him call her that. Even though it triggered confusion and anxiety about where this was going between them.

"I know you're resisting the idea of having a long-term relationship with me," he said, "but I'll do whatever I can to seduce you to my way of thinking."

He nuzzled her temple, sending tingles through her.

"Like reminding you that a relationship with me includes some very special benefits. Specifically, having two men to please you."

She snuggled against his big, warm body, her breath quickening at what was to come.

"Tonight is about the three of us," he said. "And reminding you just how aroused and excited Dylan and I can make you. How intense the pleasure we can give you. How exhilarating the orgasms."

He smiled, his voice deepening to a low rumble. "And with two of us, how *many* we can give you at one time."

Chapter Twenty

Stevie's vagina clenched at the thought of the two she'd already experienced this evening . . . and in anticipation of more to come.

Reid ran his hand along the back of her head and drew her in for a kiss. His lips moved on hers, drawing her need to the surface. To feel him touching her naked body. To open to him as he pressed his cock against her slick opening and swallow it inside her.

"I want you to understand just how much the two of us can give you," he murmured against her lips, then his mouth brushed her cheek in a gentle caress.

When his lips captured hers again, his tongue glided deep as his hands cupped her behind and he pulled her tightly to his body, his thick cock cradled against her. She wanted to rock her body against him. To push him onto the patio chair and straddle him, just like she had Dylan in the cab, and drive his thick cock deep inside her.

When he released her lips, she gazed into his cobalt-blue

eyes—her own half-lidded—and murmured, "So why isn't Dylan here?"

He smiled. "Because he's getting ready for your surprise."

He took her hand and led her back into the apartment, then down the hall to the master bedroom. As soon as he opened the door, she sucked in a breath at the sight of Dylan completely naked, spread-eagle on the bed, his head at the foot of the bed hanging over the edge, and his cock at full mast, pointing straight toward the ceiling. Her pulse pounded in her ears and all she could think about was wrapping her hands around that glorious erection of his. Then her lips.

Reid laid his hand on the small of her back and pressed her farther into the room. Her gaze never leaving Dylan, but gliding over his body, she realized his ankles and wrists were bound and held fast.

"How did he get like that? Is there someone else here?"

Reid chuckled. "No. His ankles were easy to do alone, and as for his wrists, he just had to attach the bands around them, then pull on the restraining straps. They tighten easily with a pull on the loose strap, but to loosen them is another matter."

Reid walked to the bed and grabbed a strap near Dylan's right hand and pulled it, tugging Dylan's hands farther apart.

"There, that's better." Reid turned back to Stevie. "Why don't you sit down and have a glass of wine?"

He gestured to the two upholstered armchairs by the round table at the window, both turned to face the bed. An open bottle of wine and two full glasses sat on the table.

She sat down in one of the chairs and picked up a glass, then sipped. The heat warming her throat was nothing compared to the heat pumping through her body.

Reid slipped off his jacket and tossed it over the back of the couch, then he unzipped his suit pants. He drew out his enormous, fully engorged cock and wrapped his hand around it while he stepped closer to the bed.

He knelt on the cushioned bench at the end of the bed and pushed his cock to his belly, then draped his balls over Dylan's mouth. Dylan's tongue glided out and heat flooded Stevie's core at the sight of him licking them. Reid arched his neck, pleasure washing across his face, then he lowered them into Dylan's mouth. Dylan drew one soft sac inside and suckled, to Reid's approving groan.

Heat melted inside her at the sight of Reid's soft flesh inside Dylan's mouth. After a few moments, Reid shifted away, then dropped his cock forward and pressed it to Dylan's lips. Dylan opened and, with his head hanging over the bed, Reid was able to glide right down Dylan's throat. Reid drew back, then glided deep again.

Stevie could feel moisture trickling down her inner thigh. Oh, God, it was so hot watching the two of them.

After a few more thrusts, Reid stood up, moved to the side of the bed, and sat down. Her breath caught as he wrapped his hand around Dylan's erect cock and pressed it to his lips. Reid locked his gaze on Stevie's as he swallowed the big cockhead in his mouth and sucked on it like a lollipop.

"Oh, God, that's so sexy." The intense need in her hoarse, desire-coarsened words surprised even her.

Reid's mouth slipped from Dylan's cock, his hand still around it. Stroking.

"We knew you'd like this. We'll do anything you want us to," he murmured.

"Anything?" The possibilities that flashed through her mind sent her heartbeat racing.

"We're both excited by the fact that you like to watch us. That it *arouses* you so much. So we're happy to do anything you ask."

Would they actually fuck each other if she asked them to?

From the sincere look in their eyes, she knew they would, but she wasn't sure if they were ready for that. And just knowing they would do that for her was a powerful turn-on.

"I want you to run your hands over Dylan's body. To tease him."

Reid ran his hands down Dylan's legs, to his ankles, then glided back upward, stroking the insides of his thick thighs. He stroked around his testicles, without touching them, then over his stomach. Then his fingers lightly brushed Dylan's thick cock, making it twitch. Then Reid cupped Dylan's balls in his hand and he caressed them lightly. He leaned forward and licked Dylan's taut, sculpted stomach while he moved his hands along Dylan's thick, pulsing cock.

Reid's lips covered Dylan's nipple and he suckled softly, to Dylan's groan.

Stevie couldn't help herself. Her fingers found the slick flesh between her legs and stroked. She couldn't believe how wet she was, already soaking the back of her dress.

"Oh, God, I want to see you both with a cock in your mouth."

Reid tugged Dylan's body upward until his head was flat on the bed, then stood up. She watched in awe as he stripped off his shirt, exposing his broad chest and muscular arms, then he dropped his pants and boxers to the floor.

He walked to the end of the bed and knelt on it, then lowered his cock into Dylan's mouth, who opened wide to accommodate him. Reid leaned over and grasped Dylan's erection firmly in his hand and guided it to his lips. She watched in fascination as the thick cockhead disappeared into Reid's mouth.

She kept stroking herself, pleasure rippling through her, conscious that both men watched her as they sucked each other's cocks.

"This is so hot," she murmured. "I want you to make each other come."

Each man pulsed deeper on the cock in his mouth, their throats moving as the shafts stroked inside. Stevie stroked her slick flesh, pleasure rising inside her as the men's actions aroused her more and more.

Both their gazes, locked on her fingers, blazed with heat.

"God, I'm so close to coming," she cooed, feeling the burn rising inside her.

Dylan started to groan around Reid's cock and Reid pulsed faster on Dylan. Dylan arched against Reid's face as he pivoted his face forward and back, taking Reid deeper. A growl rumbled from Reid's throat, then he jerked against Dylan's mouth, clearly releasing his load into it. The sight sent pleasure exploding within her and she moaned out loud. Then Dylan groaned, Reid's emptied cock flopping from his mouth as he came inside Reid's.

Her head flung back as she continued to ride the wave of bliss.

When her orgasm finally waned, she opened her eyes and saw both men's gazes locked on her. Reid was lying on the bed beside Dylan, his head near his hip, his legs over Dylan's outstretched arm.

She lurched to her feet and surged to the bed. She kissed Dylan, swirling her tongue into his mouth, tasting Reid's essence. Then she arched over him, straddling his body as she moved closer to Reid. He sat up and she kissed him, tasting Dylan's semen on his tongue.

"Oh, God, that was so exciting." She grabbed Reid's hand and pressed it to her. "See how wet I am." Her slick flesh was resting on Dylan's belly and she glided forward and back to ensure he felt it, too.

"What do you want us to do now, baby?" Reid asked.

"I want you to . . ." She sucked in a breath. "To strip me and tie me down like Dylan is, then fuck me until I scream. Then do it again. And again."

Reid chuckled, then grabbed the hem of her dress and tugged it upward, peeling it from her body. She was totally naked now, her bosom heaving.

Reid released Dylan's wrists, then Dylan sat up and helped Reid release his ankles.

Then suddenly Stevie found herself pressed flat to the bed, with one man securing her wrists and the other her ankles. Reid had loosened the restraining straps when he released Dylan, but now he pulled on the straps and her arms were pulled wide. When Dylan did the same to her ankles, she sucked in a breath, feeling vulnerable and exposed.

And wildly aroused.

Suddenly, both men were licking her breasts, then both their mouths moved over her nipples and they suckled. Big hands moved between her legs and stroked her slick flesh. The fingers tangled together and slipped inside her as the men continued to suck her hard, aching nipples.

Her insides quivered.

"Oh, God, that feels so good," she cried.

Dylan left her nipple to the cold air, his fingers slipping free of her, too, as he found her neck and nipped the tender skin. His fingers toyed with her damp nub as he sucked on her neck. Reid glided downward, his mouth finding her clit as his fingers still pulsed into her opening.

She couldn't stand it any longer.

"Oh, please," she keened. "I need a cock inside me."

Both men shifted and Dylan's cockhead slid into her mouth as Reid's large tip pushed against her opening. As she sucked on Dylan, Reid thrust deep inside her.

She gasped, sucking in air around Dylan's shaft. He pushed deeper, filling her throat. Then he drew back and slipped from her mouth. He leaned down and suckled her nipple, pinching the other with his fingers, as Reid drove inside her again.

"Oh, fuck me, Reid. Fast and hard. I'm so close."

Reid drove deep again, then again. His cock drove into her like a piston. Deep. Hard. Fast.

She arched against him.

"I'm. Going. To. Come." She sucked in a breath, feeling dizzy.

"Do it, baby," Reid said, his voice gravelly. "I want to see you orgasm."

Pleasure swamped her and she gasped. He kept pounding into her, his big cock driving deep and hard.

"Oh, God, yes!" She arched forward and wailed. Tingles danced across her body and she shuddered as ecstasy claimed her.

Reid groaned and erupted inside her.

Before she could catch her breath, Reid slipped from her body and Dylan drove inside her. His hard cock stroking her sensitized passage sent her over the edge again, wailing as a new, intense orgasm shot through her.

Dylan rode her hard, driving her pleasure higher and higher. When he exploded inside her, she gasped, shattering in a mind-numbing cataclysm of bliss.

As she lay panting on the bed, Reid grinned and pressed his impossibly rigid cock against Dylan's and slid inside her, too. They moved together in a slow, languid pace, almost lulling her into a relaxed state, but then the feel of both hard cocks, growing more rigid inside her with each stroke, sent heat pulsing through her once again. Her pussy squeezed them intimately, making them both moan in unison.

They sped up . . . pushing inside her . . . stroking her sensitive flesh . . . until she flipped off the edge again, groaning at the intensity of yet another orgasm pulsing through her, catapulting her over the edge of ecstasy.

They both released inside her again, and she wondered how it was possible.

Then they collapsed on the bed beside her, one on each side. They snuggled closer, their necks resting on her outstretched arms, as they nuzzled her temple.

God, how could she ever give this up?

Stevie woke up lying on her back, the two men's bodies pressed against her, one on either side. One of her arms was sprawled across Dylan's stomach. He was also on his back, his semi-rigid cock snuggled against her wrist. He'd kicked aside the covers leaving his sexy, naked body fully exposed.

Her other arm was against Reid's chest. He was lying on his side, his arm around her waist, and she realized he was gazing at her.

"You been awake long?" she asked, conscious of his vivid blue eyes intent on her.

"About five minutes." He smiled. "I've just been watching you sleep. Thinking how nice it is you're here." He stroked a hair from her face, the tender touch tugging at her heart. "How much I'd like you here every day."

She drew in a breath. Oh, God, she loved being with him, too.

This time with him—and with Dylan—had been the most exciting time of her life. And it wasn't just because of the sex. Both these men seemed to understand her. Sometimes even better than she understood herself.

And Reid . . . Her heart swelled. She couldn't deny she was in love with him.

His gaze grew more intense, as if he could read it in her eyes.

"Good morning," Dylan said, his eyes still closed.

He shifted his body and his cock brushed against her arm. His eyelids fluttered open, a smile curling his lips, as his cock grew more rigid. He took her hand and wrapped it around his thickening shaft.

"Oh, yeah, this is the way to wake up in the morning."

"Dylan, I know you're quite enjoying yourself there," Reid said, gazing at Dylan's growing cock, Stevie's fingers cradled in his hand, holding the big shaft, "but Stevie and I need to talk. Would you mind taking care of that in the shower? By yourself?"

Dylan glanced to Stevie's face, then Reid's, and he rolled away, his cock sliding from her fingers.

"Oh, sure. Use me for your *dirty, erotic* fantasies, then send me on my way once you're done with me." His hand stroked his big cock as he walked toward the bedroom door. "Not even a blow job to ease the pain of rejection," he grumbled, but then he glanced over his shoulder and she saw a big grin on his face. "Of course, if you need me again, just give a shout and I'll be at your service."

Once the door closed behind him, Stevie turned to face Reid again.

"You look like you want to talk," he said.

She sat up, pulling the sheet around her chest. "The other day . . . you said that you love me."

"That's right. I do love you." He took her hand and pressed it to his lips, sending warmth spreading through her. "Stevie, I know you said you're not interested in a relationship. And I'm not trying to pressure you. But I'm going to tell you how I feel."

He stroked her cheek, his cobalt eyes staring at her with heart-wrenching warmth.

"That means I'm going to say I love you," he continued. "And I'm going to tell you things like I wish I could wake up to your beautiful face every day. To hold you in my arms every night."

He leaned in and kissed her. Even though it was a whisper-light brush of his lips, the tenderness of that touch sent a tumultuous blast of emotions through her.

When he drew back, the poignant emotion in his eyes melted her heart.

"And to be honest, I intend to do everything I can to convince you we should be together. But I know I have to move at a speed you're comfortable with."

"I'm just afraid of leading you on," she said, her voice quavering.

He brushed his lips over her knuckles, his blue eyes filled with concern. "Are you working up the courage to break this off?"

"No, it's not that. I'm just trying to figure things out. I've thought about myself and my life in a certain way for a long time, and then I met you and . . ." She shrugged. "Everything changed. I grew up believing all wealthy people were a certain way. But you aren't like that." She glanced at the en suite door. "And neither is Dylan."

She squeezed his hand. "You are caring and generous and . . ." She felt tears prickling at her eyes and blinked them back. "You truly seem to care about me."

"Of course I care about you." His warm, husky words

wrapped around her heart and squeezed. "I told you. I love you."

Reid stared into Stevie's eyes. He could almost believe her barriers were crumbling. That maybe she was thinking things might work between them.

"Sweetheart, as I said, I don't want to pressure you, but are you considering the possibility of us having a longer-term relationship after all?"

She bit her lip. "Reid, I'm really trying to work this out. When you say you love me, I think about the fact that my family loved me, yet they never seemed to care about my happiness. And Sean loved me, but he still walked away. For the good of the family."

She shook her head.

"But you . . ." Her voice quivered with the intensity of her emotions. "You truly seem to want to make me happy."

He pulled her into his arms and held her tight, his heart aching at her pain.

"Fuck, Stevie. I hate how your family treated you. That they made you feel small and unloved. You deserve so much better."

She rested her head against his chest, and he held her snugly against him, loving her so close to his heart.

"Reid, I want to give you what you want. I want to be the woman who can commit herself to you. To return your love. You deserve that and so much more. But . . ."

Just as hope had started to blossom, her "but" stole it away. He tipped up her chin, his gaze locking with hers.

"You told me you weren't breaking up with me."

"That's not where I'm going." She sat up and cupped his face in her hands, stroking his cheek tenderly. "I'm confused. You've shaken up my entire world. It takes time to give up a lifetime of beliefs and I don't want to keep you in limbo."

"So what are you saying?"

"I think I need some time to myself. To let me clear my head and see where I really want my life to go."

"Stevie, I'm in love with you and I know that scares you, but I believe you feel the same about me."

His arms curved around her waist and he drew her in close.

"If you need time to come to terms with that, as much as I hate the thought of being apart from you, we have to give you that time. I have a lot of things to get done in Philly, especially now that we have this new contract with Raphael, so how about I go back there for a while and you can stay here and do that thinking?"

"Actually, a friend is helping me find an apartment and says there'll be something available in a few days. Until then, I'll be staying with him."

Reid's chest tightened. "*Him?*"

Chapter Twenty-one

Stevie rested her hand on Reid's arm.

"Look, it's not Sean I'll be staying with if that's what you're worried about. It's my friends Derrick and Jon. They're a couple."

His clenched jaw relaxed.

"Okay, I wish you'd stay here, but I get it. You need time and space." His eyebrow rose. "So I'll go back to Philadelphia and wrap up some things. Then I'll come back into town on . . . let's say three weeks from Thursday, and we'll meet somewhere and talk. How does that sound?"

"That sounds perfect."

He took her hand and locked gazes with her.

"But I want you to promise you'll be there."

"I promise. How about I pick you up in my cab in the evening? Say seven? Then we can go somewhere for a drink."

He smiled. "That would be great. I don't know where I'll be, so why don't you pick me up outside the Empire State Building."

She returned his smile. "Okay, you're on."

* * *

Over the next week, Stevie spent a few nights staying with Jon and Derrick, enjoying spending time with them after her shifts. Then they helped her move her stuff into a delightful apartment in a classy neighborhood where she could stay for a couple of months. It was owned by a friend of Derrick's who was away on business overseas. Derrick had contacted him and he was fine with Stevie staying there until she found a place. In fact, he was happy to have someone to keep an eye on it.

The move didn't take long since all she had were clothes. Before she'd lived with Hank, she'd rented a furnished place, not really wanting to accumulate a lot of stuff. And she didn't want anything from the apartment she'd shared with him. Those were memories better left behind.

As the weeks went by, she found she missed Reid terribly.

And Dylan, but for different reasons.

The sex between the three of them was sensational. And addictive. But what she had with Reid . . . her heart pounded. She really did love him.

She sat on the couch sipping her lemonade as she watched the same classic movie she'd seen with Reid and Dylan when they'd been at Raphael's lake house. Which was making her miss them all the more.

Even though she had let go of her concerns about being with a wealthy man, she still worried about her independence. Standing on her own two feet and earning a living.

But there had to be a way she could make it work out.

A way she could meet her need to be self-reliant while still being with Reid.

The music rose as the final scene played itself out on the screen and she found herself dabbing tears from her eyes, feeling a little silly that she was affected so much by an old movie.

But there was nothing wrong with a happily-ever-after and she longed for that herself. And in her heart, she knew she would only find it with Reid.

Her heart swelled and at that moment, she just *knew*. Whatever it took, she would find a way to be with Reid. She knew Reid would do anything to make things work between them. All they had to do was figure it out.

Together.

The next few days, she found herself smiling all the time. Looking forward to when she'd see Reid again. She hadn't told Jon and Derrick about her decision. In fact, she hadn't told them that Reid had gone to Philadelphia for a few weeks, so every time Jon texted her asking how it was going with her and Reid, she just told him she hadn't seen him in a while. He probably had the idea that they'd broken up by now and she wasn't about to correct that. It was just easier that way.

And no matter what, she didn't want anyone else to know about her decision before Reid did.

In fact, it would make it all that much more fun when she showed up at Jon and Derrick's door with both Reid and Dylan, announcing the three of them were an item. She grinned at the thought.

When the day finally came that she would be meeting

Reid, she was excited. Waiting until seven o'clock was torture. Luckily, Sean called and invited her out for an early dinner so he could see her one more time before he headed back to Chicago in a few days.

"Sorry to keep you waiting," Sean said when he arrived at the table. He ordered an imported beer from the waitress.

"It's okay. I'm glad you invited me." She smiled. "I'm happy that we can be friends."

"Of course. I'll always care about you. All I can say is that Reid is a very lucky man."

She sipped her glass of wine. She didn't want to talk about her and Reid, because if she did, she might blurt out her decision. A decision that was going to change her life. A decision she could barely keep contained, she was so happy.

But that news was for Reid first.

"You are still seeing him, aren't you?"

"He's been out of town for a while," she said, noncommittally.

He nodded. "I'm sorry it didn't work out."

"No, it's not that, it's just . . ." She tightened her hand around her glass. "No, nothing. It doesn't matter."

"Stefani, if you want to talk about it, I'm here for you."

"No, really." She smiled, so close to letting her happiness spill free. "I'm fine."

"But it's what friends do," he said.

"Okay, if you really want to be my friend, then why don't you call me Stevie? That's what my friends call me."

"Okay, Stevie." Then he broke out in laughter. "Oh, man, that's strange."

She laughed and opened her menu. "I've heard that the gnocchi here is fabulous."

The waitress dropped off Sean's beer and they ordered their dinners.

He didn't bring up Reid again and they had a nice dinner talking about old friends and some of the good times they'd shared. He also told her that he was planning to move to New York the following month because of a new business venture. They exchanged e-mails and he said he'd let her know when he'd settled into his new place.

As they were sipping their coffee after dinner, her phone beeped. She pulled it from her pocket and confirmed it was her six thirty reminder to meet Reid.

"I have an appointment at seven, so I have to get going. Can I give you a ride?"

"Sure. My hotel's just a few blocks down the road."

He paid the bill, she grabbed her bag, and they stepped outside.

As they walked to her cab, Stevie zipped up her jacket against the drizzle that had been going on for hours. Elation swelled inside her because it was time to go meet Reid.

Sean climbed in the backseat and she started the cab.

She checked her mirrors, then moved into traffic, being extra cautious with the wet weather. It only took a couple of minutes to travel the few blocks to where she was dropping off Sean and she pulled over to let him out.

"Good-bye, Stevie," Sean said. "And don't forget to keep in touch."

It still felt odd to hear him call her that. She smiled.

"I will."

He closed the door and she drew in a deep breath, her stomach fluttering at the thought that she'd be seeing Reid in just a few minutes. The long weeks apart had seemed like an eternity.

The rain was falling harder, so she turned her windshield wipers to a higher speed. As they swished across the glass, she checked the traffic. There was a lull and she pulled away from the curb and accelerated.

The green light ahead was probably going to change soon, but she thought she could make it. She sped up a little more, but as she got closer, the light turned amber. She started to slow down, but in a flash, a pickup truck pulled out from a side street, clearly intent on beating the traffic light. He screeched around the corner and was on her bumper. The driver slammed on his brakes, but with the slick pavement, he didn't stop in time. The impact jerked her cab forward, then it slid into the intersection.

She glanced in the mirror to see Sean running along the sidewalk toward her and—

Something crashed into the side of the cab, slamming her sideways.

An explosion of pain tore through her.

Everything went black.

Chapter Twenty-two

Reid glanced at his watch. Fifteen minutes late. Stevie must have been held up with a fare.

Standing below the Empire State Building, on the corner they'd agreed upon, he stepped to the side to avoid the streams of people making their way down the sidewalk. Some had umbrellas while others walked swiftly to escape the misting rain.

Beside him a vendor sold roasted chestnuts, their sweet scent mixing with the smell of wet city streets.

He wiped rain out of his eyes and scanned the faces of passersby, searching for Stevie.

He could hear sirens a few blocks over and an ambulance raced by, lights flashing. He heard some people walking by talking about an accident a block down.

Maybe that was why Stevie was late. Traffic backed up by the accident.

He waited patiently, but after a half hour he texted her. When she still hadn't shown up or answered his text after an hour, he dialed her number, but got her voice mail. He left a message.

Ten minutes later, he pulled out his phone.

I'm going back to the penthouse. Text me.

Disappointment and anger washed through him. Had she decided to go back to her ex-fiancé without even giving Reid a chance? Without even meeting him face-to-face to tell him?

Breaking her promise.

He grabbed a cab and was soon riding the elevator to the penthouse.

"So how did it go?" Dylan asked as Reid walked into the living room. "You couldn't talk Stevie into coming back here with you tonight?"

Reid slumped on the couch. "Stevie didn't show."

Over the following week, Reid's anger grew as Stevie held her silence, not responding to his texts or phone calls. Finally, he called her cab company and asked for her specifically. They told him she wasn't on duty, which was odd since he knew she worked every day and he'd called right in the middle of her usual shift. He tried again the next day and the next.

Dylan talked to some connections he had and found out that Stevie hadn't been doing shifts through the company for the whole week. Reid kept trying to call her, but her phone always went to voice mail. Then one day, after several weeks, he found that her cell phone service had lapsed.

God damn, he could think of only one reason for all of

this. Stevie must have decided to go back to Sean and they'd
returned to Chicago.

Her brain felt foggy. She heard voices around her but
couldn't make out the words. A hand held hers, but she
didn't know whose and . . . she drifted off.

A voice called her name and she drifted through the darkness, wondering who he was. Where he was. It seemed like
a friendly voice . . .

She was surrounded by darkness, but she could sense someone was near. An ache pounded through her. She didn't
feel like she could move.

But she was tired of the darkness.

With great effort, she forced her eyelids to open.

It was dark in the room. She was lying on a bed. She
tried to sit up, but her muscles would not obey.

As things came more into focus, she felt a sharpness in
her arm. She glanced at it and saw a needle taped to her skin
attached to an IV.

How long had she been here?

Why was she here?

She turned her head, and was hit with a wash of
throbbing pain and dizziness. Someone was sitting in the
chair beside her bed, near the window. He looked to be
asleep.

"Hello," she tried to say, but her voice came out hoarse
and barely audible. She tried again.

"Stevie?"

The man sat upright.

"Oh, my God. You're awake."

It was Jon.

He took her hand and the feel of it, although sending a little pain lancing through her arm, anchored her.

She needed this human contact. She tried to squeeze his hand, but she didn't have the strength.

He stood up and leaned over her, his face, although smiling, filled with concern.

"It's okay, sweetie," he said. "You've been through a lot." He stroked her hair from her face and her eyelids fluttered closed.

He continued to hold her hand as she faded into the blackness again.

Stevie could feel the warm sunlight on her face and she opened her eyes. She was in a hospital room and a nurse was opening the drapes. Outside the glass she could see blue sky and the branches of a tree near the window, leaves fluttering on a soft breeze. A small bird landed on a branch, then hopped along it, twittering, then flew away again.

"You're awake." The nurse, a lovely young woman with long sandy-brown hair tied behind her head smiled. "How are you feeling?"

"Things hurt," Stevie managed to say. She hadn't taken inventory of what, but her body just seemed to be unhappy.

"I'll have the doctor come and talk to you. She might

modify your pain medication." She rested her hand on Stevie's arm. "Are you okay or would you like me to get something for you now?"

The pain wasn't extreme and Stevie hated taking medication.

"No, I'll be okay." She tried to sit up and groaned at the sudden shooting pain through her hips.

"Just relax. Let's try this." The nurse pressed a button, and with a buzz, the bed tilted upward slowly. She stopped it at a comfortable angle, then adjusted the pillows behind Stevie. "How's that?"

"Good, thanks."

The nurse patted her arm. "Okay. I'll go talk to the doctor. In the meantime, do you feel up to seeing a visitor? There's a gentleman who's been here every day since you got here."

"You mean my friend Jon?" Stevie vaguely remembered seeing him when she'd woken up briefly.

"No, Jon is very nice and he's been here a lot, too. Often with his friend Derrick. But I mean another gentleman. He's always dressed in a nice suit and he's a very take-charge kind of man."

Stevie's heart fluttered. Reid was here?

"He comes in every day and talks to the doctor," the nurse continued, "then sits by your side for hours. Between the three of them, there's always been someone here watching over you." She smiled. "The only reason he's not here now is because he went to get a coffee. He should be back in a minute. Do you want to see him?"

Did she want to see Reid?

God, yes. But, no. She didn't want him to see her help-less in bed.

"I'd like to sit up," Stevie said, shifting forward despite the pain. "Maybe you could help me into a chair." She tried to move her legs to the side of the bed, but . . .

The nurse rested her hand on Stevie's chest and pressed her back, her face filled with compassion. "Honey, I'm sorry. You'll have to stay put."

Why couldn't she seem to move her legs?

"Stevie. My God, it's good to see you awake."

The deep male voice was familiar, but it wasn't Reid's.

Sean continued into the room, a paper coffee cup in his hand. He placed it on her side table and pulled a chair close to the bed, then sat down, his face beaming with a smile. The nurse slipped away quietly.

He took her hand and squeezed lightly.

"You had us all pretty worried. It was touch and go there for a while. The doctors weren't sure you were going to make it."

She shook her head, vaguely remembering that night . . . the car hitting her cab . . . the pain.

"How long have I been here?"

"You've been in a coma for a while, Stevie. It's been weeks since the accident."

Shock washed through her.

"How badly am I hurt?" she asked. She tried again to move her legs and anxiety lurched through her when she had no success.

"I'll let the doctor answer that. She'll be able to explain all the details."

She gripped Sean's arm. "I don't need details right now. I just need to know . . . will I be able to walk again?"

Sean's mouth compressed into a flat line. "Stevie, the doctor—"

"Sean . . ."

He drew in a deep breath. "They're not sure yet."

Her world came crashing down around her. If she couldn't walk . . .

Oh, God, she wouldn't be able to drive, either.

How would she take care of herself?

She rested her head back against the pillow and consciousness faded.

"Stevie. Stevie?"

The insistent voice drew her from the darkness. Her eyelids fluttered open to see Sean sitting by her side. Jon stood behind him and smiled as soon as he saw her eyes open.

"Hi, Stevie," Jon said. "I'm going to go call Derrick so he can come in for a visit. He'll be so happy to see you awake finally."

Sean squeezed her hand. "And the doctor will be here in a minute to talk to you."

She nodded, a little disoriented. A glance at the window told her it was early evening.

"Sean, did . . . ?" Her voice was hoarse and he lifted a cup with a straw to her lips.

"Here, have some water," he urged.

She sipped, then nodded. "Has Reid been here to see me?"

He frowned. "No."

Her heart ached.

"Stevie, I thought you weren't seeing him anymore. Your friend Jon was under the same impression." He squeezed her hand. "Damn, Stevie, if I had known . . ." He started to stand. "I'll call him right now."

She clung to his hand. "No, don't do that." She shook her head. "I'm sorry, I'm just disoriented."

So it wasn't that Reid didn't care. It was that he didn't know.

He must have been worried when she didn't show up.

But weeks had gone by. Maybe more, because she was sure Sean was downplaying things until the doctor spoke to her. By now, Reid was probably angry. He'd certainly suffered the worst of the pain.

So leaving him in the dark was the best thing.

Because she didn't want him to see her like this. Helpless. Unable to fend for herself.

Maybe never able to take care of herself again.

She knew that as soon as Reid found out what had happened to her, he'd insist on taking care of her. It was the kind of man he was. But she couldn't be that kind of burden.

That was no way to start a relationship.

Chapter Twenty-three

After Stevie spoke with the doctor, she started to take stock of how bad things were. The doctor was hopeful Stevie would be able to walk again—which was fabulous news—but not before extensive physiotherapy.

Unfortunately, her cab was totaled. And she didn't know when, if ever, she'd be able to drive again.

The doctor cautioned her that even if they got her walking, she still might not be able to function at a full-time job for a while, let alone the long shifts she'd done driving the cab. She'd had a bad concussion and it could be over a year before she'd be fully recovered from that.

So she decided to sell the medallion. It had plummeted in value since she'd bought it—bringing in about a third of what she'd paid for it—but the money would help her get by for a while once she got out of the hospital. And it'd help her pay Sean back, since she was sure he'd paid extra to have her in a private room at the hospital. She knew he would refuse her money, but she would insist.

It was important for her to stand on her own two feet. Both figuratively and literally.

Stevie glanced up from her laptop as Sean opened the door of the apartment and walked into the living room carrying a bag of groceries and a bouquet of fresh flowers. He'd texted her to let her know he was coming over, even though he came by at this time every day.

"I still have the last flowers you brought me," she said.

"That was a week ago and they're looking pretty strag gly." He smiled. "Anyway, I like bringing you flowers."

Sean had been wonderful. Luckily, he'd already been planning to move to New York to start a new branch of his business, so he moved a littler earlier, refusing to leave her. He'd stayed by her side through the physiotherapy, then he'd gotten her set up in the new apartment Derrick had found for her. It was small, but fine for her. And the rent was man ageable. For a while.

Sean had stayed with her at first, until he was sure she could manage on her own. It was so odd having him sleep on her couch in this small place when he had a huge lux ury apartment of his own. But she refused to stay at his place, and he'd refused to leave her alone.

Which she was happy about, because it had been a rough few months after she'd first moved in. Her walking had still been pretty shaky and it was difficult to do even the simplest things, like making a straightforward meal. She still needed a cane to get around, and hadn't gone out on her own yet. Sean came by every day to take her out for a walk.

Tomorrow, however, she planned to make her first outing on her own.

She was sitting sideways on the couch leaning against a pillow, but when Sean returned from the kitchen after putting away the groceries, she turned so she was sitting up. He sat down in the chair.

"So how's the book going?" he asked.

She smiled. "Slowly. But I'm loving every minute of it."

She'd signed up for an online course, and had even connected with some other writers through a writing group to do critiquing of each other's work.

She closed the computer and put it on the coffee table.

He smiled. "I see you've been cooking."

"If you call heating up a frozen lasagna cooking, then yeah. Dinner will be ready in ten minutes," she said.

"I saw a salad in the fridge, too. Don't diminish what you've accomplished." His smile widened. "You really have come a long way."

"And tomorrow I plan to walk all the way to that little diner around the corner on my own."

"That's great."

She saw the concern in his eyes and knew he wanted to suggest coming with her. But they both knew that the main thing she needed to do was gain confidence in going out on her own. And she couldn't do that if he was acting as her safety net.

"I saw an old friend of yours today," he said.

The way he stared at his hands made her shift uneasily. "Who?"

"Dylan Cole. He recognized me from Raphael Allegro's party."

Her stomach tightened. "You didn't tell him about the accident, did you?"

A few weeks after she'd left the hospital, she'd admitted to Sean that she'd been going to meet Reid that day. She'd had little choice when he told her she'd been calling out Reid's name in her sleep. But she'd explained that she didn't want to see Reid now. That she didn't want to be a burden to him. Sean had tried to talk her into letting him contact Reid, but she'd made him swear not to.

"No, of course not. He said that Reid tried to call you for weeks. When he got a message saying your phone service was canceled, he assumed you had come back to me and that we'd returned to Chicago."

Shortly after she'd woken from the coma, she'd asked Sean to cancel her cell service. The phone had been smashed during the accident and she'd decided to wait a few weeks before getting a new one. And she hadn't wanted Reid calling her.

"What did you tell him?" she asked.

He shook his head. "I told him we were seeing each other. I kept it vague, but he clearly interpreted it that we're together."

She nodded. That was good. Then Reid would give up on her.

Sean's chocolate-brown eyes turned to her. "Why don't you let me tell them what happened? Right now Reid's angry, but once he knows . . ."

"Yes, once he knows, he'll feel sorry for me . . . and he'll want to take care of me."

His eyes glowed with compassion. "And what's wrong with that?"

"I don't want him to look at me like an invalid. And I certainly don't want to be a burden to him, which is exactly what I'd be. It's not fair to him. If he found out he'd feel like he had to swoop in and take care of me. That's just how he is, but I can't let him. I need to be able to take care of myself."

Fear raced through her at the thought. She didn't know how she would take care of herself. She was physically capable of doing the basics, but she couldn't hold down a job. Not with the lasting effects of her concussion. And even if that weren't the case, she couldn't get a job waiting tables or working in a store. She wouldn't be able to take being on her feet that long.

The money would run out eventually.

She bit her lip. She'd figure something out. She was strong and smart. There was some way she could do this without relying on others.

All she knew for sure right now was that she did *not* want Reid Jacobs to see her broken and helpless. And she certainly didn't want him to feel obligated to pick up the pieces.

Stevie sat down in the booth at the diner and tucked her cane between herself and the wall below the window, then set her bag in front of it. She was tired, but it was a good tired. She'd walked all the way from her apartment on her own. It had been slow going, but she knew it would get better every day.

The waitress came by and poured her some water from a jug, then took her order. Stevie opted for the soup, salad, and half-sandwich special. She pulled a book from her bag and read until the food arrived. She had thought about bringing her laptop so she could work on her latest writing assignment, but she hadn't wanted to carry the extra weight. Not this first time out.

After she finished eating, she lingered over a coffee, catching up on her e-mails and texts. She texted back and forth with Jon for a bit, then finally decided it was time to start the trek home.

She signaled the waitress for her check, then fished in her bag for her wallet.

As the waitress approached the table with the check in her hand, someone behind her spoke.

"I'll get that."

She froze, then slowly glanced around to see Reid.

Her stomach flopped over and she feared she'd lose her dinner.

The waitress handed him the bill and continued on her way.

Reid sat down across from her, grim-faced.

"Hello, Stevie."

"Hi." Tension stretched between them. "I can manage the check."

"I have no doubt, but surely you'll let an *old friend* treat you to dinner. We are friends, aren't we?"

"Reid . . ."

"Or maybe I'm wrong about that. Friends don't make promises they don't intend to keep. Like meeting to discuss something as important as the rest of their lives." He frowned. "I mean, I get it. You decided to go back to your ex-fiancé. But you could have done me the courtesy of talking to me about it first. Or even letting me know you weren't going to show up that day."

"I'm sorry, Reid. Something happened that . . . I just couldn't get in touch with you."

His eyebrow rose. "Why? Was your phone broken?"

She pursed her lips. "As a matter of fact, it was."

He scowled. "And what about the next day? Or the day after that? Or the next week?" He leaned in close, his eyes simmering with anger. But beneath that anger she saw an intense, gut-wrenching pain.

"I was worried sick about you," he continued, his voice almost shaking. "I couldn't believe you'd just walk away without a word. Especially after *promising* you'd meet me." His fist clenched, crumpling the bill that was still in his hand. "But, apparently, I was wrong."

Oh, God. Seeing firsthand how much she'd hurt him tore at her heart. She should say something, but . . . there was nothing she could say that wouldn't make it worse.

She stared at her hands. "I'm sorry, Reid."

He nodded. "You're sorry. Well, that makes it all better, doesn't it?"

He stood up and pulled his wallet from his pocket, then dropped the check on the table with a twenty-dollar bill on top of it.

"I hope you and Sean are very happy together."

Her heart clenched as he strode to the door. Once he was outside, she watched through the window as he got into a town car that had been waiting for him. It drove away.

Her stomach ached it was clenched so tight. She felt tears swelling in her eyes, but she blinked them back as best she could.

The waitress came by and collected the check.

"Can I get you anything else, hon?" she asked. She was an older woman with kind eyes. "Another cup of coffee, maybe?"

"No, thanks."

The woman started to count out change from her apron pocket.

"No, keep that," Stevie said.

"Thanks," the waitress said then moved on to a table with new arrivals.

Stevie sat for a few minutes, sipping her water, buoying herself up for the walk home.

Sitting in the back of the town car while it moved through the city traffic, Reid pulled his buzzing cell phone from his pocket, still reeling from the painful interaction with Stevie.

He'd thought he'd had it all together. That this meeting with her would allow him to find closure. But he hadn't been prepared for the assault of emotions that had rocked him to the core.

"How did it go with Stevie?" Dylan asked when Reid answered the call.

"Fuck, it was bad. I couldn't have been more of a jerk."

"Maybe you should go back and apologize."

"No. I'm sure she doesn't want to see me again. And what would be the point?"

"You didn't tell her that Sean told me where she'd be today, did you?" Dylan asked.

"No. He made you promise we wouldn't and I honored that."

Reid couldn't quite figure out why Sean would let Dylan know that Stevie would be at the diner this evening. Maybe he'd anticipated that Reid would do just what he did—act like a jerk—and that would ensure Stevie never wanted to see him again. But why would Sean chance it? Unless maybe he was tired of Stevie and was hoping for a way out.

He shook his head. He'd already thought through all these scenarios, plus a dozen others, and he knew that all the ones that meant Stevie and Sean weren't happy together were just wishful thinking on his part.

"Okay," Dylan said, "we'll have a drink when you get back and you can tell me all about it. In the meantime, I need the information about that meeting tomorrow with our new client. Something else has come up and I may need to shift some things around."

"Yeah, okay. Just a minute." Reid pulled out his wallet and looked inside.

Damn it. The piece of paper with the notes he'd jotted down was gone.

Chapter Twenty-four

Stevie drew in a deep breath. It was time to go. She picked up her bag and set it on the end of the table, then reached for her cane.

Before she could stand up, the waitress hurried to the table. "The gentleman you were talking to . . . he left this behind. He must have pulled it out of his wallet along with the twenty." The waitress handed her a slip of paper. "It looks like a note for a meeting of some kind. There's an address, phone number, and a time written down. It might be important. Can you give it to him?"

Stevie shook her head. "I won't be seeing him again, but I can give you his cell number."

Stevie still remembered it. Along with so many other things she wished she could just forget.

The waitress gave her a pen and Stevie jotted the number down on the back of the slip of paper.

"Just don't call him until I'm gone. Okay?"

"Oh, it looks like it won't be necessary." The waitress's gaze was on the door. "He's back."

Stevie's chest clenched and she shoved the cane under the table. It rested at an angle against the bench and she hastily pushed her bag in front of it as best she could as Reid strode to the table.

"Sir, I think this is yours," the waitress said, as she held out the slip of paper.

"Yes, thank you." He took the paper from the woman and watched her walk away.

Then his gaze fell to Stevie. Thankfully, he didn't seem to see the cane.

"Stevie, I'm sorry about earlier. I didn't behave very well."

"It's okay. I understand why you're angry."

"That's no excuse. May I sit down?"

"I'm . . . uh . . . I was just leaving."

"It'll just take a minute."

She tried to push the cane sideways under the guise of moving her bag, so his leg wouldn't bump into it, but she didn't succeed and the cane fell to the floor.

"What's that?" Reid leaned over and picked it up, then drew it from under the table. His gaze darted to hers.

"Oh, yes, I think someone left that behind. I'm sure they'll come back for it."

His eyes narrowed. "I really doubt someone would leave without their cane. Stevie, is this yours?" he asked point-blank.

She bit her lip. "Okay, yes, I had a bit of an accident, but I'm fine. It's really nothing."

"Really?" He searched her face for a moment, then nodded. "Okay, well, I'll walk you out."

She froze. "No, it's okay. I think I'll have another coffee before I go."

His eyes narrowed. "I thought you were ready to leave."

"I was but . . . I changed my mind."

"Okay, good. I'll sit with you until you're ready to go."

She frowned in exasperation. "I'd rather you don't. I'd like some time to myself."

Relief washed through her as he nodded.

"Okay. But I really feel like a cup of coffee, so I'll just sit at the counter."

She frowned. "Reid, why are you doing this?"

Reid locked gazes with her. "Because I want to know what you're not telling me."

If she just had a sprained ankle or something similar, why would she be trying to hide it?

She sighed.

"Fine. I walk with a bit of a limp. I'm sure you figured that out from the cane, but I just didn't want you to see, okay? So will you leave now?"

"Why? What happened?"

She brushed his question aside with a shake of her head. "It doesn't matter. It's none of your concern. Now, will you please let me go?"

"Of course." He stood up, then offered his hand to help her up.

She scowled. She refused his hand and pulled her bag—which was like a mini backpack—over her shoulders, then pushed herself to her feet, keeping her hand on the table for balance. She reached for the cane he was still holding.

When he gave it to her, he gestured for her to precede him. She hesitated, then seemed to realize there was no way she'd win insisting he go first, so she took a step forward.

Shock surged through him as she started to move. She had trouble lifting her feet and shuffled more than walked, leaning heavily on her cane. His gut clenched at the realization that she'd actually been hurt quite badly.

His throat closed as if gripped by a steadily tightening hand. He flashed back to that night. Sirens blaring in the distance. An ambulance with its flashing lights racing past him. Then it dawned on him . . .

Fuck, that ambulance had been for her.

When she approached the door, he rushed ahead to open it. Her face was downcast, but he caught a glimpse of tears glittering in her eyes.

Once they were outside, she started to move down the sidewalk, but he caught her arm.

"Now I understand why you didn't contact me that night. That's when you had the accident, isn't it?"

She stared at him, saying nothing, but her eyes gave her away.

"How bad was it?" he asked grimly.

"I told you, it wasn't bad."

"Stevie, you can barely walk after all these months. You must have been in critical condition."

She shook her head. "It doesn't matter. I'm okay now."

Damn, he'd been such an idiot. He should have known that only something unavoidable—something tragic—would have kept her away. He'd thought the worst of her while she'd been lying in a hospital room, fighting for her life.

He squeezed her hand. "I'm so sorry."

She tugged her hand away. "Don't be sorry. It wasn't your fault. It wasn't anyone's fault."

"Stevie, let me help you."

Her jaw twitched. "I don't need your help. I can manage perfectly well on my own."

He rested his hand on her arm. "I know you can, sweetheart. I just . . ."

Pain washed through him at the thought that he might lose her again. She was so full of pride and he didn't know how to convince her it was okay to accept his help.

"Stevie, please don't shut me out again. I don't know why you chose not to contact me after the accident . . . and we can put that way on the back burner for now . . . but please talk to me."

She clutched tightly to her cane, looking a little wobbly. "I'm sorry, Reid I really am, I never meant to hurt you."

Stevie's heart ached at the sadness in Reid's eyes. She regretted snapping at him when he'd offered his help. That hadn't been fair of her. This was a shock for him and he was doing his best.

"This is my ride," he said, gesturing to the town car waiting at the curb for him. "Let me give you a lift home."

"No, thank you. I'll walk."

"You really won't take a ride?"

"No. But please don't take it the wrong way. This is my first time out on my own. I promised myself I'd walk from my apartment to the diner and back again. With no help. It's important to me that I do it without anyone to lean on."

He squeezed her arm.

"But, Stevie, you'll always have me to lean on. Whether you take advantage of that or not. I will always be there for you, anytime you choose to call me."

Dampness pooled in her eyes. She knew what he said was true, and it touched her. Especially after what she'd put him through over the past few months.

"Thank you, Reid, I . . ." Her throat closed up and she just nodded her head as she drew in a deep breath. "I appreciate that and I don't mean to offend you. I just really need to do this on my own."

"All right. I understand that. But can we talk later? Maybe have a drink together?" He smiled warmly. "After all, it sounds like this is an accomplishment to celebrate."

She hesitated. But everything in her heart told her to accept.

"If you'd like to stop by later," she said, "you could come up and have a drink."

His smile broadened. "You couldn't keep me away."

Chapter Twenty-five

When Stevie arrived at her apartment building, she was disappointed that Reid wasn't there waiting for her. She'd said later, but she'd been sure in his usual style, he'd push that to the limit. She'd definitely thought he'd be as anxious to see her again as she was to see him.

And to talk.

She sighed and opened the glass door, then hobbled to the elevator. She got off on her floor and walked down the hall. As she started to tap in the combination for the lock, the doorknob turned and the door opened.

Her breath caught.

"Hello." Reid stood inside her doorway facing her.

She laughed, a little giddy at seeing him again. "I'd ask how you got in, but I know you have your ways."

She walked in and he closed the door behind her. She rested her cane against the shelving unit by the door and slipped her bag from her shoulders, then put it on one of the shelves. When she turned around, there was Reid, smiling at her.

He rested his hands on her shoulders and moved closer. When his lips brushed hers, she felt a rush of heat. He deepened the kiss, his tongue gliding inside her mouth and she welcomed it with delicate strokes of her own.

He stepped her back against the wall, his fingers gliding through her hair. His body was so big and masculine. So welcome.

Oh, God, she'd missed him.

His hips pressed tightly to hers, his cock swelling beneath the fabric. At the exciting feel of his thick, hard shaft against her, she groaned softly.

"Oh, fuck, Stevie. I'm sorry." Reid pulled back so fast she almost toppled over, but he steadied her in his arms. "Did I hurt you?"

"No."

"But you cried out."

She smiled at the concern in his eyes and stroked his cheek.

"That's because I was enjoying it."

He searched her face, doubt in his eyes, then scooped her up and carried her into the living room. He set her gently on the couch.

"I'm afraid the place is a little small," she apologized, "but—"

His mouth covered hers, stopping her words.

"I don't care about that. I just care that I'm with you." He stroked her hair back over her ear. "Why didn't you tell me sooner? I could have helped."

She shook her head, her stomach tightening into knots.

"I didn't want to be a burden."

He took her hand, and the gentleness of his touch . . . the softness in his eyes . . . tore at her heart.

"I love you, Stevie. Taking care of you would never be a burden."

He drew her hand to his lips and the tender kiss echoed through her soul.

"What if it had been me that had been hurt?" he asked. "Would you have considered it a burden to be there for me?"

She gazed into his cobalt-blue eyes, trembling at the thought of something happening to him.

"Of course not. I would do everything I could for you."

"Then let me do that for you. Don't deny me the chance to be the man you need."

She stared at him, a small part of her crying out that she didn't need anyone. But in these past few months, she had learned that she was strong, even when she was physically weak. That she could push past what seemed like insurmountable odds, like learning to walk again, even when the doctors doubted she ever would.

Accepting help wasn't a weakness. In fact, it took a lot of strength to allow herself to trust that much. And if there was anyone she could trust, in her heart, she knew it was Reid.

"Reid, I'm so sorry."

He frowned. "Does that mean you still won't let me help you?"

"No, I mean I'm sorry I pushed you away. I should have contacted you." She took his hand and he closed his fingers around hers. "That day . . . when the accident happened . . . I was on my way to you. To give you my answer."

"And that answer was yes." He said it with such confidence, she wasn't sure if he actually knew it in his heart, or was just willing it to be true.

She couldn't help but laugh. "Yes, it was."

But then her fragile hold on her emotions crumbled and tears streamed from her eyes.

"Aw, sweetheart," he said in a heartbreakingly tender voice.

He opened his arms and she slid into them. As his arms wrapped around her, he pressed his lips to her temple.

"Just tell me you'll let me help you, sweetheart. That's all I'm asking right now."

Her head rested against his chest, the sound of his beating heart soothing her.

She nodded, blinking back the tears. "Thank you, Reid," she whispered.

He tightened his arms and she felt so cherished.

She drew in a deep breath, the loving warmth quivering through her changing to something else. She drew back and gazed up at him. His blue eyes, filled with tenderness, turned to her.

She rested her hand on his cheek. "You said you wanted to be the man I need."

"Yes." He said the word with a sweet gentleness that tugged at her heart.

"I do need you." She rested her hand on his chest and trailed her fingers down his warm shirt, leaving no doubt as to the kind of need she meant.

He took her hand, drew it to his mouth, then kissed it. "Maybe we should have that drink you promised me." "It can wait until later," she murmured.

She stroked his cheek, then hooked her arms around his neck and drew him closer so she could nuzzle his jaw.

"How much later?" he asked.

She raised an eyebrow, a gleam in her eyes. "Tomorrow?"

"Stevie, I don't know . . ."

Her lips found his again and she pushed her tongue into his mouth and swirled.

"You said you'd be the man I need. And I need this. I need to be with you." She gazed deep into his eyes. "Don't you want me?"

"Oh, God, sweetheart. Of course I do."

His lips found hers and she pulled him with her as she leaned back on the couch. The feel of his body over hers, his hand gliding down her side, set her heart racing. He cupped her breast and she arched against his palm.

She unbuttoned her shirt and pulled it open. She wore a simple white lace bra underneath, but his eyes lit up as he gazed at her. He sat up, perched on the edge of the couch beside her and cupped both her breasts. The warmth of his hands around her took her breath away.

She hadn't been with a man in months. Not since the last time she'd been with Reid. And not since the accident. She was a bit anxious, but she knew Reid would be patient and guide her through it with a gentle hand.

His fingers slipped from her breast and stroked down her belly, then he unfastened her jeans. He pulled down the zipper, the raspy sound sending tingles through her. Soon he'd be touching her there. Where she ached for him.

But a little panic set in because . . . when he pulled down her jeans . . .

The scars . . .

She knew she needn't worry. Reid wouldn't walk away because she wasn't perfect. But she wasn't quite ready to face his reaction yet, whatever it would be.

She slipped off her shirt, then arched forward and unfastened her bra. Then she peeled it away. His gaze fell to her swollen nipples and sparks danced in his cobalt-blue eyes. He cupped her soft mounds and caressed them. When his thumbs glided over her hard buds, she whimpered.

He leaned in and took one in his mouth, his thumb continuing to tease the other.

"Oh, God, yes." Her fingers curled around his shoulders, a deep need pulsing through her.

"Reid, it's been so long. Please make love to me. I want to feel you inside me."

He kissed down her belly, then grasped her jeans and eased them downward.

When they were partway down her thighs, his gaze locked on her scars and he stopped. The shock in his eyes as his gaze followed the lines marring her body tore at her heart.

"My, God, Stevie. What am I doing? You've been hurt."

"That was months ago. I might not be able to walk perfectly, but that doesn't change how I feel. What I want." She stroked her hand through his hair. "And I want you."

He nodded and drew her jeans the rest of the way off.

His gaze traveled the length of her legs and back again and she could see he was disturbed by the extent of her scars.

"Reid."

His gaze shifted to her face, his eyes filled with shock and sadness.

"Kiss me," she urged.

He dipped his head to hers and kissed her. She wrapped her arms around him and responded with passion, deepening the kiss. Gliding her tongue into his mouth and coaxing.

She felt the fire ignite in him again and he drew her tighter to him, then he lifted her in his arms.

"Where's the bedroom?" he asked.

She pointed and he carried her to it, then laid her on the bed. He sat down beside her, and very gently drew her small lace panties down, paying total attention to her legs rather than her newly exposed flesh. She wanted to arch upward to pull his attention back, but she patiently held herself still.

When he discarded her panties and turned back to her, she smiled.

"So did you miss seeing me like this?" she asked.

The depth of need in his eyes took her breath away.

"Of course I did." His hand stroked over her breast, then down to her waist. "I could hardly sleep at night thinking of you. Wishing you were naked in my arms."

"Then do something about it." She took his hand and guided it lower.

With their gazes locked, she cupped his hand over her intimate flesh, then pressed his fingers into her folds until he could feel her dampness.

"Oh, fuck, Stevie."

As if he couldn't help himself, he stroked her slick folds. Heat shimmered in his eyes and he dipped his fingers deeper.

Oh, God, the feel of his thick fingers inside her was divine.

"Oh, yes, Reid. That feels so good," she encouraged.

He glided deeper still, his fingertips gently stroking the walls of her sensitive passage.

She ran her hand over the bulge in his pants, wanting to feel the thickness of it. Wanting him to drive it inside her.

But he drew her hand away and moved to the end of the bed, then parted her legs. He knelt on the bed and caressed her inner thighs, his touch gentle and a little uncertain. Then he stroked over her intimate flesh again. She moaned softly, wanting his cock inside her so badly.

"Reid, I want you."

"I know, baby. I want you, too."

He leaned forward and his lips brushed her sensitive flesh. When his tongue burrowed into her, she moaned. Her fingers curled in his hair as he licked her slit, then he opened her soft folds with his thumb and . . .

"Oh, God, yes!" She arched against his tongue as it rasped over her clit, sending quivering waves of pleasure radiating outward.

He suckled and teased. Then he slid two thick fingers into her slick opening. They pulsed inside her. She trembled at the delicious sensations.

Pleasure rose inside her as he kept sucking and pumping.

She arched. It had been so long, and she was so close.

"I want you to come, baby," he murmured against her slick flesh. "I want to know I've made you happy."

"Oh, so happy," she moaned.

His tongue swirled and his fingers drove deep. Over and over again.

"Yes! Oh, God!" The white-hot wave of pleasure crashed through her, swirling over every cell, her nerve endings singeing. She gasped, clinging to his head . . . then moaned as the orgasm claimed her.

When she released him and lay panting on the bed, he kissed her belly, then across her hips and down her legs. She gazed down to see him staring at her scars as he brushed his lips over them in light kisses.

She opened her arms to him. "Come and make love to me."

He prowled upward, but lay down beside her. "I think that's enough for now."

He pulled her into his arms and snuggled her against his body. The hard column of his cock pressed against her hip.

"I think your body has different ideas."

It twitched gently against her. She wrapped her hand around it and stroked, but he captured her wrist and drew it away.

"Stevie, I'm not going to make love to you now." He stroked her hair, and his solemn gaze locked on hers. "It's not that I don't want to. I just . . . need a little time to get used to the idea. I . . ." His lips compressed. "I don't want to hurt you."

Chapter Twenty-six

At Reid's words, Stevie's throat tightened.

She stroked his cheek, loving the raspy feel.

"I'm not made of glass." She nuzzled his neck, then dragged her teeth across the stubble on his chin. "I won't break. And in fact"—she grinned and rolled over, presenting him with her ass—"I can take quite a bit of punishment."

His hand stroked over her ass, but then he rolled her back again.

"It's not going to happen right now." His expression was resolute.

She frowned. "Okay, but I'm going to feel you inside me one way or another."

She stroked down his tight abs and grasped his cock. God, it was so hard and throbbing she didn't know how he could deny himself.

"Stevie . . ."

"Surely, you don't think you can hurt me if I do oral sex, do you?"

The haunted look in his eyes dissipated as a slow smile spread across his face. He stood up and then helped her sit up, watching as she slowly pushed her legs off the side of the bed and to the floor. Then he positioned himself in front of her.

She smiled as she wrapped both hands around the big cock presented to her. She stroked, her insides quivering at the feel of the thick shaft gliding between her fingers. His breathing accelerated as she pumped him faster. She swallowed his big cockhead into her mouth, watching the growing need in his eyes, and suckled as she cupped his balls in one hand, continuing to stroke with the other.

His hand glided over her hair.

"Oh, fuck, Stevie, I'm so close."

She was tempted to pull off him and offer her pussy instead, hoping he'd be so close to the edge he wouldn't resist.

But she didn't.

She squeezed him tightly in her mouth and sucked deeply, continuing to stroke him.

"Oh, God damn!"

He jerked forward as his cock erupted into her mouth. She suckled and swallowed, delighted she'd made him come.

A moment later, he dropped to his knees in front of her and held her close, his big arms around her, and his lips captured hers in a passionate kiss. Then he lifted her onto the bed and drew her against his body, pressing her head to his chest. He held it snugly against him, the quick beat of his heart pounding in her ear.

"God, I've missed you." He held her tighter, as if he was

afraid she might slip away. His lips brushed her temple, sending tremors through her. "I love you so much."

"I love you, too," she heard herself whisper before drifting off to sleep.

Reid hardly slept that night, holding Stevie close to his body, fretting at how he'd let her down.

He hadn't been there for her after the accident, to help her deal with the difficult healing process, both emotionally and physically. And even last night, he'd been so thrown off by her extreme difficulty walking, and then the sight of her scars . . . his gut clenched . . . by her physical vulnerability and his need to protect her, even from himself . . . that he'd denied her what she had really wanted.

To be physically intimate with him.

Sure, he had relented enough to give her an orgasm, and then, when she'd insisted, to allow her to give him one, too, but . . . she'd wanted more.

She'd wanted him inside her.

How badly had he screwed things up by denying her that? Had he scarred her emotionally, making her feel unattractive? Or too fragile in his eyes?

He stroked her hair from her face, his fingers following the strands down her back. Lightly so he didn't wake her.

He couldn't lie here any longer. In agony with her snuggled so close. Not wanting to wake her. Not wanting to face making the same mistake again.

Because he still didn't know . . . not for sure . . . if he could do what she wanted. As much as he wanted her . . .

he yearned to slide his aching cock inside her . . . he wasn't sure if he could do it.

He eased away from her and slid from the bed, careful not to wake her, then pulled on his boxers and walked to the kitchen. Once he had a hot cup of coffee, he went into the living room and sat down, staring out at the dawn sky. The clouds were bathed in a pink glow from the rising light of the sun, still below the horizon.

It was still early and Stevie would probably sleep another couple of hours.

He wanted to check his e-mail, but he'd left his phone in the bedroom. He walked down the hall, hoping to slip in and out without waking her, but at the door, he heard her voice. She must be talking to someone on the phone.

He wanted to give her privacy for her conversation, so he went back to the living room and picked up his coffee, then finished the last of it. He decided he'd grab a shower, then join her in the bedroom again.

He walked to the bathroom, but hesitated at the door. He would love to take her in the shower with him. To soap her naked body and stroke every part of her. But he didn't know if her legs would hold her stable enough. And he didn't want to chance her falling and getting hurt.

He stepped into the shower and let the warm water spill over him. He took a long shower, reluctant to return to Stevie in case he found out he couldn't get past his debilitating protectiveness.

Finally, he turned off the water and pulled back the shower curtain. He dried himself off and combed his hair, then wrapped a dry towel around his waist. He opened the door, then walked to the bedroom. As he reached for the doorknob, he heard Stevie's voice.

Was she still talking on the phone?

Then his stomach tightened as he heard a man's voice.

Someone was in the bedroom with her. And the only one who made sense was her ex-fiancé, Sean.

Fuck, he hadn't confirmed that the two of them weren't together. When he'd found out that the accident was the reason she hadn't shown up that night . . . and then when he'd seen this small apartment . . . He was sure Sean wouldn't live in a small place like this with her. If they were living together, since the man had money, it would be in a large, luxurious apartment.

But despite all of that, maybe she was seeing Sean.

He was an idiot. He *knew* they were still in touch because it was Sean who had told Dylan that Stevie would be at the diner last night.

He paced to the living room, unsure of what to do. Should he slip away and leave them to it?

A strong resolve settled into his gut. No. He would fight for her.

He turned to stride back to the bedroom, when he heard someone tapping the combination into the lock on her door. He knew it wasn't the superintendent because when he'd talked the man into letting him into the apartment last night, the man had had a key.

The door opened and . . .

What the hell?

Sean walked into the living room.

As soon as he saw Reid standing there, he stopped cold.

"Damn, I'm sorry, I should have realized. I didn't mean to intrude."

Sean walked to the coffee table and set down the cloth bag that appeared to contain some groceries. A smile turned up the man's lips.

"As much as I wish she would have chosen me," Sean said, "I'm glad that you two finally connected. She's so clearly in love with you, but with her fierce pride, she wouldn't allow herself to be taken care of by you or anyone else. That's why she didn't let me contact you, and I had to honor her request."

Shock still held Reid immobile. "But you told Dylan last night—"

"I only told him where she'd be. I know that's pushing the limit—a lot—but I had to do something." Sean's gaze locked with Reid's. "I want her to be happy. And you're the man to do that."

He offered his hand to Reid and they shook. Then Sean turned and left.

Reid turned toward the hall.

It clearly wasn't Sean in the bedroom, so who the hell was it?

He strode down the hall and stopped at the door, ready to thrust it open and storm inside. But he drew in a deep breath and knocked on the door.

"Who is it?" Stevie called.

"How the hell many men do you expect to walk into your bedroom?" he said as he flung the door open and stepped inside.

Chapter Twenty-seven

To Reid's total surprise, Dylan stood by the window talking to Stevie. She was still in bed—naked—but she was sitting up with the covers tucked around her.

She giggled. "Well, I was pretty sure it was you."

"Hey, man," Dylan said. "Stevie called me and told me you two reconnected last night. Then she asked me to come over."

"Really?" Reid glanced at Stevie. "Does he know about the accident? How badly hurt you were?"

"She told me," Dylan said somberly.

"And I told him I really need a man and that you were a bit . . . reluctant. So he said he'd come over and . . ." She grinned. "Cheer you on."

"Or show you how it's done," Dylan said with a smile. "In case you've forgotten."

They both glanced at Reid and he drew in a breath. Could he allow Dylan to give her what he couldn't?

Stevie smiled invitingly. "Maybe if you both come over here and—"

"No," Reid interrupted. "You're right. I think maybe Dylan should show me how it's done."

Stevie glanced at Reid's face. He was struggling, she knew that. She'd called Dylan and asked him to come over, thinking maybe he could talk to Reid. Help him figure things out. But when Dylan had teased him about showing him how it was done, she was surprised Reid had accepted the offer.

She glanced at Dylan and he shrugged, then nodded. Dylan knew Reid pretty well, so if he thought it was okay . . .

She settled herself a little higher on the pillows, and after one last glance at Reid, who stood leaning against the doorway, she turned to Dylan.

"Dylan, I'd love to see you naked." With that, she dropped the sheet to her waist.

Dylan's appreciative gaze took in her naked breasts and he smiled.

"Whatever you want." Dylan stripped off his shirt, revealing his muscled torso accented with tattoos that continued across his thick biceps.

Then he dropped his jeans to the floor. His swelling cock was already stretching the fabric of his boxers and she watched hungrily as he tucked his thumbs under the waistband and pushed them down. When he stood up, she couldn't stop staring at his thick, rigid erection.

"It's beautiful." Her voice turned throaty as she said, "I want to feel it inside me."

Dylan walked toward the bed, a big smile on his face.

Then he pulled the covers the rest of the way off her and scooped her into his arms. She curled her hands around his neck as he carried her across the room, into the living room, and sat on the couch, with her sitting across his lap. Reid followed them and stood watching.

"Can you kneel over my lap?" Dylan asked. "Will that work?"

She smiled. "Yes."

He wrapped his hands around her waist and helped her turn toward him and rest her knees on either side of him. He nuzzled her neck. Electricity fluttered across her nerve endings and she arched toward him. His hands glided up her back and he pressed her closer, then captured her lips. She cupped his face and kissed him.

When their lips parted, she smiled. "I'm wet and ready. I really need your cock inside me."

His fingers stroked over her intimate flesh, then slipped inside to feel her slickness.

"Fuck, you are. I could slip right in." He glanced over her shoulder, at Reid behind her.

Reid nodded as Dylan glanced at him, clearly seeking his approval.

Dylan wrapped his hands around Stevie's waist again and lifted her, then pressed his cock to her opening. Reid could see the big shaft pushing into her as he lowered her onto it.

"Oh, God, that feels so good," she murmured, then rested her head against Dylan's chest.

Dylan stroked her hair, then gathered it together and

drew it forward over her shoulder, leaving her back naked. Dylan stared at Reid, and with a slight gesture of his head, signaled for him to come over.

At the thought of joining them, Reid's cock jolted, desire flooding through him. He dropped his towel to the floor and stepped behind them. Stevie started to rock her hips and Reid could just imagine Dylan's cock moving inside her.

God, he wished he was deep inside her right now.

He knelt behind her, his own cock twitching with need, and he stroked her back lightly. He ran his hands downward, then cupped her ass. He squeezed it, knowing that would cause more friction as Dylan moved inside her, and she groaned.

"Reid, come closer," she murmured.

He pressed close to her back and she slid one of her hands from around Dylan's neck and curled it around Reid's. She leaned back against him and drew his hand to her breast. He cupped the soft flesh and caressed gently to her needy moans. Dylan pivoted his hips forward and back and Reid watched their joined bodies move together. Reid stroked his hand down her stomach, then pressed his finger into her folds until he found her clit.

"Oh, yesss . . ." she moaned.

Dylan picked up speed, his big cock gliding deep into her. She was angled back, resting on Reid's chest now as Dylan fucked her, Reid stroking the bundle of nerves that gave her such raw pleasure. She turned her head and found Reid's lips, pulsing inside his mouth with her tongue as she kept rocking against Dylan.

"Ohhhh," she murmured against his lips. "Make me come."

Reid's cock was hard against her back, throbbing with need, and the words practically made him come on the spot.

Dylan picked up speed and Reid swirled over her clit, then began to vibrate his fingertip against it.

She sucked in a breath, then began to moan again. Low and gravelly at first. Then louder and louder as her face blossomed into bliss.

God, it was the most beautiful sight in existence. Watching her come. Her face glowing in ecstasy.

Dylan jerked against her, groaning his release.

Finally, Stevie collapsed on Reid's chest and he wrapped his arms around her. He nuzzled her temple, listening to her rapid breathing, delighted to be sharing this intimacy with her. Dylan leaned forward and kissed her. She smiled, glancing from one to the other of them.

"That was a great team effort," she said. "But only two of us are happy." She pushed herself onto her knees and leaned forward, resting her hands against Dylan's shoulders. "Now what about you, Reid?" she asked.

Her gorgeous pussy was open to him. Exposed and waiting for his throbbing cock to push inside her.

He could, he knew, drive into her and take his pleasure. Even give her an echo orgasm, but he wanted their first time together again to be more special than that.

"I don't want to do this right now, Stevie."

She seemed to stiffen, then she eased her body onto Dylan's lap and gazed over her shoulder at him. The devastated look on her face made his heart stutter.

"I don't mean I don't want you, baby. I do," Reid said. "I want nothing more than to feel you around me right now."

"Then do it," she pleaded.

"I want it to be special. I don't want it to be . . ."

"An afterthought?" She bit her lip, uncertainty washing across her features.

Dylan watched the two of them as he eased her onto the couch beside him so she was facing Reid.

"Oh, God, I'm an idiot," she whispered hoarsely. "I shouldn't have been with Dylan first."

Reid realized he was doing it again. He knelt in front of her and pulled her into his arms, finding her lips and taking them in a passionate kiss.

She wrapped her legs around his waist. His cock was nestled between their bodies, so warm and cozy. He tucked his hands under her ass and stood up, lifting her with him. She clung tightly to him as he carried her to the bedroom again. She kissed him, her mouth moving with passionate abandon, sending heat zinging through him.

Somehow he made it into the room without plowing into a wall and he set her on the bed. She refused to let him go, her tongue swirling inside his mouth, her arms clinging tightly to his neck. He pushed them both farther onto the bed and stretched out over her. She finally released his neck and then her hands were wrapped around his cock and before he could stop her, she was dragging his cockhead over her slickness.

Then she pushed him inside.

"Oh, God, that's . . ." His breath caught as her body

welcomed him with a tight hug, her internal muscles squeezing around him as his shaft pushed deep inside her.

Once he was fully immersed, he just stared into her eyes, feeling as dazed as she looked.

She cupped his cheeks and brought his lips back to hers, then kissed him again.

"You feel so good inside me," she murmured, her eyes glittering.

"Fuck, the feel of you around me is indescribable. I could die happy in your arms right now."

She ran her fingers through his hair. The feel of her fingertips stroking him was so sweet and tender.

He drew back in a slow, even stroke, watching her eyes grow glassy. Then he slowly eased forward.

Her eyelids fell closed and a delighted smile curved her lips. He nuzzled her neck as he pushed in deep. Then he drew back again. Slowly. Stroking her insides.

"Oh, yes," she murmured in a throaty whisper, clinging to his neck.

"Do you like that, baby?" he asked as he glided deep again.

She opened her eyes and locked with his. "You don't know how much."

He couldn't believe he was inside her again. Making love to her. Possessing her body.

As she gasped softly, the poignancy and sweetness of the moment faded, transforming into urgent need.

She gripped his cock tightly within her body, stroking his throbbing shaft as he glided into her faster. At her throaty moan, his animal hunger urged him to thrust quicker. Deeper.

"Yes, that's what I want. Fuck me, Reid. Hard and fast."

Fuck, what is she doing to me?

He couldn't help himself now. He was driving into her, riding her with rapid thrusts. His cock pumping into her, his hips thrashing against her pelvis.

He felt the heat swell inside him, burning through his body. His blood boiled and his hard cock ached as it never had before.

Her hands tightened around his neck.

"Oh, yesss   oh, God, Reid, I'm going to come now."

Her voice faded to a squeak, then she moaned. It was as if her whole body exhaled the sound, filling the room with the echoes of their passion. Her hips arched against him, taking him even deeper.

"Ah, fuck, baby." Then his tightly coiled need released, hot seed erupting from his cock. Filling her body.

The feel of it seemed to drive her pleasure higher, her moans turning to wails. He kept pounding into her as she rode the wave of bliss. Until slowly, her wails faded to moans.

Finally she fell back on the bed, still clinging to him tightly.

She sucked in air and he smiled down at her. She pulled him in for a kiss then let him ease back a little and gazed into his eyes with a smile.

"See, I didn't break."

He laughed. "God, I love you, baby."

"I love you, too," she whispered back.

Chapter Twenty-eight

Reid smiled at her. "I'm glad you're finally able to admit how you feel about me."

"Yes. And on the day of the accident I was on my way to tell you."

At the reminder of that horrible event, he held her closer, kissing her on the forehead and stroking her back. "We've been through hell to be together, and now I'm never going to let you go. I'll *always* be here for you, Stevie."

"And I love you for that, but I don't want you to feel you have to take care of me. I need to figure out how to take care of myself."

"Stevie, you've recovered from a coma. You've learned to walk again when it looked like that was impossible. You've moved into this place and you are taking care of yourself."

"I still need help. More than I feel comfortable taking. I can't hold down a job right now. And my money will finally run out." Damn, she hadn't wanted him to know all that.

"Sweetheart, I would love to help you. And there's nothing wrong with accepting help." He stroked his fingers through her hair. "In fact, that's one of the joys of being in love. Being able to help each other."

The glowing warmth in his cobalt-blue eyes . . . the love shining there . . . made her throat close up. He loved her and . . . oh, God in heaven, she loved him so much.

A slow smile spread across his face, as if he could see the love swelling from her heart.

He took her hand, then pressed it to his lips and kissed it like something cherished.

"Stevie, these past few months . . . when I thought I'd lost you forever . . . I've never suffered so much pain. And then seeing you yesterday . . . and discovering that you had suffered real, physical pain . . . that you almost died . . ." He squeezed her hand. "God, I wish I could have been there for you."

Guilt washed through her, but she'd done what she'd thought was the right thing. "I'm sorry, Reid."

"Baby, that's all behind us now. I just want to make sure we're never apart again. I love you and I can't stand the thought of being without you again."

He drew away, then sank to the floor and settled on his knees, his blue gaze locked on hers. She drew in a breath as he took her hand.

"Stevie, will you marry me?"

Shock jolted through her. Then . . .

Elation.

The thought of marrying Reid . . . of being with him always . . . filled her heart with joy.

But . . .

Could she really allow herself that?

"But I can barely walk," she protested. "And I can't just live off your money."

He squeezed her hand, gazing at her with a gentle smile.

"Sweetheart, walking and money aren't the most important things in life. What about love? And wanting another person so much you'd do anything for them?"

Her heart ached. She knew he would do anything for her.

"I love you," he continued, "and I don't want to be without you. Please don't deny me what I so desperately want . . . and what you do, too, I'm sure . . . because of pride." He squeezed her hand. "Come and live with me. Be my wife."

She stared at him, trembling.

"You can take all the time you need to recover. Then when you're able, if you want to go back to work, you can do that. If you want to drive a cab, I'll buy you one. If you want to pursue your writing more seriously, you can do that, too. I bet with your drive and determination, you'll write a bestseller first time out and be making more money than me."

She laughed. "Yeah, wouldn't that be nice."

She loved that he believed in her so much.

He pushed himself onto the bed again and slid his arm around her. He nuzzled her neck.

"And to sweeten the pot, you know Dylan comes as part of the package. You and I will be married, but he'll be in our bed anytime you want him."

Oh, God, it was so clear he loved her with a depth she could never have conceived of. And everything he said about what was important in life . . . He was right, and she knew in her heart that the only reason she needed to prove her independence was because she had never been able to trust love before. She'd been hurt too deeply by the people closest to her.

And she knew, right down in the depths of her soul, that Reid would never hurt her like that. Would never abandon her. Or put his needs ahead of her own.

Because he did truly love her.

Joy swelled through her as she realized that she didn't have to fight it anymore.

"Well, of course, then I'll say yes."

His jaw dropped open and he seemed in shock.

"Why are you so surprised?" she asked. "You provided some well-thought-out arguments."

"Yeah, but I guess I didn't think that the Dylan argument would be the one that actually convinced you."

She laughed. "It wasn't, but offering him certainly made the idea totally impossible to resist." She curled her hand around his neck and pulled him in for a sweet, poignant kiss. "But the real reason I said yes is because"—she smiled and stroked his hair—"I love you so much. I just couldn't resist you any longer."

He laughed with joy then pulled her into his arms. "Oh, God, I love you, too."

His lips merged with hers and he rolled on top of her again. She could feel his cock rising and she arched against him.

As he swelled, she rolled him back and pulled herself on top of him, then sat on his hips. She undulated, gliding her intimate flesh over his hardening cock.

"Oh, fuck, baby. There's nothing I'd rather do than be inside you right now."

She grinned. "What about being inside me at the same time as Dylan?"

His lips turned up in a broad smile. Then he shouted, "Dylan, get in here. We need you."

She arched against Reid, longing for him inside her.

Dylan walked in the door and grinned at the sight of the two of them.

"Room for one more?" he asked.

Stevie leaned forward and kissed Reid. Then she glanced over her shoulder.

"Only for you." She smiled in joy. "Come help us celebrate our engagement."

"Really?" Dylan's face lit up. "That's fabulous."

Dylan surged toward the bed as she wrapped her hand around Reid's cock and pressed it to her opening, then glided down on him. His enormous cock filled her all the way. Dylan grabbed a bottle of lube, then a moment later knelt behind her and his hard cockhead pressed against her back opening.

"Oh, yes, Dylan. Fill me."

He eased forward, gliding into her slowly. Stretching her.

Once he was all the way inside, the three of them paused, just enjoying being so intimately close.

Then Reid wrapped his hands around her waist and

guided her to move. All three of them moved in unison. Their cocks moved inside her. Gliding in and out. The sensation of their thick shafts stroking her sensitive passages was intensely erotic.

They sped up and she moaned softly.

"Do you like us both inside you, baby?" Reid asked, his gaze locked on her face.

"Oh, yes."

Dylan laughed and stroked faster, his cock gliding inside her tight passage.

They both began to thrust and pleasure coiled inside her, then quivered throughout her entire body.

"Fuck, baby, I'm going to come."

At Reid's words, she felt bliss rise within her and she moaned, the ecstatic sensations surging through her.

"Ah, fuck!" Dylan jerked against her, filling her with his heat.

Then Reid groaned and she felt his seed erupt inside her.

She wailed, clinging to Reid's shoulders. Riding the intense, pulsing orgasm until she was flying into oblivion, her consciousness shattering.

Then she collapsed on Reid's chest, his heartbeat against her ear, and she knew he was her anchor. With him she would always be loved.

And at that moment, she realized it wasn't really independence that she needed, but respect. And she had that with both Reid and Dylan.

Both of them respected her determination and her creativity. She knew with their support and encouragement, there would be no barrier she couldn't overcome.

She squeezed her internal muscles around their two cocks.

She knew that both of them would do whatever they could to make her happy. And she would do the same for them. And she knew that she was already starting to fall in love with Dylan, too.

She couldn't imagine a happier future than being with these two incredible men.

Don't miss Opal Carew's next red-hot romance

Heat

Coming June 2017
from St. Martin's Press